CHASING SUNSET

What Reviewers Say
About Missouri Vaun's Work

Spencer's Cove

"Just when I thought I knew where this story was going and who everyone was, Missouri Vaun took me on a ride that totally exceeded my expectations. ...It was a magical tale and I absolutely adored it. Highly recommended."—*Kitty Kat's Book Reviews*

Take My Hand

"The chemistry between River and Clay is off the charts and their sex scenes were just plain hot!"—*Les Rêveur*

"The small town charms of *Take My Hand* evoke the heady perfume of pine needles and undergrowth, birdsong, and summer cocktails with friends."—*Omnivore Bibliosaur*

Love at Cooper's Creek

"Blown away...how have I not read a book by Missouri Vaun before. What a beautiful love story which, honestly, I wasn't ready to finish. Kate and Shaw's chemistry was instantaneous and as the reader I could feel it radiating off the page."—*Les Reveur*

"*Love at Cooper's Creek* is a gentle, warm hug of a book."—*The Lesbian Review*

Crossing the Wide Forever

"*Crossing the Wide Forever* is a near-heroic love story set in an epic time, told with almost lyrical prose. Words on the page will carry the reader, along with the main characters, back into history and into adventure. It's a tale that's easy to read, with enchanting main characters, despicable villains, and supportive friendships, producing a fascinating account of passion and adventure."
—*Lambda Literary Review*

Birthright

"The author develops a world that has a medieval feeling, complete with monasteries and vassal farmers, while also being a place and time where a lesbian relationship is just as legitimate and open as a heterosexual one. This kept pleasantly surprising me throughout my reading of the book. The adventure part of the story was fun, including traveling across kingdoms, on "wind-ships" across deserts, and plenty of sword fighting. …This book is worth reading for its fantasy world alone. In our world, where those in the LGBTQ communities still often face derision, prejudice, and danger for living and loving openly, being immersed in a world where the Queen can openly love another woman is a refreshing break from reality."
—Amanda Chapman, Librarian, Davisville Free Library (RI)

"*Birthright* by Missouri Vaun is one of the smoothest reads I've had my hands on in a long time."—*The Lesbian Review*

The Time Before Now

"[*The Time Before Now*] is just so good. Vaun's character work in this novel is flawless. She told a compelling story about a

person so real you could just about reach out and touch her."
—*The Lesbian Review*

The Ground Beneath

"One of my favourite things about Missouri Vaun's writing is her ability to write the attraction between two women. Somehow she manages to get that twinkle in the stomach just right and she makes me feel it as if I am falling in love with my wife all over again."
—*The Lesbian Review*

All Things Rise

"The futuristic world that author Missouri Vaun has brought to life is as interesting as it is plausible. The sci-fi aspect, though, is not hard-core which makes for easy reading and understanding of the technology prevalent in the cloud cities. ...[T]he focus was really on the dynamics of the characters especially Cole, Ava and Audrey--whether they were interacting on the ground or above the clouds. From the first page to the last, the writing was just perfect."—*AoBibliosphere*

"This is a lovely little Sci-Fi romance, well worth a read for anyone looking for something different. I will be keeping an eye out for future works by Missouri Vaun."—*The Lesbian Review*

"Simply put, this book is easy to love. Everything about it makes for a wonderful read and re-read. I was able to go on a journey with these characters, an emotional, internal journey where I was able to take a look at the fact that while society and technology can change vastly until almost nothing remains the same, there are some fundamentals that never change, like hope, the raw emotion of human nature, and the far reaching search for the person who is able to soothe the fire in our souls with the love in theirs."—*Roses and Whimsy*

Writing as Paige Braddock

Jane's World and the Case of the Mail Order Bride

"This is such a quirky, sweet novel with a cast of memorable characters. It has laugh out loud moments and will leave you feeling charmed."—*The Lesbian Review*

Visit us at www.boldstrokesbooks.com

By the Author

All Things Rise

The Time Before Now

The Ground Beneath

Whiskey Sunrise

Valley of Fire

Death By Cocktail Straw

One More Reason To Leave Orlando

Smothered and Covered

Privacy Glass

Birthright

Crossing The Wide Forever

Love At Cooper's Creek

Take My Hand

Proxima Five

Spencer's Cove

Chasing Sunset

Writing as Paige Braddock

Jane's World: The Case of the Mail Order Bride

CHASING SUNSET

by

Missouri Vaun

2019

CHASING SUNSET

ISBN 13: 978-1-63555-454-0

This Trade Paperback Original Is Published By
Bold Strokes Books, Inc.
P.O. Box 249
Valley Falls, NY 12185

First Edition: August 2019

CREDITS
Editor: Cindy Cresap
Production Design: Susan Ramundo
Cover Design By Tammy Seidick

Acknowledgments

People ask me sometimes, where do you get your ideas? Most of the time I have no idea. It's just this magical thing that happens, usually in the shower when I have nothing to write on, or when I'm driving to work. But in this case, I remember the exact place the idea for *Chasing Sunset* happened.

I was sitting at the base of the Eiffel Tower (not the one in Paris, the one in Vegas). A group of us were having drinks near Paris Las Vegas one night during the annual GCLS convention. There were no novels in the pipeline for me so I turned to my friend and beta reader, Jenny Harmon, and asked…what should I write about next? Jenny immediately said, a road trip romance. Being someone who loves cars *and* road trips I thought this was a terrific suggestion. So, thank you, Jenny!

Many thanks to the BSB team for making these stories real and sharable. Rad, Sandy, Cindy, Ruth, and Paula, thank you for all the support.

There are a couple of other people I should mention with gratitude in my heart. One of them is Brian Miller for always answering my questions about sports cars and for being an all-around great guy. And thank you to Connie Ward, who shared photos and some details of her 1962 MG Roadster.

A big thank you to Rachel Black. You generously shared your experience as an actor and that was invaluable. You made this story so much better.

Thank you to my beta readers, Jenny, Vanessa, and Alena.

I'm grateful for my supportive and loving wife, Evelyn, who always supports me through the creative process. Thirty thousand words in, when I worry none of the plot points are going to come together, she's always there for me with encouragement.

I'll just add one note in closing. In case anyone wonders when you get to this portion of the story. Yes, I did drive across the Mississippi River three times, all in a row, on two different occasions—once in Vicksburg and once in Memphis.

On a road trip, once you're west of the Mississippi, anything can happen.

Dedication

For my grandfather, who taught me to drive.
I've loved road trips ever since.

CHAPTER ONE

Somewhere over Nebraska, halfway through the second Diet Coke, Iris Fleming began to question all her life choices. Possibly it was the generally unpleasant experience of modern air travel in coach. Maybe it was simply that she'd expected to be somewhere else in her life at this point.

Her mother would love it if she moved back to New York, found a nice investment banker, and settled down to have kids. But Iris wasn't quite ready to give up on her acting career, or Southern California. She hadn't broken the news to her mother yet, but after her most recent failed relationship, she might be ready to give up on men. As for the kid thing, she was moments away from turning thirty, and her biological clock hadn't started chiming yet. There was a possibility it never would. The idea of motherhood was a concept she might like to explore, someday.

Iris had always thought she'd stick with acting and try to make a successful go of it, until she turned thirty. Now that thirty had almost arrived, she was pushing that timeline back, at least another five years. This role she was about to test for might just be the game changer she'd been waiting for. This was the last stage before getting the role. She'd be on camera in front of the people who would have the final say, the producers, creator, and showrunner. This could be the part that finally elevated her career beyond spots on TV shows and the occasional national commercial.

Some people got into acting seeking fame. That wasn't why Iris had originally gotten into the business, but she wouldn't say no to a little fame. Especially if it had a side dish of fortune.

Fox and Friends rudely and abruptly cut into her thoughts.

The elderly woman next to her kept accidentally hitting the video controls for Iris's monitor with her elbow. The mildly amusing sitcom she wasn't really watching switched to Fox News abruptly every twenty minutes whether Iris wanted it to or not.

Iris touched the woman's arm to get her attention.

"Oh dear, I've done it again. I'm so sorry."

"It's all right," Iris said for the tenth time.

Equally bothersome was the guy across the aisle who wouldn't stop talking to his seatmate about his 5 Series BMW or his numerous ski trips to Europe. Iris had resorted to watching TV with headphones simply to drown him out. He'd insisted on talking to her while they queued up on the Jetway to board the plane, even though she'd been wearing earbuds. A clear indication that she didn't really want to talk to anyone. It wasn't that the guy was terrible looking. Although, a few hours a week at the gym wouldn't hurt. But after her ex, Kent, she was done with men for a while. Not in the mood.

Yeah, air travel in coach pretty much sucked.

Iris wanted to make this cross-country flight as stress free as possible. She'd dressed for comfort in boyfriend jeans and an oversized T-shirt and tried her best not to stress over the reason for the trip.

They were only moments away from starting the descent into Atlanta.

"Are you flying home?" Her seatmate was searching through her purse.

"No, I live near LA." Iris removed her headphones. She'd missed too many gaps in the sitcom to follow the story anyway.

"I was in Los Angeles visiting my daughter." The woman's eyes lost focus, as if she were visualizing something. "I love the weather, but everything is just too perfect there."

The woman was right. The only problem was that perfection was an illusion. Iris had the perfect career, the perfect rental house, and the perfect boyfriend. In reality, none of it was perfect, especially the boyfriend part. She'd chosen to ignore all the red flags, all the weird uneasy stomach twinges that let you know something wasn't quite right.

Denial was her only excuse.

Denial was a great place to visit. Denial could easily justify finishing a pint of ice cream all by yourself or that French fries were technically a vegetable. Yes, denial was a great place to visit, but you shouldn't live there. Bad things happened when you stayed too long. But that was the problem wasn't it? Denial was only obvious from the other side, after you passed through it. Denial's talent was disguising itself as confirmation that everything was okay. Thus, the rethinking of life choices. Iris sank into the headrest and closed her eyes. She took a few deep breaths and tried to relax.

As if it wasn't stressful enough to read for casting agents in LA, now Iris had agreed to fly to Atlanta to meet the creative team for a new series. This way she could be nervous and jet-lagged at the same time. Great plan. Normally, everything happened in LA, but they were filming this show in Atlanta, and the creative leads were big shots from some dystopian Netflix miniseries that had won every award possible. Iris and the other actor in consideration for the female leads were being flown to Atlanta to read for the producer and the director.

She'd considered spiking what was left of her Diet Coke with something stronger, but the drink cart never materialized, and now the tray tables were stowed. She craned her neck from the aisle seat, but it seemed no one was coming to claim her empty soda can.

"We've begun our initial descent into the Atlanta airport. Please remain in your seats for the—" The captain's announcement cut off abruptly as the aircraft jolted sharply.

The almost empty Diet Coke slipped from her loose grip. It rolled past her seat toward the back of the aircraft. Iris grabbed for the seat's armrest as the plane lurched violently downward. At the edge of her peripheral vision, she saw the Diet Coke can whoosh across the carpet toward the front of the plane. Several other free-range beverages joined the fray, toppling along the carpeted aisle.

The plane was falling from the sky!

Not in a nosedive, but rather, belly first, it dropped like a cement block. Iris sensed the heaviness of the Boeing 737 in every fiber of her being as gravity yanked the aircraft toward the ground in a free fall.

Had the plane encountered a wind shear?

Had the engines stalled?

No, she could feel the vibration of the turbo jet engines through her fingertips as she white-knuckled the armrest. Her stomach lunged upward and lodged in her throat, threatening to eject everything she'd eaten earlier.

They'd been close to the Atlanta airport. Seatbacks were in their upright and locked positions. Touchdown was so near. Five minutes out, the runway was a dark asphalt line cut through a sea of broccoli topped hardwoods.

The deafening whine of the engines invaded her senses. She squeezed her eyes shut and held her breath as the torque of the descent caused the seat belt to cut sharply into her lower abdomen. They were going to crash. Surely, they were going to crash. The plane was falling too fast, too close to the ground. Iris's twenty-nine years of life flashed like heat lightning through her mind, silent and searing. Had she done anything important? Lasting? Obit-worthy? Probably not.

Then suddenly, the landing gear made contact. With bone-jarring finality and air brakes screaming, they hit the tarmac. A duffel bag ejected from the overhead bin, narrowly missing her head. Mr. Chatty across from her wasn't as lucky. A rolling bag struck the side of his face wheels first, and blood ran down his cheek, soaking into the collar of his white dress shirt.

They were alive; the plane was on the runway.

The deafening wind noise across the braking flaps seemed louder than usual. A moment of stunned silence filled the aircraft cabin as the plane slowed, then the joyful sounds of relieved passengers. Some wept, some cheered, somewhere at the rear of the compartment an infant cried. Lots of luggage had haphazardly tumbled from the overhead bins upon impact. The pilot was saying something now, but Iris couldn't hear the words above the white noise of panic that still swirled inside her head.

The drop toward the runway had probably lasted less than a minute, but Iris was sure she'd lost a year of her life. She closed her eyes and took several deep, slow breaths.

As she waited for her heartbeat to slow to a normal rate, Iris silently considered all the reasons why she shouldn't have made the trip. The most recent near-death experience now taking the top spot on that list. An endless loop of second-guesses and what-ifs had been cycling through her head during the entire flight from Los Angeles to Atlanta. There was nothing quite as potent as a cheating boyfriend to tank your self-esteem. The breakup with Kent had definitely *not* been a confidence boost. But ambition had overruled uncertainty, so here she was. She wanted to do something more lasting, something that would negate the need to be cast for commercials simply to pay the bills.

"Thank you, Jesus."

Iris blinked several times, suddenly aware again of the elderly woman in the seat next to her.

"Thank yew, Jeezus," her seat mate said it again, her southern accent more noticeable the more times she repeated the phrase.

"Are you all right, ma'am?"

"Ask me again when we're off this airplane." There was good-natured humor and relief in her words. She turned to Iris. "What about you, honey, are you all right?"

"Yes, shaken, but okay." Iris swept her fingers through her hair, a habit that usually helped ground her when she was nervous.

The woman riffled through her large handbag as the plane taxied across the tarmac. She produced two red striped peppermint candies and offered one to Iris.

"Peppermint. It settles the stomach." She crinkled the plastic wrapped candies between her fingers.

The small gesture of kindness reminded Iris of her grandmother and how she'd kept peppermints in her purse to quiet Iris during evening mass. The sight of the candy swept Iris back to childhood and the itch to break free.

"Thank you." Iris unwrapped the candy and popped it in her mouth. She was fairly sure it was going to take more than one small mint to settle her tattered nerves, but she was grateful for anything that would kill the taste of fear lingering in her mouth.

She sucked the candy gratefully, rolling it over with her tongue as she watched the flight attendants methodically move through the cabin. Fallen luggage was gathered up and stowed overhead as the aircraft lumbered toward the terminal.

Iris wondered how long it would take to drive back to California after the audition, because there was no way she wanted to get back on an airplane again anytime soon. Maybe a cross-country road trip was the perfect way to celebrate her impending thirtieth birthday.

CHAPTER TWO

A name and an address flashed across the screen of the cell phone at the edge of the dresser, followed by a pickup time. Taylor Finn leaned closer so she could read the details. She returned to her reflection in the mirror as she finished buttoning the tailored pale blue shirt. The light starch made the collar stand up nicely. She reached for the charcoal jacket that matched her dress pants, slim through the hips and tapered at the cuff. She couldn't bring herself to wear a black suit and drive a limo, such a cliché. Dark gray was close enough. It was warm tonight so she opted for black wingtips with no socks to finish the ensemble. She slipped her wallet into her back pocket, then reached for her phone along with the car keys.

Finn trotted down the steps of the one-room cabin and followed the gravel path to the main house. Her family had owned the Hideaway Haven since the forties. Nestled in the foothills of the Blue Ridge Mountains, Hideaway Haven was a collection of small, rustic cabins peppered among old growth poplars and maples, with a few conifers thrown in. The vintage roadside getaway was about an hour outside Metro Atlanta. Finn had taken over one of the cabins for herself. If all the units filled up, she moved into the main house, which also doubled as restaurant and registration. Her parents occupied the entire second floor. But lately there'd been a drop in reservations. It seemed everyone did VRBO these days, which was taking a toll on small roadside motels.

Her mother rarely left the main house in case someone unexpectedly needed a cabin for the night. She glanced up at Finn when the bell over the door chimed.

"You need a haircut." Her mother only looked up briefly. Her salt-and-pepper hair curled around her face, the curls more textured due to the summer humidity. She was wearing a well-worn apron over a floral blouse and dark Capri pants, with old-school women's Keds tennis shoes. A television in the dining area near the kitchen blared CNN. Her mother had taken a seat nearby. She sipped iced tea and shook her head at the news. "That man. How did she ever agree to marry that man?"

"Maybe she knew he'd be president one day." Finn pulled a Coke from the cooler next to the wall and used the opener mounted on the side of the classic icebox to pop the cap.

"Even still, she should've known better."

"You've gotta quit watching the news, Mama. Nothin' good ever comes of it." Finn took a long swig of the icy cola. The carbonation burned her throat a little, but it was refreshing.

"Don't quote your father to me. Lord knows he tells me his own self plenty often enough." Her mother shook her head and sipped her tea, never taking her eyes off the newscaster. "Now there's a good-looking man."

"He's gay, Mama." Finn leaned against the registration counter. She ran her fingers through her hair, pushing it off her forehead. She'd put product in it to give it a casually tousled shape, but the front was getting a little long. Her mother didn't like it when it fell into her eyes.

"I know he's gay. Most of the handsome ones are. Except for George Clooney. Now there's a man I'd like to meet some day." A commercial came on, and her mother hit the mute button and rotated in her direction. "Where are you off to?"

"I'm working tonight. Driving to Atlanta. I'll probably be back really late."

"How much longer are you going to do that job? You are wasting your time. You could make something of yourself."

They had this conversation at least once a month. Finn could set her calendar by this discussion. When was Finn going to quit driving rich people around and get a real job, a job with a future?

"We've been over this, Mama. As long as it takes." Finn pushed the door open, not waiting for her mother's reply.

The screen door banged loudly. She stood for a moment and finished off the last bit of cola. She tossed the bottle into the recycle bin and strode to the garage behind the main house. The extra-long black company car lurked in the shadowy interior of the carport, which was walled on three sides but open at the front. There were three bays in the carport—one for the limo, one for her mother's ancient Volvo sedan, and one for her most prized possession, a 1958 MG MGA Roadster. She tugged at the gray canvas cover to make sure it was snug as if she were tucking in an infant for the night. In truth, this car *was* her baby, just not the sort of baby her mother preferred. Her mother wanted Finn to have an actual infant, a toddler who'd call her Grandma, not an overly pampered vintage sports car.

One night at dinner, Finn actually got the nerve to remind her mother that she was gay and she wasn't going to sleep with a guy. So a baby happening was highly unlikely. They never talked about sex so this was a radical breach of southern protocol. To which her mother responded by suggesting Finn didn't have to keep a man, just sleep with him so she could have a baby. Finn was speechless, and she was pretty sure the conversation had ruined her father's appetite. He sat back in his chair with wide eyes. He pushed away the plate of his Wednesday favorite, meatloaf, and scowled at them both.

Regardless, it didn't seem that a baby was in her future.

Cars were the only true love Finn had ever committed to. If asked, she'd have had a hard time pinning down the origin of her love affair with automobiles. Even her first memory of Christmas was asking her mother for a toy truck. Her mother had given her a dollhouse instead. She'd promptly traded it to her cousin Jeffrey for a case of Matchbox cars. Jeffrey preferred dolls and clothes. This wouldn't be the last Christmas she and her cousin swapped gifts. He'd grown up to be a very stylish man, currently living in Midtown Atlanta with his boyfriend.

Given the choice, Finn had pretty much always set her sights on anything with wheels. The first bicycle she ever owned was an intoxicating taste of freedom. She rode the wheels off that thing. It wasn't long before she began customizing the bike. Changing out the handlebars, removing the fenders, almost as if she were customizing a stock car for racing. Then she and her brother, Trey, built ramps for jumping over things in the backyard. Until one day when she'd failed to tighten the handlebars properly. They came off mid jump. Trey broke his arm, and Finn was grounded for a month. She was twelve and Trey was ten. Good times.

Finn stood next to the town car's driver's side door as she removed her jacket, folded it, and placed it on the passenger seat. She reached for her aviator style sunglasses in the console and put them on as she settled in behind the wheel. She might as well be comfortable for the drive to the city. Besides, she didn't want to have to run the AC. In the early evening she preferred to drive with all the windows open. The smell of fresh cut grass wafted through the car, and the soothing rhythm of cicadas sang their roadside summer melody as she drove along the tree-lined scenic byway.

A dog had his head out the window of an approaching car. Finn couldn't help smiling. He was a big collie, his long hair fluffed in the wind. His mouth was open and his tongue was out. He looked like he was smiling. Dogs couldn't drive, but they definitely understood the joy of cars. Yeah, dogs got it.

The sleek black limo looked completely out of place in rural north Georgia. Almost as out of place as her roadster. Almost as out of place as she did sometimes. Unincorporated Watts Mountain wasn't exactly an ideal community for a butch lesbian. Her mother preferred the word tomboy. Finn wasn't crazy about either label. She simply was who she was. She was who she'd always been. And whether she fit in or not, this was home.

Watts Mountain was founded in 1834, and it was really more of a hill than a mountain. But from here you could see the beginnings of the Blue Ridge Mountains a half hour's drive away. The community's only claim to fame was a post office that closed in 1967. Oh, and Watts Lake, conveniently located only a few miles from Hideaway Haven.

Watts Mountain had a small grocery at Turner's Corner. That intersection had the only three-way stop sign. The grocery had a single gas pump that occasionally ran dry because the Turners, who owned the store, weren't the best at managing their inventory. They had the necessities, beer, chips, and deli sandwiches. And there was a little mail center and gift shop across the highway, housed in the original train depot. From back when a train actually ran along this neglected section of track.

The necessary items for a picnic at the lake were readily available, including recycled inner tubes for flotation enjoyment. But for any other needs, like a date or a movie, well, that required a drive to the metro area. The suburbs of Atlanta now stretched miles and miles past the Perimeter, which was an eight-lane motor speedway populated by rednecks with shotguns in the gun racks of their pickups and yuppies in BMWs and Audis. Atlanta was booming and the city had the traffic to prove it.

Her mother was annoying at times, as most mothers could be, but she was right, and Finn knew it. Driving a limo was never supposed to be a long-term plan and yet, somehow, three years after taking the position she hadn't made any real progress toward her goal. She needed to get serious about doing the career she really wanted to be doing.

Working for the limo service was like a velvet coffin. She was comfortable, and shuttling high-end passengers paid the bills. The tips were good; other perks were sometimes good too. Especially the kind that didn't involve money. It seemed that Atlanta had more than its share of bored divorcees in need of a ride. Remembering one recent afternoon made Finn smile. Elaine Caufield was in her forties, bi-curious, and gorgeous. And she never made Finn feel like a dumb kid, even though at twenty-six, she probably was. Finn knew enough to know there was a lot she didn't know.

The last three weeks, Elaine had asked for Finn by name, special request, for her shopping excursions in Buckhead. Then when they returned to Elaine's place they always ended up getting food delivered. Elaine was fun. Sometimes she'd pull up to Elaine's large brick home and help carry shopping bags into the house. She'd head toward the door and Elaine would touch her arm and simply say, *stay*.

Stay, the word some people longed to hear only made Finn want to leave, to move, to go. She feared being stuck, hindered in some way from moving on, tethered by responsibility for another's happiness.

Even still, when Elaine had asked, she'd stayed. But she never spent the night.

Yeah, this gig was a velvet coffin all right. And if she wasn't careful she'd wake up in a few years and find that she was in the exact same spot. She hated to admit it, but her mother might actually be right this time.

CHAPTER THREE

The casting director, Katherine, was an elegant woman probably in her early fifties. Her hair was pulled up into a knot, and she wore glasses with dark, thick rims, like some New York fashion designer.

"Hi, we're set up on the soundstage." She shifted the clipboard she was holding and extended her hand to Iris.

"Hi." Iris took Katherine's hand.

"You can wait in here until we call for you." Katherine motioned toward the door of a small waiting room.

No one else was in the waiting area. There was a water dispenser and cups and two love seats facing each other. Iris sat on the edge of the nearest sofa, her hands folded in her lap. She tried to relax. She'd changed into something more professional. Ditched the T-shirt for a silk blouse, but kept the jeans. She didn't want to look like she was trying too hard, or was too desperate, but she also didn't want to look as if she'd just rolled out of bed either.

Iris was oddly unsettled. Was it just residual ragged nerves from her near-death experience? Or was it reading for the part? No, she'd done readings a hundred times. The director either thought you were right for the role or you weren't. And she knew the material well. She'd already read through the sides numerous times. It was almost as if her uneasiness was from some other source. It was the sort of tingly sensation you got when something big was about to happen.

She rolled her shoulders and exhaled slowly.

Iris tried not to get down on herself when directors passed her over for someone with longer legs or poutier lips or larger breasts or whatever they were looking for that she didn't have.

She placed her palm over her stomach hoping it would settle. If this weird tingly feeling wasn't nerves, then what was it? Her agent, Judith, had mentioned this part almost as a joke because Iris had never done science fiction. Iris didn't watch *Star Trek*—none of the generations. She wasn't even sure she could describe the difference between *Star Wars* and *Star Trek*, although she knew enough to know they weren't the same. One of them had something to do with feeling a force and the other one didn't.

Zombies also did not appeal to Iris, despite their undead success with ratings and fans. Zombies had invaded Hollywood in a way that Iris couldn't quite wrap her head around.

The idea, no, the compulsion to read for the lead role in this new science fiction series had been too strong to ignore. It was like she'd received some message from the ether compelling her to do it.

For starters, this character was the bad girl of the show. A bad girl fighting for a noble cause. Robin Hood in outer space.

Iris had only ever played good girls—the sister, the best friend, the cheerleader, the popular girl, the girlfriend who died young of cancer. She had the sort of look that meant she normally didn't get cast as anything but the boring good girl. She wasn't edgy or extreme or extravagant. She felt typecast and desperately wanted to prove to the studios that she could do more. In this *bad girl* role, she'd use weapons and fight alien creatures. There'd be actual stunts and hand-to-hand combat scenes. Also, this particular character was bisexual. Judith had concerns about Iris's comfort level with an on-screen sex scene with a woman, but that would be the least taxing element. Iris had dated women before, but Judith didn't know that. Iris tried to keep her personal life personal, as much as possible in Hollywood anyway. Judith didn't need to know everything and certainly neither did her fans. Social media was invasive enough without feeding the frenzy. The social media posts following her breakup with Kent had been bad enough. This might be the one instance when she was happy that he was more famous than she was. Fame had its drawbacks. Women loved his reckless, exciting persona, and he was a shameless flirt. He'd always explained it away as simply part of the stunt driver mystique. That, of course, was true, but also complete bullshit. And on some level, she'd known that about Kent long before the relationship ended.

Whenever possible, Iris liked to control the optics and any news about her life. She was not particularly a risk taker and that path had served her well until Kent. He was the one time she'd veered outside her comfort zone, and their relationship had ended badly.

"Are you ready?" Katherine stood in the half open door.

"Yes." Iris tried to reroute her thoughts. Away from Kent and back to the part she was about to play.

"Thanks for traveling to do the reading." Katherine glanced over her shoulder as she opened the door to the soundstage.

"No problem. I was happy to get the call back." Her first two readings had been in LA. She wasn't going to make the trip unless there was a fair chance she'd get the part. Initially, Judith had cautioned Iris that it was a long shot. She wanted to prove to Judith that she could land a leading role. The past eighteen months, she'd been getting mostly supporting roles so she was beginning to feel the pressure from the agency to bring in more money. Getting cast for this part would raise her game in their eyes.

The soundstage was basically a room with a camera. There was a six-foot table in the center of the room, and everyone was already seated. She recognized one of the men at the table as the director. She'd seen photos of him online. The other guy must be the producer or the writer, she wasn't sure. There was also another woman at the table besides Katherine, who she assumed might be reading opposite her for this scene.

Everyone looked up as Katherine introduced Iris.

She knew the drill. People could be rude right to your face. If you weren't the person they wanted or your reading sucked, they'd start checking their phones right in front of you. But for the most part they wanted you to be perfect to make their job easier.

The cameraman, Brian, was a skinny guy with a cropped beard and ball cap. He stepped past Iris and adjusted the camera stand.

Katherine handed her a few sheets of paper with the sides she'd be reading. She had a copy of the script and had already read through it numerous times. She'd been practicing in preparation for today.

Another woman took a seat at the table. She was introduced as Sarah, the showrunner. So far, the creative team seemed balanced between men and women, which felt right, since the two lead roles were for women. Eric Gilet, the director, sat next to Iris. He looked to be in his mid forties. He wore horn-rimmed glasses, probably more for looks than need. He was handsome, more because of his self-confidence than his looks, which weren't bad, but Iris would have described them as only a little above average. She'd gotten used to sizing people up quickly in LA. It was a habit that had saved her more than once, but she feared she was quickly becoming jaded. Looks really couldn't tell you everything about a person, but they gave good clues.

"This is Camille Greggory. She'll be reading Cleo's part for this scene." Katherine motioned toward Camille.

"Hello." Iris and Camille shook hands.

If she got the part, Camille would be one of her character's love interests. She'd be testing with Iris to gauge chemistry between the two actors. Camille had flawless brown skin and dark hair that curled up just where it touched her shoulders. Her eyes were beautiful, large, honest. Iris thought Camille was pretty, but not in the sort of way that she'd feel overshadowed by her or attracted to her. Camille wasn't her type. She definitely liked to be the only femme in a relationship.

She smiled and made eye contact for a moment with her audience around the table.

"Can you state your name and then read the first scene?" Katherine shuffled papers and jotted something down.

"Iris Fleming, reading for the part of Jade in *Athena.*"

Eric leaned back in his chair with his arms crossed as if he were already judging her. The other guy, who looked like a rumpled frat boy in an untucked pink oxford shirt and a Red Sox cap, was the producer. Eric stood up and circled the table, pausing for a moment by Brian and the camera stand. After a few seconds, he walked over and whispered something to Katherine. Katherine nodded and then returned her attention to Iris.

"We'd like to start with page two. In this scene, you've just discovered that Cleo, one of your crewmates you thought you could trust, has betrayed you."

Iris nodded.

"Begin whenever you're ready. You have the first line." Katherine nodded. As the casting director, Katherine had done her part. Eric, the director, would take things from here.

In a conversation scene it really helped for someone to read with you. She was happy that an actor would read opposite her, rather than the casting director flatly reading lines.

Iris took a moment to settle. She looked down at her hands in her lap. She and Camille had rotated their chairs so that they were facing each other, their knees almost touching. She closed her eyes and let the room drop away, focusing her energy on conjuring a sense of hurt and anger, which wasn't that hard. All she had to do was picture Kent, and the night she'd found him in bed with someone else.

She took a deep breath, opened her eyes, and nodded, signaling to Katherine that she was ready.

"Maybe you can explain it to me." Iris glared at Camille.

"Look, I never meant for you to get caught up in this." Camille averted her eyes as if she were hiding something.

"That's the problem, Cleo, you never think. Or if you do, it's only about yourself." Iris exhaled and focused on Camille, as if she were the least trustworthy person on Earth. "And now there's no way to undo what you've done." Iris stood and paced. It helped to imagine the scene in her head. Jade and Cleo were in the bowels of a space ship named *Athena*, stolen from a military installation, making their escape from Earth. They were supposed to be on a rescue mission, stealing the ship for a higher purpose, saving the galaxy and all that, but now Jade knew she'd been played.

"Look, you'll get a share. I'll see to it personally."

"You'll see to it personally? And I'm supposed to trust you? When everything you've told me about this mission has been a big fucking lie." Iris altered her voice. She wanted the pitch to be lower, stern, and commanding, the voice of someone not intimidated by the situation. "Has everything else been a lie too?" She softened her words and allowed a slight tremble for the last line, as if she were afraid of what the answer would be.

"You mean us?"

"If you have to ask, then I assume the answer is yes." Iris was strong again, solid, sure.

"I never meant to hurt you, Jade."

"Too late."

Iris let the scene slip away and waited for further instructions. The showrunner swiveled in her chair. It was impossible to read her body language.

"Thank you, Iris, that was great. I think you had good emotional range in that scene." Eric shuffled script pages. "Can you read from scene three?"

"Sure." He wanted her to read other scenes. That was a good sign. She opened the bottle of water in front of where she'd been sitting and took a few sips.

Camille and Iris read through scripted scenes for another forty-five minutes. The more she knew about Jade, the more she liked the character, and the premise of the show. A rogue crew of mostly women, attempting to effect positive change in a future where Earth was no longer habitable and humans had scattered across galaxies in order to simply survive. She wanted to be part of this show for sure.

CHAPTER FOUR

The Sovereign Building's gleaming, curved profile was one of Atlanta's more architecturally unique high-rises. It was one of the most exclusive luxury condo complexes in the city. It always reminded Finn of the sort of building a stuntman might jump from with a hang glider.

Finn eased the town car next to the valet stand. She gave the valet her name so that he could ring Geoff Botha, her client for the evening.

Like his father, Geoff had a South African accent, he was in his late twenties, and based on her limited interaction with him, Finn had already determined he was sort of an entitled dick. Geoff's father was one of Finn's regular clients. He was older, distinguished, and much more pleasant to chauffeur than his son who she'd only met on one other occasion en route to a family wedding.

She walked around the car to open the door for him when Geoff appeared. He was about Finn's height, close to six feet, and was dressed in a dark suit similar to hers. Like Finn's, his was also Italian cut, to accentuate his trim physique. She knew already he'd had a few pre-dinner drinks. No wonder he didn't want to drive himself.

He looked back toward the revolving glass door, and a few seconds later, his date stepped through. He obviously hadn't been polite enough to wait for her. His date was very attractive. She was wearing an ivory blouse and a black pencil skirt, her long legs accented by impossible heels. Her brown hair framed her slender face with soft waves dropping past her shoulders. He winked at Finn after he watched his tight-skirted date slide into the back seat.

This is going to be a long night.

Finn closed the door and rounded the car to the driver's side.

"Where to?" She had an itinerary for the evening, but it was always a good idea to check with passengers in case plans had changed.

"Bones. We've got an early dinner reservation, and I don't want to be late." Geoff spoke to her from the back seat.

"No problem." She glanced in the rearview mirror. He slouched back with his arm around the woman, who rested a manicured hand on his thigh.

Bones was a pricey steak house with a clubby vibe. She'd been there once with Elaine. It was probably the most expensive steak Finn had ever eaten.

Traffic was moderate for a Friday night. But Buckhead was busy. Bars and restaurants would be packed based on the traffic winding along Piedmont Road from downtown. She deposited Geoff and his date a few minutes before seven and then drove around the block to look for a good spot to wait. She ended up finding a place in the parking lot of a nearby Men's Wearhouse, conveniently located next to a Caribou Coffee. She walked back to the car with her coffee and a scone. Sugar and caffeine would help get her through the next couple of hours, depending on how long dinner lasted. Geoff would text her when he was ready to be picked up. In the meantime, she had a little time to kill.

Her phone lit up with a text from her mom with a list of groceries to pick up on the way home later. She replied and then scrolled through the news feed on the screen while she sipped her Americano.

The audition lasted past six o'clock, which surprised Iris a little. She was on her way to the elevator when Eric Gilet, the director, stopped her.

"Iris, do you have a minute?"

"Sure." The elevator door swished closed behind her as she followed Eric back down the hallway.

She thought they were going back into the soundstage, but instead he opened a door on the other side of the hall and smiled as he waited for her to enter. The space looked like some sort of lounge similar to the waiting room she'd been in earlier. There was a mid century modern, stylishly uncomfortable looking sofa along one wall and a coffee table strewn with well-read magazines. Why did he want to speak to her alone?

"Your reading was good. I wanted a chance to talk to you a little about the part."

"Sure. Was there something I missed?"

Eric stood a little too close, and she took a step back.

"You and Camille have very good chemistry. That's part of what will make the show work."

"Yes, I really like the interplay between Jade and Cloe."

But it seemed like she and Eric were talking about different things.

"This character, Jade, she's very…sexual."

"If you're talking about the fact that she's bisexual I already spoke with the casting director about that element of the character. It won't be a problem."

"Great, well, I guess what I mean is that I was hoping to see even more sexual energy in the reading between you and Camille. I'm wondering if you could show me a little more of that now."

"I don't really understand what you're asking." Something about this entire encounter was beginning to make Iris uncomfortable. She glanced at the door.

"Before you leave, I thought you could show me a little more… talk through a few more lines with specific emphasis…letting your skills of seduction come through the part." He nonchalantly sidestepped so that he was standing between Iris and the door.

It was a highly unusual request, a ridiculous request. Was he making a pass? Iris was equally angered and unnerved.

"I'd prefer to do any additional acting on the soundstage."
Iris reached for the doorknob, but Eric leaned against it, resting his
weight against the door.

"If you work with me, I could make sure you own this role."

Her arm was still outstretched, her hand resting on the
doorknob. He placed his hand at the small of her back and drew her
closer. She immediately pressed both hands against his chest in an
attempt to push away from him. Now he had his other arm around
her and tried to kiss her.

"Eric, stop."

"You're an incredibly beautiful woman, Iris. I know when a
woman is attracted to me."

Delusional much?

"I said stop." She managed to wedge her elbow against his
chest, which kept her face just out of reach as he once again tried to
kiss her.

"I love the way your body feels so firm, so tight."

She kept shifting in his arms in an attempt to break his grip.
She pushed at his face, inadvertently scratching his cheek with her
fingernail.

"Fuck." He covered the scratch with his hand and glared at her.

He lost his focus for a moment and she broke free. The sudden
shift in position caused him to take his weight away from Iris's
escape route. In that instant, Camille opened the door.

"Oh—" Camille stopped in the doorway. "I'm sorry. Katherine
told me this room was free. I didn't mean to interrupt."

"You didn't interrupt." Iris's cheeks flamed, and she glared at
Eric as she reached for her purse that she'd dropped as she attempted
to deflect his advances. She swept past Camille into the hallway. Her
heart was pounding. She was completely embarrassed. She was sure
Camille would assume the worst of her.

She pushed the button for the elevator several times, impatient
for its arrival. She smoothed her hair and glanced over her shoulder
to make sure Eric wasn't going to try to intercept her again. Tears of
frustration and rage gathered along her lashes as she stepped onto
the elevator. She pivoted to touch the button for the lobby just in

time to see Eric standing in the hallway. His expression was dark as the doors closed.

Iris covered her face with her hands and tried to calm down.

Once in the lobby, she fumbled with the keys to the rental car. Her hands were shaking. She needed to get the hell out of this building and away from Eric Gilet. A wave of humid air swept past as she exited the air-conditioned lobby.

Now what?

Eric Gilet had turned out to be a complete dick. He'd been so smugly sure of his physical charms. If Camille hadn't opened the door how far would he have tried to take things? Had she done something to give him the impression she was interested? No, she was sure she hadn't. She'd been completely focused on Camille during the reading. Maybe that was what had gotten him so worked up. That thought made her angrier.

She hurried to her rental car and halted at the garage exit ramp to survey the street. She turned right to head downtown. She almost ran a red light a block from the garage. She slammed on the brakes just as a pedestrian stepped into the crosswalk.

"What the fuck?" he yelled and gestured with his hands.

Clearly, she was too rattled to drive. She scanned the street for somewhere to pull over.

The Peachtree Diner looked well lit and warmly inviting so she turned in.

CHAPTER FIVE

Finn eased the stretch limo over to the curb, just in front of the valet parking stand. Geoff and his date exited the restaurant as she pulled up. From Geoff's body language she knew right away he'd had too much to drink. Finn could also read the signs enough to know that Geoff's companion was ready for this date to be over. Good. Finn wasn't really in the mood for a long night anyway.

She held the door open as her two passengers slid into the back seat. Traffic along Peachtree was stop-and-go as they left the restaurant.

Muffled but agitated voices from the passenger compartment caught her attention. The car's interior had recessed lighting, just bright enough to see what was happening. There were bench seats along the sides of the stretch limo, with mini bar accessories on each end. Geoff and his date were at the far end of the passenger compartment. From what she could see, just glancing in the rearview mirror, he was trying his best to make it to second base, while his date put up defensive moves with her hands.

Finn gripped the steering wheel a bit tighter, rolling her knuckles forward as if she were making a fist. After a minute, Finn glanced into the rearview mirror again, and she didn't like what she saw. She'd never been in a situation quite like this. There had been times when guys had too much to drink and they got obnoxious, even women on bachelorette outings could get annoyingly rowdy, but this…this was different. It seemed like a line was being crossed, and she didn't feel right just watching it happen from the driver's seat.

She scrolled through scenarios in her head for what to do. Each would have consequences.

At any moment, Finn expected Geoff to ask her to raise the window that separated the passenger compartment from the driver's seat. Finn ran through repercussions in her head because she had no intention of honoring that request when he made it.

Movement captured her attention again as the young woman in the back seat attempted to deflect Geoff's advances, which were becoming more aggressive. Their voices were muffled, but it didn't take a genius to figure out that the woman did not want Geoff's hand between her legs. The woman's defensive moves were becoming more frantic and Geoff's more insistent.

"Hey! Driver! Close the window," Geoff shouted from the back seat.

"No! Geoff…I said stop!" The woman pushed against his forearm.

Finn heard the words clearly that time. She clenched her jaw, checked traffic quickly, and pulled over. She took a deep breath as she strode around the car to the rear passenger door. Geoff was drunk enough that she figured he hadn't even noticed the car had stopped. He seemed genuinely surprised when she hauled him from the back seat by his jacket collar.

"What the fu—"

Finn's fist answered his unfinished question.

"Fucking hell." He writhed at her feet, cradling his bloody nose.

When he made a drunken attempt to get up she punched him in the nose again. She was fairly sure she'd broken it that time. She wrung her hand in the air to ease the pain of her stinging knuckles and silently thanked her brother for all those boxing lessons so long ago. Geoff moaned and rolled onto his side, pulling his knees up toward his chest like an oversized baby.

The woman, her blouse and skirt slightly askew, watched with wide eyes through the open door from the back seat. Finn stepped over Geoff and leaned partway into the car. She handed the woman a handkerchief from her jacket pocket before she closed the door. She drove away, leaving him in a heap on the sidewalk.

"I need a cup of coffee. How about you?" Finn glanced up at the mirror. It was late, but she knew of an all-night diner not too far away.

The woman nodded from the back seat of the limo as she dabbed at tears with Finn's linen handkerchief.

❖

This was definitely not Iris's night. First, Eric's unwanted and aggressive advances, then some random guy took a seat at the counter and kept trying to engage her in conversation. She was upset and in no mood to make small talk with a flirtatious stranger.

After a few minutes in the car, still rattled from her encounter with Eric, she'd decided food was what she needed. Food and a chance to regroup.

Yes, coffee and food were what she needed.

A near-death experience and a handsy director and now an overly friendly stranger. She was seriously beginning to dislike Atlanta.

"What can I get you, hon?" A waitress, probably in her thirties, with a coffee pot in one hand leaned against the counter in front of where Iris was sitting.

"Can I get a coffee?" It was still early on the West Coast; she knew she wouldn't be going to sleep any time soon.

"Here's a menu." She handed Iris a shiny tri-folded menu with one hand and filled a mug with the other. "You look familiar."

"Do I?" Iris knew she didn't know this woman, but she didn't want to be rude.

"Did you come in here last week with a little boot on and one of those wheelie things?"

"Excuse me?"

"You know, the wheelie cart they give you when you've got a broken foot." The waitress braced her hand on her hip and studied Iris.

"It wasn't me. Maybe you've confused me with someone else."

This happened sometimes. People thought they recognized Iris, but more than likely they'd seen her on TV. She wasn't going to reveal that she'd done TV shows and commercials. That sort of sharing led to more sharing and conversation, which she was definitely not in the mood for. She was barely keeping it together and had no intention of bursting into tears, in a diner, in front of the waitress.

Beside her, thankfully, the overly chatty stranger tossed some bills on the counter and left. Iris's shoulders began to relax a little.

"I remember now." The waitress was back, her face brightened. "You were at karaoke the other night. You sang that Pat Benatar song." She set a small porcelain cow filled with cream in front of Iris. "You were good too." She smiled and nodded as she walked away.

Iris never did karaoke, but she wasn't in the mood to argue. She added cream to her coffee and scanned the menu. She was angry. She'd wanted the part on this show so badly. She'd felt so good about her work this afternoon. But now there was no way she could take the job even if they offered it.

Could she?

No.

Even if they offered it to her, Eric would be impossible to work with now. He'd either come on to her again or he'd make her life miserable for turning him down. And who knows what Camille thought she'd stumbled into. Did Camille think Iris had a thing going with Eric? That would be equally bad. The cast would think she had some favored position with the director. They would assume she only got the part because she'd slept with Eric before the show even got off the ground.

The whole situation was a disaster.

Not only did she want this part, but financially, she needed it.

She'd been lucky enough to land a national commercial that aired during the Super Bowl. That one job paid enough to keep her afloat for several months. It made her bank account solvent but definitely did *not* make her feel artistically successful. She needed to find steady work soon or she should seriously reconsider her career. The thought of moving back home, a failure at twenty-nine, was not high on her list of future plans. Thoughts swirled in her head as she waited for the waitress to return.

❖

Finn parked the limo behind the Peachtree Diner, near the dumpsters, so that she wouldn't take up three spaces out front. She checked her phone, expecting any moment to get a text message from her boss saying she was fired. Maybe Geoff was too drunk or too embarrassed to call it in. At any rate, she hadn't gotten the ax yet, but she knew it was going to fall soon.

"We can get something and then I'll drive you home." Finn opened the door. "I'm Finn, by the way."

"Thank you." She accepted Finn's hand as she slid out of the back seat. "I'm Ashley."

Finn held the door of the diner for Ashley. A waitress at the counter motioned for them to take a seat. Finn angled toward a booth near the door.

"Two coffees." Finn held up two fingers.

A moment later, they were sipping coffee and sharing a slice of apple pie. Well, mostly Finn was eating the pie, but she'd offered to share it with Ashley.

"Thank you for what you did." Ashley sniffed and dabbed at a tear with her napkin. "I'm sure you think I'm a fool for going out with him."

"We've all made bad decisions about beautiful people." Finn forked another healthy bite of pie from the center of the table.

"He is good-looking, but when he drinks, he's such a..."

The waterworks were starting again. Ashley was just a wee bit tipsy, and it was probably making her more emotional. Finn had done her best to cheer Ashley up, but nothing was working. It wasn't like Ashley was her problem anyway. She'd simply rescued Ashley from a jerk, and as soon as she finished this pie she'd drive her home and that would be the end of it.

Ashley was crying for real now. Finn wasn't great with big emotional displays, especially in public and especially when they weren't her fault. She was an innocent bystander.

A couple seated at a nearby table turned and scowled at Finn like angry parents, as if whatever was wrong was all her doing. She smiled thinly around her mouthful of sweet apple pie. She could guess what they were thinking. How could she eat at a time like this, seated across from a woman crying her eyes out?

And then some absolutely gorgeous blonde seated at the counter rotated and glared at her too. Great. This whole scene was beginning to turn ugly and the pie wasn't even that good.

"Hey, Ashley…do me a favor and stop crying."

Ashley sobbed louder.

Iris signed the receipt for her Cobb salad and tried to ignore the scene playing out behind her. But the poor woman was obviously in distress, and her date seemed as if she couldn't care less. The woman with long hair had obviously been crying before they got to the diner; her mascara had seeped all under her eyes. She looked like a sad debutante who'd been caught in a rainstorm. Her companion was very attractive in her own way, but not feminine at all. Iris would have described her as androgynous leaning toward butch. She was wearing a gray suit with a dress shirt. She had tousled short dark hair and an air of casual self-confidence, bordering on cockiness.

The butch woman's demeanor reminded Iris a little of her ex, Kent.

She was immediately annoyed.

No, furious was more accurate.

Why were women always put in positions like this? Why did people think they could just take advantage of women without consequence? Why had no one come to her defense? Several other patrons had noticed this woman's distress and no one had taken action. Well, she'd seen enough.

Iris strode across the room toward the door, weaving past a few empty tables. Every aggravated, agitated cell in her body began to vibrate as if she might explode. The indifferent, clueless expression on the butch woman's face was like a match to a fuse. When she neared the booth where the two women were sitting, the dark-haired woman in the suit looked up as if she were about to say something. In that instant, on impulse, Iris picked up the glass of water in front of the woman and threw it in her face. She made a quick exit, not waiting for the fallout.

Ashley abruptly stopped crying, sniffed, and regarded Finn with wide eyes.

"Do you know her?"

"No, I've never seen her before in my life." Finn wiped her face with a handful of napkins and then dabbed at her soaked shirt.

"She does a really good Pat Benatar." The waitress held a towel out to Finn, as if getting dowsed with water by an angry stranger was a completely normal occurrence. "Can I get ya'll anything else? Maybe a little more water?"

"No, thank you, just the check." Finn scowled at the waitress.

Was everyone out to ruin her night? She was just trying to do her job, do the right thing, and drive home. Now, she was probably going to get fired and some total stranger had just thrown a drink in her face. What else could go wrong? Probably best not to ask that question.

CHAPTER SIX

Iris fumbled with the key fob for the rental car. She was so upset about everything. Her frustration had spilled over, and she couldn't help throwing water in that smug woman's face. She'd never done anything like that in her life. She backed out and eased into traffic, taking deep breaths in the hopes that the adrenaline in her system would ease. She'd give anything to be able to go back in time. Now that she'd had some time to think, there were a million things she wished she'd thought to say to Eric. But all of those things would likely remain unsaid. She squeezed the steering wheel until her knuckles turned white, then she exhaled slowly.

While she ate she'd decided not to go to the pre-arranged hotel. She didn't want to be anywhere that Eric could easily find her. The production company had booked her room for two nights. When she'd searched on her phone for hotels, a ton of options had come up in the metro area, most part of big hotel chains. She'd headed in the general direction of the first few she'd found, but there'd obviously been a wreck or something. All lanes on Piedmont Avenue were completely stopped, red taillights blazed ahead as far as Iris could see.

Forget this. She wasn't going to waste any more time sitting in traffic.

She managed to do a six-point turn and then a U-turn to head in the opposite direction.

If she was going to be stuck here for a couple of days she might as well get out of the city a little. She pulled off into the oval glare of the nearest convenience store and searched for an alternative place to stay. She expanded her hotel search and located what looked like a charming vintage place just off the highway about forty-five minutes away. And the best part was that there was no red on this route, all green, the traffic looked clear.

She hit start for the directions. The destination was almost an hour away. Maybe by the time she arrived she'd be calm enough to get some sleep.

The farther she drove from the northern suburbs the more traffic thinned. It had been a long time since she'd been in a place this dark. LA extended forever, into the desert even. Only at the coast could you escape some of the electric glow of the city and then only if you faced the dark Pacific.

When she'd first moved there from New York City she'd loved that there was always something to do. The constant parties made the adjustment to the West Coast more bearable, less lonely. All the social noise was a distraction from loneliness but not a cure. In the past year, the shallowness of Hollywood had begun to wear on her, especially since her breakup with Kent.

Her roommate, Maggie, was her closest friend in California. She wanted to call Maggie and relay the encounter with Eric, but it was earlier on the West Coast and she knew Maggie was still at work. She'd call once she got settled for the night, and hopefully Maggie would make her feel less crazy about everything.

She checked her phone. Twenty more minutes to her destination. The highway had narrowed to two lanes and was now winding through a more rural area, dotted with modest frame houses set far from the road, small squares of light from the windows poked holes in the dark. Iris was reminded of summers spent with her grandparents in Connecticut. She smiled for the first time since leaving the soundstage.

Finn was happy to put the night behind her. She'd dropped Ashley in Midtown, and there was so much traffic, due to a wreck, that it was late by the time she made it back to her cabin. The lights were off in the main house, and at least one spot had been rented in her absence. A car with Ohio plates was parked in front of the cabin next to hers. They probably underestimated how long it would take to reach Florida. That seemed to be the only reason anyone from Ohio ever did a layover in rural Georgia.

Damn.

With everything that had happened she'd forgotten to pick up the groceries her mom had asked for. She'd turned her phone off because she knew what was coming from her boss and didn't really want to deal with it after the evening she'd had, getting a drink thrown in her face was just icing on the cake.

What the hell was up with that woman anyway?

Finn wracked her brain for a clue but had none. She was certain she'd never met the woman before. She'd have remembered her for sure. She was gorgeous...like, supermodel gorgeous. And then she fled the diner before Finn even had a chance to find out what she'd done to piss her off.

Whatever.

She'd add that to the ever-lengthening list of *things that made no sense.* The world was full of them, and it did no good to spend too much brain power trying to sort them out. Finn was okay with not knowing everything. In fact, she was happily in the dark about many things. She liked to keep her life simple and avoid complications whenever possible.

She tossed her keys on the table near the tiny kitchenette area, along with her phone. The dark phone screen was what reminded her she'd forgotten her mother's grocery request. She hung her jacket over a chair and scanned the mini fridge for something to drink. She never drank while driving and now felt that she needed something to dull the edge of all the caffeine she'd consumed. She rubbed the knuckles of her hand as she leaned into the fridge. Finn hoped Geoff's face was as sore as her hand.

Three beers lurked behind a loaf of bread and a half-empty jar of peanut butter. She popped the cap off one of the beers and took a long swig. As she took another long pull on the microbrew, she tugged her shirttail free and kicked off her shoes. The day had been far too long.

She was walking into the bedroom, but stopped mid stride when she heard a rapid knock at the door. That was odd. It was late.

Finn opened the door and almost spewed the mouthful of beer when she saw who was standing on the doorstep. She fought the urge and swallowed with a loud gulp instead. The woman who'd tossed the drink in her face looked up from the stoop, her eyes blinking into the glare of the porch light.

"Did you come to apologize?" Finn leaned her shoulder against the doorframe and took another sip of her beer. She tried to feign nonchalance.

Fate, it seemed, had a sense of humor.

"I…oh…what…how are you here?" The woman was as surprised to see Finn as Finn had been to see her. She was wearing a robe over something; Finn couldn't quite see the details. She hugged herself and glanced nervously over her shoulder. "I heard something."

"So the answer is no then?"

"What?"

God, she was beautiful. Long blond hair cascaded around her face. Toned, shapely legs extended below the hem of the robe that only reached mid thigh. She was sexy and elegant at the same time. There was an openness, an innocence in her expression that Finn would have described as somewhere on the verge between girlhood and womanhood.

"As in, no, you're not here to apologize." Finn didn't really need an apology. She was mostly just happy to get a chance to solve the mystery of who this woman was.

"I'm sorry I bothered you. This was all a bad idea." The woman turned to leave.

"Hey, I'm Finn, by the way. Taylor Finn." She was hoping to at least get the woman's name before she disappeared again.

"I'm Iris." Iris glanced back toward the dark woods surrounding the small row of rustic cabins. "Did you hear that?" She'd been about to leave but now took a few steps closer to where Finn was standing. The doorway cast an oasis of light against the darkness.

Finn decided, in addition to being gorgeous in the empirical sense of the word, Iris also had a particular and mysterious charm. She knew she was staring, despite her efforts not to.

"There...there's the sound again." Iris jumped.

That time Finn heard it too. A scuffle and then a clanking sound. Something was probably rummaging in the trash cans behind Iris's cabin. Finn slipped on her shoes and reached for the flashlight that hung just inside the door.

"Come on. Let's take a look." Finn stepped past Iris.

"Are you sure? What if it's a bear?" Iris took a few tentative steps. She was barefoot. She must have been in bed when she'd walked over to Finn's cabin.

"If it's a bear we'll run for it."

"Is that a joke? I thought you were never supposed to run from a bear."

"Don't worry, I'm sure it's not a bear." Finn squinted into the dark as she swung the flashlight in an arc at the edge of the woods. *I hope.*

It was easy to act all chivalrous and butch in the face of a curious raccoon looking for a late night garbage snack. But she didn't particularly want to deal with a black bear. They were mostly harmless but could be cantankerous under the right circumstances.

Finn eased closer to Iris's cabin. There was a good bit of tree debris on the ground so it was almost impossible to step without making crackling noises.

"Be careful." Finn pointed down. "You're barefoot."

Iris was gingerly trying to follow Finn. She'd been spooked but obviously not so scared that she didn't want to see for herself what was making all the noise. Brave and beautiful, two of Finn's favorite qualities.

The light from Finn's flashlight landed on two glassy eyes surrounded by black fur. It was a bear. She wasn't about to get between this fellow and whatever he'd found in the trash.

"Oh, shit." She took a step back and bumped into Iris.

"What? What do you see?"

"It's a black bear." Finn tried not to alarm Iris. "Let's move away, back up—"

She turned and attempted to shoo Iris toward her cabin.

"Ow! Ow!" Iris urgently whispered as she lifted her foot. Pain was evident on her face. "I stepped on something." She hopped on one foot, holding the other.

The bear was curious now. He tipped the whole trash can over. It fell against the can next to it in a clanging, clattering, chain reaction of falling garbage.

"Hold this." Finn handed Iris the flashlight.

"What...what are you doing?"

"How much do you weigh?" Finn slipped one arm under Iris's knees and lifted her up.

"Never ask a woman that question, even in an emergency situation."

"Noted." It had been a rhetorical question anyway. Iris was petite and looked as if she weighed a hundred pounds soaking wet. Finn could bench press that on a bad day.

Iris wrapped her arm around Finn's neck as they made haste back to her cabin. The door was still open. She slipped sideways through the door and kicked it closed with her foot. She angled toward the small sofa in the sitting area and set Iris down.

"Sorry, I just...I didn't mean to assume..." She realized she'd sort of acted on instinct and now she'd delivered Iris, spooked and barely dressed, to her secluded cabin in the woods.

"It's okay." Iris seemed a bit shaken.

"Here, let me see your foot." Finn knelt in front of her and gently explored with her fingertips.

CHAPTER SEVEN

Iris felt as if she'd fallen into some strange fairy tale. A maiden in distress saved by a dark-haired chivalrous stranger. Finn was kneeling in front of her, gently probing her injured foot.

"I think this is what got you." Finn held up a small sharp shard of a leaf. It looked like a broken dead leaf off a holly bush.

"Thank you." When Finn brushed her fingers along the edge of her foot, Iris shivered.

"Are you cold? I could get you a blanket."

"No, I'm fine." Iris swallowed. Her throat felt dry. "Could I possibly have some water?"

"Sure." Finn got to her feet and returned with a glass of water, but then hesitated. "Wait, can I trust you with this?"

"I promise only to drink it."

Finn smiled as she handed over the glass.

Iris studied her in the warm glow from a nearby lamp. Finn seemed so real, in a very perfect, unreal sort of way. She was wearing dark, slim-fit dress pants and a tailored light blue shirt, untucked, cuffed to her elbows. Her skin was golden brown, probably from time in the sun, and when she looked up, her eyes were most definitely blue. Finn's eyes were stop-you-in-your-tracks bright blue. A shade so intense that if she'd seen Finn on film she'd have assumed they only looked that way onscreen because of some post-production magic. The intensity of Finn's direct eye contact stirred her insides, unsettled her, as if something unexpected and carnal might happen at any moment if she stayed too long.

"Thank you." She took the glass from Finn and couldn't help feeling just a little twinge in her stomach from Finn's direct eye contact. She probably *should* apologize.

While Iris sipped, Finn slid a kitchen chair over and sat down across from her.

"Was that your girlfriend? The woman you were with at the diner?" Iris regretted blurting out the question almost immediately, but she was dying to know. Fate had obviously thrown them together for a reason. Now she had to find out why.

"Ashley? No." Finn shook her head as she reached for her unfinished beer and then glanced at Iris. "Would you prefer a beer?"

"I'm fine with water, thanks." She waited for Finn to fill in a few more blanks.

"I drive for a limo service, and Ashley was half my fare for tonight."

"What happened to the other half?"

"I left him with a bloody nose on the sidewalk for being a dick."

"So that's why Ashley was crying?"

"Yeah, when her boyfriend drinks he apparently becomes a handsy asshole. I felt compelled to eject him from the car." Finn had a far-off look in her eyes as she sipped her beer.

Iris found herself drawn to the small bit of smooth skin exposed by her open collar.

"I'm sorry I threw that drink in your face." She was aware she was in a very short nightgown and robe. She tugged it closed and angled her knees to the side. "I had a very bad day and…and I jumped to conclusions when I saw her crying. I'm sorry."

"Apology accepted. I'm sure from where you were sitting things looked different."

"Yes, but I still shouldn't have done that. I honestly don't know what came over me." Iris swept her fingers through her hair and looked away, taking in the room.

"So, you had a bad day too?" Finn's question was soft, kind.

"Yes. The worst."

"Would it help to talk about it?"

For some reason, Iris didn't really want to talk about what had happened with Finn.

"Not really."

"I'm a good listener. And besides, you don't want to go back to your cabin until our bear friend leaves, right?"

Iris's heart rate spiked. She'd been so distracted by Finn that she'd forgotten about the bear outside her cabin.

"Maybe I will take that beer after all."

"You've got it." Finn rummaged in the mini-fridge and returned with a beer for each of them. "Drink it slow. These are my last two." Finn smiled as she sipped. "I wasn't expecting company."

"Do you live here?" Iris realized there was actual food on the counter in the kitchen, and the rustic space had a definite lived in vibe.

"Yes, for now. It's kind of a temporary thing that's turned out to be, well, not so temporary." Finn looked around the room and then back at Iris. "My folks own this place so I've been renting this cabin for a little more than a year."

"It's cute."

"Speaking of this place...how is it you ended up here? Don't take this the wrong way, but you don't really seem like the woodsy type."

Iris laughed.

"I mean, maybe you're the best sort of woodsy type and I have no idea what I'm talking about." Finn fidgeted in her chair.

"No, you're not completely off base. It's been a long time since I spent any time in the woods. I didn't feel like staying in the city. I wanted to get away, and Hideaway Haven came up in my search. I just took a chance that this would be a nice place. The reviews online were all really good."

"So, Iris...I didn't get your last name."

"Fleming."

"Iris Fleming, what brings you to my neck of the woods, pun intended." Finn grinned.

Finn was definitely flirtatious, but in a friendly, non-aggressive way. Iris felt at ease in Finn's company and they'd only just met.

Finn was so *not* from the Hollywood scene. Her openness, her realness was refreshing. She wasn't trying to impress Iris or make herself seem more than she was. Finn wasn't trying to sell herself. Iris decided she liked Finn. She also found her good looks and easy confidence attractive. When Iris had first seen Finn at the diner she'd compared her to Kent, but she realized after a few minutes of conversation that Finn was nothing like Kent.

"What's funny?"

"Why do you ask?"

"You were smiling." Finn cocked her head and regarded Iris with curiosity.

"Oh, nothing. In answer to your original question, I was in Atlanta to audition for a part in a new series."

"You're an actor?"

"Yes." Finn obviously didn't recognize her. Iris felt more at ease.

"That's great. Did you get the part?"

"I don't know, and even if I did I'm not sure I'll take it."

"I'm sensing this is all part of your very bad day?"

"Yes. The director is an ass. I'm not sure I can work with him."

"That's too bad."

"Yeah, it is. I really wanted to be part of the series." Iris smiled thinly and sighed. "Enough about me, tell me more about you. You drive a limo? Out here in the woods?"

Finn smiled broadly, and the cutest dimples appeared on each cheek.

"I can see how that might look, but actually all my clients are in the metro area. I just don't care to live in the city. Plus, I was trying to save money to get to LA."

"Really? Why?" She had a hard time picturing Finn there.

"Well, I really want to be a stunt driver, and the best schools for stunt driving are in LA."

"My ex-boyfriend was an actor and a stunt driver."

It was almost as if Iris said the word in slow motion as Finn focused on her lips. The B word, ex-boyfriend echoed inside Finn's head. She'd had the distinct feeling that Iris was attracted to her.

Maybe she was, despite the boyfriend thing. Finn usually had pretty good instincts about when a woman found her attractive.

"A stunt driver, really?"

"Kent Kenny."

"You dated Kent Kenny?" Finn sat forward in her chair. Kent wasn't just any actor. He was a damn good driver and did almost all of his own stunts, or so she'd read. If someone was going to have a boyfriend he'd be a good one to have. What were the odds? This was definitely some weird twist of fate.

"You know him?"

"Anyone who follows stunt driving in movies knows who he is. He's good."

"And he knows it." There was a hint of frustration in Iris's statement. She glanced up at Finn. "Sorry, not your fault, but I'm not a fan of stunt drivers."

"Unless they save you from a bear." Finn tried to lighten the mood.

"Maybe."

There was obviously more to this story.

Finn had seen photos of Kent. He was super good-looking. He probably could have any woman he went after. Iris was definitely his equal in the looks department. She didn't know Iris, but a knot settled in her stomach that someone, even Kent, would treat her badly. Was every guy an asshole? Today it seemed they'd had more than their share of rich party boys gone wrong.

"Do you think he's still out there?"

"Who?" Finn had been lost in thought.

"The bear?"

"Oh, yeah, the bear." Finn had been conspiring some way to win her over, but Iris probably just wanted to get back to her own cabin and go back to sleep. Unfortunately, now Finn was wide-awake, despite the lateness of the hour.

Finn opened the door and stepped into the dark with the flashlight. She didn't have to take too many steps to realize the bear was still foraging. His back was toward her as his entire head was inside an overturned trash can. She was definitely going to revisit the subject of bear-safe trash bins with her father.

She trotted back to the doorway where Iris waited, hugging herself.

"Is he still there?"

"Yep." Finn was determined to cheer Iris up. "Maybe we should just plan to hang out here for a while. Want to watch a movie or something?" Getting her mind on something else would probably help Iris feel better.

"You don't have a TV." Iris scanned the room.

"But I have a laptop. And I've got Netflix." Finn smiled.

Finn motioned with her thumb toward the bedroom, as if she were trying to hitch a ride.

"Come on, we can lounge in here and watch something until Mr. Bear finds somewhere else to forage." The look on Iris's face told her she'd gone one step too far. "Hey, I didn't mean anything by that."

Iris looked at her with piercing brown eyes that shot right through her.

"I just meant the bed is easier for lounging. That sofa is pretty small. And uncomfortable."

"Are you sure I'm not keeping you from sleep…or something else."

"No, seriously. I never have company here." She realized she was possibly revealing more than she'd meant to. "I mean, it's nice to have company."

"What? Do you have trouble coaxing women back to your cabin in the dark woods?"

"Um, well…" The truth was she didn't bring women to her place because she was next door to her very nosy and opinionated mother. That was just plain asking for trouble in all kinds of ways that Finn had no intention of dealing with.

"Sorry, I didn't mean to give you a hard time."

"You didn't, really." Finn waved her off. Her usual charms seemed to have no effect on Iris. It didn't matter. Why was she trying so hard? Because Iris was beautiful? Finn had been with beautiful women before, and they were a handful—needy, self-involved, high-maintenance.

Finn tamped down her enthusiasm. She was simply trying to help Iris out, not make a move. She waited to see which way the wind was going to blow, but she wasn't going to beg her to stay over. Especially when she knew this had nowhere to go.

"Well, maybe I will stay for a little while. If you're sure you don't mind."

"I wouldn't have offered otherwise."

Iris followed her to the bedroom. Finn pulled the covers back on one side.

"Here, you can get under. You must be cold. And I'll sit on top."

"Such a gentleman." Iris joked as she slid under the covers.

"I try." Although she felt like it was probably all going to waste on a straight girl.

Finn balanced her laptop with one hand and logged in with the other before handing it to Iris.

"Pick whatever looks good. I'll see if I have some chips or something to snack on. And how's your beer?" Finn was in full *I don't care* mode now.

"I still have some left, thanks." Iris didn't seem to notice.

Finn stepped into the kitchen. Why was she suddenly in a bad mood? There was an exceptionally attractive woman in her bed right now. How had such a bad night taken such a spectacularly good turn? Probably best not to ask the fates too many questions for fear they actually might answer. She returned with a bowl of chips along with what was left of her drink. She kicked off her shoes and sat next to Iris, her legs stretched out in front of her. She was determined to enjoy the view, regardless of the evening's outcome.

"What'd you find?" Finn dipped her head toward the screen.

"How do you feel about watching a classic?"

"Whatever you want." Finn actually meant it. She'd have a hard time watching the movie with Iris next to her anyway.

"A classic it is then." Iris hit play and settled the laptop between them. "Doris Day always cheers me up."

Iris smiled as she reached for a few chips. One of those smiles that made Finn's stomach somersault. She'd do her best to look at the screen and not Iris, but that was going to be difficult. Who was she kidding? She did care, at least a little.

❖

Finn found it strange to be in bed with a woman she hadn't even kissed. Well, not really *in bed* in the traditional sense of that phrase, but still. An hour into the movie, she'd sensed Iris settle, and then after a little while she was asleep. Finn let the movie run on her laptop even though she'd long since stopped watching it. She rolled onto her side, propped on her elbow, and studied Iris.

So serene. The room was dark except for the glow of the screen. It cast Iris's delicate features in subtle highlights. Wow, Iris was so beautiful.

Was it bad form not to wake Iris? She was sure the bear had moved along by now. Finn considered it for a moment and decided she wouldn't disturb her. Iris had mentioned that she'd had a rough day, so Finn decided to let her sleep.

Sleep was tempting Finn as well. She closed the laptop softly and rolled onto her back, leaving the computer on top of the blanket in the center of the bed. She wasn't sure how long she lay in the dark contemplating the ceiling when sleep finally found her.

CHAPTER EIGHT

Iris woke with a jolt. Where was she? She blinked, her chest rose and fell rapidly making the crisp sheet rustle. Oh, right, the cabin. The room wasn't completely dark. A pink hue edged in through the partially open drapes. She moved her hand beneath the covers and bumped the corner of something hard. Finn's laptop was on top of the blanket between them. She must have fallen asleep watching the movie.

The laptop was closed, so at some point, Finn must have closed it and decided not to wake her. She turned her head just enough to see that Finn was asleep, still fully clothed.

Iris rubbed her eyes and tried to figure out what time it was. She didn't relish the thought of traipsing from Finn's cabin to hers in her nightgown and robe. She slowly sat up and rotated her feet over the side of the bed, careful not to wake Finn.

Iris stood at the foot of the bed for a moment. What was the protocol in a situation like this? It hadn't been a date, but somehow it felt a little like one. And surely Finn had rescued her from a fearful, fitful night had she been left to wait out the bear in her own cabin. Maybe she should leave a note. She looked around the bedroom but didn't find anything readily available to write on, and sifting through a stranger's dresser drawers seemed like a bad idea.

Finn was sleeping soundly. Iris stepped nearer and looked down at Finn's relaxed features. She looked so innocent. All of the swagger from the previous night was missing from her face. In sleep, Finn's guard was down and Iris thought she was adorable. Sexy even. There was an alluring serenity in her expression that made Iris want to reach over and tenderly stroke Finn's face.

Instead, Iris moved the laptop to the dresser and pulled the unoccupied blanket from her side of the bed over to cover Finn. Then she quietly let herself out into the crisp just-now-dawn air. Dew clung to every leaf. Large droplets pelted her from the broad leaves overhead as she scurried to her cabin. This time she was careful to avoid the ground near the holly bush as she passed.

It was still very early so as soon as she was inside, Iris tossed her robe onto a chair and burrowed under the covers in her own bed. She'd sleep a couple more hours, find coffee, and figure out what was next. After all, today was her birthday.

Finn stretched, yawned, and then remembered Iris was next to her. A fleeting rush of excitement evaporated the instant she realized Iris was gone. Like discovering on Christmas morning that none of the presents under the tree were yours. Not that that had ever happened to Finn, but she was pretty sure the disappointment as a result of Iris's absence was what it would feel like.

She rubbed her eyes and then checked her phone on the nightstand. It was only eight thirty, not so late that her mother would give her grief for sleeping in. She sat up so that she could look out the bedroom window. Iris's rental was still parked in front of the cabin next door. Finn launched out of bed and hustled through an accelerated version of her usual morning ritual of showering and getting dressed. She checked out the window for Iris's car once more as she ran her fingers through her hair with molding paste to calm it down and arrange it into some semblance of orderly chaos.

Luckily, her mother was nowhere in sight when Finn bounded into the kitchen and retrieved two cups of coffee. Hmm, cream or no cream? Sugar? She pondered these questions. They'd shared a bed, in the most platonic way possible, but she had no idea how Iris preferred her coffee.

Finn opted for a small tray and loaded it with cream, sugar, spoons, and two of her mother's buttered biscuits from the stove for good measure. Might as well bring a small jar of strawberry preserves. What good were biscuits without jam? Cabin two was about to get room service.

Nothing had happened last night, but Finn's ego couldn't quite let the idea of it go. There was something about Iris that had captured her attention in a big way. She hoped coffee delivery turned out to be a welcomed gesture. She should be thinking about how she'd just gotten herself fired and how she needed to be looking for another job, but Iris was a much more pleasant distraction.

It was nine o'clock now. Was that a reasonable time to deliver coffee? Finn's courage waned for an instant, her hand hovered, then she swallowed and knocked. She didn't knock very loudly. If Iris was still in bed she could easily keep sleeping.

Finn held onto the tray with both hands and shifted her weight nervously from foot to foot. Should she knock again? She glanced over her shoulder as a car passed along the road. When she turned back, Iris was standing in the open door. She was pressing her damp hair with a towel; she'd obviously just showered. Iris smiled and Finn's nervousness puddled around her feet and then rose again and settled in her stomach.

"Hi." Iris was wearing the short, sheer robe from the night before. It wasn't much of a robe, more of a robe-like suggestion.

"Hey." Finn raised the tray in Iris's direction. "I thought you might like some coffee."

"I had no idea this cabin came with room service." Iris was teasing. "Or did you receive my psychic wave from next door?"

"I just wanted to see you...I mean, you know, before you left." Finn hadn't meant to blurt out the truth.

"I'm glad."

"You're glad?"

"Yes, why wouldn't I be?" Iris continued to squeeze lengths of her hair with the towel, tilting her head for a better angle. "I didn't want to wake you earlier, but I considered it, so that I could thank you for last night."

Oh, so Iris only wanted to say thank you. Well, that was still an improvement from having a glass of water thrown in your face.

"You can take the tray if you like." Finn didn't want to assume she was getting invited in.

"But there are two cups?"

"I was..." She didn't really know what to say. Barging over with coffee for a near stranger first thing in the morning now seemed a bit presumptuous.

"Come in." Iris stepped aside to make room for Finn. "It'll just take me a minute to get dressed. Please, come in."

As Finn slid past, she got the most delicious scent of Iris— her hair, her skin, whatever she was wearing, Finn loved it. Some yummy mixture of coconut and vanilla and sunshine, yeah, sunshine.

Finn sat at the table in the kitchenette area and stirred cream into her coffee. She heard the blow dryer in the other room. After a few minutes, Iris joined her. She'd changed into shorts and a distressed V-neck T-shirt that was worn thin and soft and drew Finn's attention to every curve. She struggled to return her gaze to Iris's face.

"I think that cream has been adequately stirred." Iris smiled as she sat down.

She was right. Finn had been so distracted she'd stirred her coffee at least a thousand strokes. She cleared her throat and set the spoon on the tray.

Iris thought Finn was charming this morning. She was wearing faded jeans, worn through in a few strategic spots, and a charcoal T-shirt that snuggly hugged her biceps and broad shoulders. The shirt was tucked in only at the front, showing just a hint of a scuffed, wide black leather belt, and she was wearing driving mocs without socks. Her long legs had been stretched out, but she readjusted when Iris sat down, as if she was assuming some stance of casual attention.

"So, big plans for today?" Finn was fishing.

"I don't need to return my rental car until tomorrow." She wasn't sure she should go into all the gory details about her flight and how she'd jokingly thought of driving back to California. "I'm just planning to relax today and enjoy my birthday." She air-toasted with her coffee in Finn's direction.

"What?" Finn brightened. "Today is your birthday?"

"Yes, the big three-oh." Iris took a bite of biscuit with the jam. "Oh, wow, this is delicious. Are these homemade?"

"Yeah, my mom is famous for her biscuits and her fried chicken. But you're deflecting. It's your birthday. We should do something." Finn hesitated. "I mean, we could do something if you want. I could show you around. We could go to the lake or go for a drive."

"Don't you have plans?"

"Maybe you haven't heard, but I'm recently between jobs, plus, it's Saturday."

"If you're up for playing tour guide, then I happily accept." Iris's phone chimed in the other room. "Sorry, let me get that. It's probably my mom."

She returned to the kitchen as she swiped the screen.

"It's a birthday text from my mom. I'll call her later." Her mother was in New York. She'd probably been waiting so as not to send Iris a message too early. She'd probably forgotten Iris was in Atlanta for work and not in California. Her mother sometimes lost track of details.

Finn finished the last bite of her biscuit.

"So, there's a lake nearby?" Iris held her coffee in both hands and rested her elbows on the table. She sipped the coffee and regarded Finn across the rim of her mug.

"It's not a large lake, but it's very pretty. It's spring fed so the water is fairly cold year-round, but there are canoes and trails to hike."

"That sounds like fun."

"We could pick up some food at Turner's Corner and have lunch at the lake."

"Turner's Corner?"

"It's the only place close by that passes for a grocery."

Finn was energized by her own plan and Iris couldn't help smiling. Sometimes not having a plan inspired the best plans. A spontaneous picnic sounded like the perfect way to spend her birthday. No expectations, no pressure.

"Am I dressed okay for a day at the lake?"

"You're perfect…I mean, yes, what you're wearing is great." Finn blushed and averted her eyes. She started to reassemble the empty coffee mugs onto the tray. "Um, I'll change into shorts and come back in say…a half hour?"

"Sounds good." She'd give her mom a quick call while she waited.

Finn picked up the tray and headed toward the door. Iris was a few steps behind. Finn attempted to balance the tray with one hand so that she could open the door, but in her haste didn't get the angle quite right. Iris reached her just in time to catch one of the empty mugs as it tumbled, but not the small serving bowl of strawberry preserves. Finn grabbed for it at the same time Iris did. They bumped into each other which caused Finn to flip the entire tray. Everything hit the hardwood floor with a clatter, spraying both of them with a light splattering of strawberry goo.

"Oh, shit." Finn still held the empty tray.

Iris stared down at the mess, then back at Finn. She started to laugh, then Finn started to laugh.

"I'm thinking your next job should *not* involve table service." Iris looked down at her legs speckled with bits of strawberry.

"I'm so sorry." Finn started to swipe at the sweet goo on Iris's thigh and then realized what she was doing. "Um…sorry about that too."

"It's okay, really." Heat rose to her cheeks, inexplicably. Finn's light touch and the tingling sensation across her skin surprised her more than the fumbled tray of dishware and jam.

"I'll clean this mess up." Finn hurried to the kitchen for a towel.

"Hey, I can do this." Iris needed a moment to collect herself. "You go change and I'll handle this."

"You're sure?" Finn hesitated.

"Absolutely. Go." Iris took the towel from Finn. "The sooner you change the sooner we get to the lake." She waved Finn toward the door. "I can manage a little strawberry jam."

"Okay…again…sorry about the mess and the thing…with my…on your leg." Finn mimicked the motion she'd made with her hand up Iris's thigh.

"Stop apologizing. It's really okay."

Finn nodded and then trotted out the door and down the steps.

Iris exhaled and leaned against the closed door.

Whoa.

Was it simply because Finn reminded her of her ex? No, aside from her initial impression of Finn, there weren't that many similarities with Kent. Maybe there was something else. Finn was definitely her type—dark hair, blue eyes, athletic. She was momentarily reminded of her high school crush, Emily Scott, a charismatic forward for the basketball team. She smiled. Oh, yes, Finn was definitely her type.

She mulled it over while she wiped the floor with the dampened towel. Then she went to the bath and stepped into the shower to rinse off her legs. Luckily, her shorts had been spared because she hadn't packed very many outfits for her three-day trip. She dried off and settled into a chair to phone her mother. She toyed with the frayed hem of her T-shirt while she waited for her mom to pick up.

CHAPTER NINE

Finn tossed her strawberry speckled jeans on the floor and rummaged in the dresser for cargo shorts. What a complete idiot. Iris made her so nervous she couldn't be trusted to walk and chew gum at the same time. *Good Lord, pull it together. She's not even gay. She doesn't even like you that way.* Finn chided herself as she pulled on khaki cargo shorts and flip-flops.

She braced against the edge of the sink and sternly regarded her reflection in the bathroom mirror. *And she's never gonna like you if you act like a friggin' crushed out goofball.*

She pointed a finger at her reflection. *Tighten up, Finn.*

Giving herself a pep talk in the bathroom mirror, so dumb, such a rookie move.

She checked the closet for extra towels and stuffed two into a canvas messenger bag, along with some sunscreen and her cell phone. For a minute, she lingered and rotated slowly in the center of the room. What was she forgetting? A baseball cap for sun and wind. She reached for her favorite, hanging on the hook on the back of the closet door. A faded blue Atlanta Braves cap, frayed at the edge of the brim. She pulled the cap on and searched the cluttered top of her dresser for keys to the MG. She hoped the sports car would win back some cool points with Iris. At this point, she was probably starting from zero.

Finn slung the bag across her chest and was just about to reach for the door when her phone buzzed. She checked the screen. It was her boss, Everett Green. Might as well take the call and get this over with, otherwise it'd be hanging over her head all day.

"Hello?" Finn tried to sound neutral.

"First off, you're fired." He didn't even bother to say hello.

"Yeah, I figured." How could she be mad? She deserved it.

"Second, bring the damn car back to the lot. Now."

"I'll bring it back tomorrow when I can get a ride home from my brother, okay?" She wasn't about to derail the birthday outing with Iris just to return the stupid limo. Especially since she was already fired.

There was silence on the other end.

"Mr. Green, I'm sorry about what happened." She didn't really feel remorse for what she'd done, but the polite thing to do was apologize anyway. Everett Green had been a good boss. He'd cut her slack on many occasions just because he was a nice guy.

"Look, Finn, I like you, and I think Geoff is an entitled ass, but you can't punch clients and work for me." He didn't really soften his tone, but Finn knew he'd have probably wanted to do the same thing under similar circumstances.

Geoff's father was a steady client so he probably had no choice but to fire her. She wanted to ask what Geoff's version of the story had been but stopped herself. There was no way he'd own up to being bested by a woman.

"I understand." There was no point arguing or trying to defend herself. "I'll have the car back first thing tomorrow."

"I'll expect you by ten." Everett clicked off.

It was a blessing in disguise. Geoff had done her a favor. She now had no excuse not to pursue the career she really wanted. No more excuses.

A noise pulled her attention to the rear of cabin two. Her father was cleaning up the bear debris. She chided herself for not thinking to do that first thing, but in her defense, Iris had been very distracting.

"Do you need help?" Her father looked up as she approached.

"No, I'm almost done." He reached for a shredded Pringles can.

"It was a black bear. I saw him last night after I came in." She adjusted the bag's strap across her chest, holding onto it with one hand. "I should have cleaned this up already, sorry."

"No big deal. I figured you got in late from work." He straightened to look at her. He was wearing a well-loved, faded John Deere cap. His coveralls had been dark blue at some point, before they'd been washed a million times and worn almost through at the knees. His boots were just as weathered. Finn's father had favorite clothes, and he pretty much wore them to rags. Once, he'd given her a sweatshirt of his for safekeeping because he feared her mother would throw it away. It was rife with holes all along the hem and at the elbows, but he wasn't quite ready to give it up.

"Where are you off too?" He tied the top of the bag he was holding.

"I'm showing one of our guests around. It's her birthday so I offered to drive her out to the lake."

"Don't you have to work today? Saturdays are usually busy for you."

"No, not today. Long story."

Thankfully, he didn't ask more about how she'd met the birthday girl in cabin two. He tossed the garbage bags into his pickup truck and slowly turned onto the blacktop. He waved. She was watching him leave as she walked toward the front of the cabin and almost bumped into Iris, again.

"Oh, sorry." She took a step back.

"Who was that?" Iris's eyes followed the truck.

"That was my dad. He's making his morning rounds."

"Did the bear leave a big mess?" Iris looked toward the back of the cabin where the trash cans had been restored to order.

"Not too bad. Dad was quicker than me with the cleanup." Finn felt for the keys inside her pocket. "Are you ready?"

"Yes. Did you want me to drive?" Iris motioned toward the rental car parked nearby.

"No, I was thinking I'd drive. You know, since I know the area."

"We're going to take a stretch limo to the lake?" Iris raised an eyebrow.

"No, I have a car of my own. Come on." Finn turned and motioned for Iris to follow. They walked past the main house and down the drive toward the three-bay carport.

Iris could see that there was a smaller vehicle parked next to the limo under a car cover. She waited while Finn pulled the snug corners free and folded the cover carefully. A beautiful, vintage, eggshell sports car was now on full display. Iris didn't know a lot about cars, but she assumed from Finn's tender care that this one was special.

"Meet Scarlett." Finn swept her hand toward the red-brown leather of the cockpit.

"You named your car?"

"And on the open road, she's gone with the wind." Finn smiled broadly.

"You did *not* just use a reference from *Gone With the Wind* about your car?"

"Yes, I most certainly did." Finn opened the passenger door for Iris. "Scarlett is impetuous, temperamental, sexy, and she'll sweep you off your feet."

Finn was so damn good-looking. Standing there holding the door for Iris, her eyes sparkled and her entire demeanor said *good time*. The perfect person to spend her birthday with. Finn's grin was contagious as Iris sank into the passenger seat. Finn closed the door and circled the car. She threw her bag and Iris's into the small trunk beneath a gleaming chrome luggage rack, then climbed in.

"This is a beautiful car." No, Iris didn't know much about cars, but this one was indisputably cool.

"My friend Ward and I added a Ford 2.3 liter inline, fuel-injected four-cylinder engine, and a five-speed manual transmission. It originally came with a four-speed." Finn rattled off details about the inner workings of the car as if Iris had any idea what she was talking about, which she did not.

"The odometer only has 9,635 miles," Finn continued. "This car has been babied."

Iris ran her finger over the soft leather along the inside of the door. The top was down, and as they picked up speed on the two-lane road, her hair began to swirl around her face. She pulled it to one side and twirled it, holding it with her hand to tame it.

The front mounted side mirrors flashed blue and green as they drove beneath the canopy of hardwoods that broke open every now and then to reveal a cloudless summer sky. The air smelled of grass and growing things.

"Have you owned the car for a long time?" Iris wondered if it was a family auto, passed down.

"I've had it for about four years. Ward discovered it under a tarp in an old boarded up barn during an estate sale. There were maps and a purse on top of the passenger seat and a mummified mouse beneath it." Finn scrunched up her nose as she told the story. "Yeah, we couldn't save the carpet, but we found a close match."

Finn downshifted as they headed into a curve, and Iris couldn't help noticing the lean, cut muscles of her forearm…and her hands. Finn had strong hands. Finn worked the clutch as she shifted again, and the roadster gained speed as it climbed out of the curve. Iris didn't care much for cars, but she decided it would be easy to fall in love with this one. The cockpit was small, intimate, and the passenger experience made her feel as if she were close to the world outside. Finn waved at a passing car. She was a local and no doubt a bit of a celebrity in this car.

They slowed and turned into a small grocery at a three-way stop. The sign on the storefront was large and looked hand-painted: Turner's Corner. A stream ran along the border of the wraparound porch. It gurgled pleasantly and light bounced off the water as it wound around several large rocks.

"I thought we'd get a few things for a picnic before we drive to the lake." Finn killed the engine.

Iris lived in Southern California now, but she'd grown up in the Northeast. In this remote outpost of the Deep South she suddenly felt a wee bit apprehensive. She was a Yankee in rural Georgia, and she worried that she stood out. But it wasn't as if she could sit in the car. That would seem even odder.

The screen door banged behind her as she followed Finn inside. The first thing Iris noticed about the store's interior was the pot-bellied stove in the center of the space. And the floorboards were traveled to the point that no varnish remained. The rest of the interior seemed to be from a later era, maybe the sixties. There was a deli counter at the back. They walked through several rows of shelves lined with general inventory: paper plates, paper towels, potato chips, syrup, cereal, all the basics.

"Hey, Finn, what are you up to today?" A full-figured woman, with medium length brown hair, probably in her forties, spoke to Finn from behind the deli counter.

"Headed to the lake." Finn studied the food behind the glass with her hands in her pockets. "This is Iris. She's visiting from California. This is Shondra."

"Hi." Iris gave a small wave. She wasn't used to being introduced to the deli personnel, but maybe in a community this small it would be rude not to be.

"California, huh?" Shondra leaned on the top of the glass case. "I've never been there but always sorta wanted to go."

"It's nice." She wasn't sure what else to say.

"What's good today?" Finn was focused on food.

"Everything." Shondra scowled.

Finn grinned. This seemed like a thing they did.

"I'll take two pulled pork sandwiches, with slaw, on Dutch crunch rolls, with…Oh, wait, I didn't even think to ask if you were vegetarian or…" Finn stopped the order midstream and turned to Iris.

"I'm okay with anything." She figured it was best to just go with whatever the locals liked.

"Great." Finn returned her attention to the case. "Can you give us a small container of that potato salad too?"

Iris was checking the drink case when two men entered the store. She gave them a quick sideways glance. They were wearing T-shirts and jeans; one of them had on a cap emblazoned with the Confederate flag. Iris mentally flinched at the sight of it and turned to check on Finn, who was chatting with Shondra.

"'Scuse me." The guy with the hat motioned toward the beer cooler. Iris hadn't realized she was standing in front of it. "Hey,

Shondra, will you make me a ham and cheese on a soft roll?" he shouted while he stood in the open cooler door.

It was probably only ten. Kind of early for beer. That's what Iris was thinking. And then she noticed that he actually grabbed two bottled Cokes. She'd made an assumption about beer-drinking rednecks, probably due to the hat. For some reason, these two good ol' boys made her a little uneasy, especially since Finn looked like the poster girl for butch lesbians. Was Georgia one of the states that tried to pass one of those bathroom bills? Or was that North Carolina? Now she couldn't remember. Iris wondered how gay-friendly a place like Watts Mountain might be for a woman who looked like Finn, someone who couldn't so easily blend in.

She walked back over to stand near Finn, feeling protective. She'd only just met Finn, but Finn had saved her from a bear, and offered to host her for a birthday outing. She figured she owed Finn whatever femme protection spell she could conjure.

Being in Atlanta one could almost forget that they were in the Deep South. Atlanta felt like an urban safe zone for outsiders. The city was a melting pot of people from elsewhere. Only a few residents she'd encountered even seemed to have a southern accent, Finn being one of them. Finn's easy, soft drawl smoothed off the corners of whatever she was saying. Finn's accent was like a gentle caress.

When she'd considered taking the role in the show she'd only really thought about the city. She hadn't considered the rest of the South or what it might be like outside the city limits. She hadn't even thought of it when she'd driven out to the cabin the previous evening. That was probably naïve.

"Hey, Finn, can you come out to the shop later?"

As she approached she realized Finn was already talking to one of the men, the one without the hat. He had a medium build. His jeans fit loose and they gathered a little over his boots. He was wearing a faded red T-shirt marred with what looked like grease or oil stains. His sandy hair fell across his forehead, and he swept it back as he faced Finn. He was only an inch or so taller than she was. He looked at Iris with wide eyes as she neared the counter, as if she were an alien, or her hair was on fire. Or possibly he recognized her from the recent Super Bowl ad, where she'd been cast as a buxom barmaid for a Doritos commercial.

"Ward, this is Iris. Iris, this is my pal, Ward."

His mouth was open, but he didn't speak.

"Nice to meet you." Iris smiled.

Still, he didn't speak.

"Earth to Ward. Snap out of it, you're staring." Finn waved her hand in front of his face.

"Sorry." He blushed and averted his eyes.

"I can come by tomorrow. I'm kinda booked today." Finn reached for the two sandwiches and the container of potato salad that Shondra placed on the deli case. "We're going out to the lake for a little while."

"Okay." He shoved his hands in his pockets. He seemed self-conscious. "I'll give you a buzz when we're ready for you."

"It was nice to meet you, Ward." Iris was glad she'd been wrong about the men, or at least one of them.

Finn never introduced the other guy. It was possible she was still on edge from her encounter with the director. Iris was definitely tuned in more than usual. She found herself paying attention to small nuances of behavior from the men she'd encountered since the incident with Eric.

Finn paid for their food. They'd grabbed chips and drinks to go with their meal. A matronly older woman ran the register at the front.

"Take a bag of ice for that potato salad and your drinks." The older woman handed Finn the change and a small plastic bag.

"Right, good thinking. Can you hold this?" Finn handed the food to Iris while she went to the drink counter at the back of the store and filled the bag with ice cubes from the fountain drink dispenser. She twisted the top of the bag into a knot as they exited.

Iris felt a little unhelpful. So far, Finn was taking care of everything and she was only tagging along. She stood by as Finn popped the trunk and tucked the bag of ice inside a small cooler with the drinks. It was the sort of tiny cooler that only held three or four drinks. The car was so small that a normal sized cooler would never have fit inside the trunk.

"Ready?" Finn held the door for Iris again.

"You really know how to spoil a birthday girl." Iris sank into the seat.

"That was my plan. I'm glad it's working."

CHAPTER TEN

Finn backed out and turned right at the intersection. The air was very warm now and humid; no doubt the lake was a perfect place to spend the day.

"Did you know the other guy that came in with your friend, Ward?" Iris was still puzzled about meeting Ward, whom Finn seemed to be friends with, but not the other guy.

"That's Jake Jensen. Local redneck, asshole."

"Oh." Iris's intuition about him had been on point.

"Yeah, he and I don't see eye to eye on much, or anything, actually." Finn glanced over. "Why, did you think he was cute or something?"

"Oh, God no. I just noticed his hat, that was all. I was surprised that someone his age would wear...um..."

"The Confederate flag?"

"Yes." She'd let the words trail off because she worried suddenly that making a derogatory comment about that bit of southern history might be offensive to a local.

"The Deep South is a complex place. Don't believe everything you read in the *New Yorker*. And yes, it is possible to have southern pride while acknowledging where our ancestors got it horribly wrong." Finn took a breath. "But only assholes fly that flag as some way to defend their whiteness. And southerners aren't the only ones who do it...as if whiteness needs defending. From whom? Other white rednecks? Stupid, ignorant, and insensitive."

Obviously, this was a topic Finn had strong feelings about.

"Ward was probably working on Jake's truck in the shop. They aren't really friends either, but sometimes a job is a job." Finn downshifted as they turned past the sign for Watts Mountain Lake.

They circled the parking lot and found a shady spot near the dock. Several overturned red canoes rested in the grass nearby.

"Want to take a spin in one of the canoes and eat after?" Finn stood beside the car waiting for her. "I don't think the food will get too warm here in the shade for only an hour or so."

"Sure. I should warn you though, it's been a long time since I canoed."

"How long?"

"Maybe since Girl Scout camp. I think I was twelve."

"You'll be fine. It'll come right back to you. Plus, the lake is so small you can't get lost. Or, if you tip over, it's easy to swim to shore."

"Good to know."

She followed Finn toward the dock. They selected a canoe and flipped it over in the grass. The paddles were tucked under the seats along with two ancient orange life preservers. They dragged the boat across the lush grass toward the water. When the aft end of the boat reached the lake, Finn climbed in with a paddle in one hand.

"Push me out. I'll paddle next to the dock. That way you can step in without getting your shoes wet."

Iris followed Finn's direction, appreciating the fact that she'd be able to keep her sandals mostly dry. She had only packed two pairs of shoes for the trip. Finn stabilized by holding on to the weathered dock while Iris gingerly stepped in. The boat rocked a little, despite Finn's focused efforts to hold it still.

"Who do these boats belong to?" Iris wondered if they were swiping someone's personal canoe. It seemed odd not to need to pay someone a rental fee. In California, nothing was free.

"They belong to the local Baptist church. Bible school starts on Monday. They won't mind if we borrow one." Finn grinned as she paddled backward to move them away from the dock.

Iris wondered if that grin allowed Finn to get away with anything she wanted. She assumed it probably did. It would be hard to resist Taylor Finn if she set her mind on something.

Finn couldn't help smiling as Iris realized she was facing the wrong direction. She tried not to laugh and make Iris feel bad about the error. She'd gotten in the canoe facing Finn, and it wasn't until she'd started to put her paddle in the water that she realized her mistake. Finn hadn't corrected her when she sat down because she was happy to look at Iris as much as possible in the short time she had. Iris was a much better view than a lake she'd visited a million times.

There was something special about Iris, and it wasn't just the way she looked. Yes, she was undeniably, distractingly gorgeous, but that wasn't it. There was something that took her breath away when she smiled at Finn. She made her feel as if she were the sole resident of planet Earth. When she smiled it was like the sun breaking through the clouds after days of rain. There was warmth there and Finn wanted to bask in it. She had plans to keep Iris in her orbit for as long as possible. And now, in the canoe, she was at Finn's mercy, a captive audience.

"Oh, I'm sorry. I've gotten this all wrong." Iris frowned.

Even when she frowned she was beautiful.

"Just stay put. You're fine." Finn paddled at a relaxed pace toward the center of the lake. "This will be better for conversation anyway. It's not like we're in a race where we need two paddlers or anything."

"Are you sure?"

"Definitely. Just relax and enjoy the ride." That sounded more flirtatious than she'd meant for it to, but Iris didn't seem to mind.

Finn was happy to have Iris all to herself for a little while. She was curious about her and had a bunch of questions queued up from the previous night. It wasn't that she was that great at small talk or conversation in general, but she'd put forth her best effort if it meant getting a glimpse into the life of Iris Fleming.

"This is a beautiful place." Iris leaned back a little, bracing her hands on either side of the canoe. The paddle lay near her legs, propped against the seat. "Although, I wish I'd brought my sunglasses. I have no idea why I left them in my bag in the car." She turned back toward Finn, shielding her eyes with her hand.

"Here, take my hat." Finn offered her Braves cap.

"Are you sure?"

"Yeah, I've got sunglasses."

"Thank you." Iris adjusted the back strap of the cap for a better fit. She trailed her fingertips in the water as the boat glided slowly across the lake. "The water is chilly."

"It's a natural, spring-fed lake, so the water temp stays pretty cool even in summer. That's why I suggested a picnic instead of swimming after our boat ride. I mean, it's refreshing, but definitely a shock at first. Plus, the swimming area is small and usually swarming with kids." Finn motioned with her thumb over her shoulder to the shoreline behind her. The bright sounds of children's voices echoed across the lake.

"Oh, yeah, I see what you mean."

"So, how long are you staying in Georgia?" Not the subtle line of questioning Finn had imagined in her head. But, too late, it was already out there.

"I'm leaving tomorrow."

"Oh, really? That soon?"

"Yes, I was only supposed to be here for a couple of days, you know, unless I get the part. In which case I'll be back for longer."

Finn's mood brightened. But then she remembered what Iris had said the night before about her bad day.

"But you mentioned something about not liking the director."

"Points for paying attention."

"I'm a good listener, remember?"

"Well, most people don't actually mean it."

"I always try to mean what I say."

"Good to know." Iris smiled. "What's next for you?"

"Besides finding a job?" Iris obviously didn't want to talk about whatever had happened.

"Yeah, besides that."

"I'm thinking on it. Obviously, I'm declaring today a personal holiday, in honor of your birthday, and plan to avoid making any adult type decisions...you know, about life, or the future, or... whatever." Finn realized she was in complete denial about the fact that she'd just gotten fired. She really was going to have to figure some things out, but not today.

"I think your thirtieth birthday is supposed to be some big milestone. At least that's what Maggie thinks."

"Who's Maggie?"

"My roommate." Iris looked out over the water. "But I really don't like to make a big deal out of birthdays. Feels like too much pressure. I like to keep my expectations in check, then I'm usually not disappointed."

"I guess that's why you didn't really have plans today."

"Frankly, my birthday sort of snuck up on me."

"My birthdays never sneak up on me, or anyone else." Finn back-paddled to turn the canoe so they could make their way toward the dock. "I make sure everyone knows my birthday is coming, and I pretty much celebrate it the entire month."

"Sounds like too much pressure."

"Only if you think of presents and cake as pressure. I think we need to work on your fun meter." Finn intentionally splashed Iris with a few drops of water as she shifted the paddle from one side to the other. Not too much water, just enough to test Iris's threshold for playfulness.

"Hey!"

"Sorry."

"I doubt that."

Finn smiled. Iris was right, she wasn't really sorry.

"It actually felt good. My legs are getting hot in the sun." Iris swept the droplets down her smooth, tanned legs.

Finn took that as an invitation to raise the stakes. As she moved the paddle she splashed Iris again. Iris responded by splashing Finn with her hand. Finn splashed her back.

"Hey! Careful! Unless you're working toward a wet T-shirt contest." Iris laughed and splashed Finn with more gusto. The canoe rocked a little from their movements.

"Is that an option?" Finn raised her sunglasses for a better look.

"Ha! You wish."

Finn laughed, dropped her glasses back to her nose, and paddled them toward the shore.

❖

Iris reached for the dock as Finn maneuvered the canoe along beside it. She climbed out, only tipping the boat a little from side to side. A woman, probably in her late thirties, wearing a broad sun hat, a tank top, and a floral skirt shouted from the dock. Iris scanned the lake to see who the woman was yelling for.

"Andrew, you get back here right this instant." She cupped her hands around her mouth and shouted again, louder this time.

There was a boy in a canoe, probably fifty feet or so from shore.

"Is that your son?" Iris couldn't help asking. The woman seemed so upset.

"Yes. He's only eight and he has not one notion of how to paddle a canoe. Which is exactly why I told him he couldn't take one out. For the life of me, that boy just will *not* listen." She tilted the brim of her hat backward and looked at Iris, with either anger or concern or a maternal mixture of both. "I'm Wanda, by the way."

"Iris." She shook the woman's hand. Southerners were so friendly. That would take some getting used to.

"I'll go get him." Finn was still seated in the canoe. She started to back-paddle.

"Oh, good Lord, thank you." Wanda spoke to Finn and then turned to Iris. "Your boyfriend is so sweet to go get my son."

Iris was going to correct Wanda's mistake, but then decided against it. Wanda was clearly too upset about losing Andrew in a wayward canoe to be bothered with momentary gender confusion.

They watched from the dock as Andrew fumbled and dropped his paddle into the lake. He reached for it with an extreme stretch and pitched the boat at a sharp angle. Iris fought the urge not to join Wanda in yelling for him to keep still. Finn was closing in on his location, but not quick enough to keep him from falling headfirst into the lake. With a splash and a yelp, the bright red canoe went bottoms up. He surfaced, but it was hard to gauge his status from the dock.

Finn watched Andrew topple as if in slow motion. She could tell by the angle of the boat that his center of gravity was way off. She picked up her pace. She was only seconds away.

"Hey, don't panic. I'm coming to get you." Finn spoke to Andrew as he bobbed in the water. He wasn't a very good swimmer, and he hadn't bothered to put on a life jacket. Typical careless kid. He surfaced and sputtered and then surfaced again, coughing. His paddle was slowly floating away along with the upturned canoe.

Finn reached for him.

"Take my hand. Don't be scared, you're gonna be okay, kid." But he wasn't buying it.

He thrashed about as she tried to grasp one of his arms. She overextended. Immediately, she registered the miscalculation. She lost focus for an instant. When he did finally capture her hand in his she was way off balance. His weight and movement toppled her and she plunged into the freezing water. She gasped, her mouth filled with water, as the cold lake took her breath.

Now both canoes were bottom side up and useless. She'd never get herself and Andrew back into her boat.

"Screw this." She put her arm around Andrew's chest and started swimming for shore with one arm, kicking furiously to aid their forward motion.

His mother was shouting something, but Finn's ears kept dipping below the surface with every stroke so she couldn't make out what she was saying. The swim seemed to take forever. Her legs and arms were shaking by the time she was able to stand in chest deep water near the dock. She half carried the boy until he was able to get his own footing. His mother met them on the grassy shore. She scooped him into a mama bear hug while simultaneously scolding him for being so careless.

"You scared me half to death!" She set him down and held his face in her hands.

"I'm sorry, Mama." He might have actually meant it too. He was visibly spooked by his experience.

Finn dropped to her knees in the grass, soaked through, and breathing hard. The woman thanked Finn profusely as Iris looked on with an amused expression.

"You're the hero of the day." Iris smiled down at her after the woman was out of earshot.

The woman tugged her son toward the parking lot. She had a death grip on his hand for sure. He glanced back once as he was pulled along.

"I'm not sure heroes are usually this winded." Finn stood up. She pulled at the wet T-shirt trying to get it away from her chilled skin. The waterlogged cargo shorts she was wearing weighed at least a hundred pounds. *Note to self: do more cardio.* She'd been working out a lot using her brother's free weights. He'd had to leave them behind when he left for life in a dorm. But obviously, she needed to add running to her daily routine.

"I guess you got your wet T-shirt contest after all." Iris was trying not to laugh.

"Oh, yeah, you're hilarious." Finn shook her head. "This wasn't quite what I had in mind."

CHAPTER ELEVEN

Finn slogged to the car where they gathered towels and the cooler. She needed a spot in the sun to dry out and warm up. They found a nice grassy area near the picnic tables, almost in the tree line. The towels were half in the sun and half in the shade, so that Iris had the option for shade since she wasn't the one who'd taken an unexpected dunk in the lake.

She hadn't planned on going swimming, but luckily Finn had worn a gray jog bra under her T-shirt. In one swift move, she swept the clingy, soggy shirt up and over her head. She felt instantly warmer after getting rid it. Iris's eyebrows arched up with surprise.

"Sorry, didn't mean to take you off guard by going shirtless."

"You didn't take me...I mean, I'm fine, I mean, you're fine."

Finn was amused. Iris looked away and fussed with smoothing out the edge of the towel she was seated on.

Iris took a deep breath and tried to settle. The sight of Finn taking her shirt off had surprised Iris, taken her breath was more accurate. But she wasn't about to admit it. Finn had the fit, leanly muscled body of an athlete, and she didn't seem self-conscious about showing it off. Her skin was smooth and tanned from time outdoors. Her washboard abs flexed as she rotated to spread her wet shirt in the sun to dry. When she turned back, there was a moment where they awkwardly stared at each other.

Iris reached toward Finn and then hesitated, her hands in midair.

"Do you mind?" she asked.

Finn shook her head. Finn looked so serious all of a sudden that Iris had to smile.

She swept her fingers through Finn's damp hair, pushing it back away from her face. She did it a second time to smooth it further.

"You let your hair fall forward, but you've got the most incredible eyes. You should show them off. They're beautiful." Iris said the last part softly, almost as if to herself.

Now, with her hair slicked back, Finn looked like some androgynous reincarnation of a modern day James Dean. Gorgeous.

"Thank you." The corner of Finn's mouth rose in a mischievous half smile. She reached for the cooler. "Should we eat?"

"Sure." Although food wasn't on her mind at the moment.

Iris opened one of the sodas and took several sips while she watched Finn unpack the sandwiches.

"I'm starved." Finn unwrapped her sandwich, poised to take a bite. "Swimming always makes me hungry."

"Hero stuff is hard work."

"Ha, very funny." Finn smiled around a mouthful.

"What about the canoes?" Iris looked toward the lake as they ate.

"We can paddle out and get them after." Finn glanced toward the swimming area. "Or we can bribe some bored teenager to do it for ten bucks."

"I vote for bribing teenagers."

"Me too."

Finn propped on one elbow, partially reclining as she ate.

This was fun. More fun than Iris had hoped for on her birthday, in a strange place where she knew no one. There was a light breeze. Just enough to cause the broad leaves over their heads to create undulating irregular shadows on the ground. A scent of something sweet traveled with the breeze. Perhaps a flower that Iris didn't recognize. She committed the scene to memory. Taking in small details so that she could return to them later. The dampness of the lush grass against her shoeless feet. The sound of children laughing. The warmth of the sun on her skin. And Finn, relaxed, lying back with eyes closed, as if they were the dearest of friends.

Iris felt a twinge of sadness that all of this would be so fleeting.

Tomorrow, she'd be leaving for Los Angeles and Finn would be staying here. And LA was a long way from Watts Mountain, in more ways than geography.

"Is something wrong?"

She hadn't realized Finn was watching her.

"No, just thinking, that's all." Iris took a bite of her sandwich. It was really good.

"You looked as if maybe you were thinking of a bad day, or *the* bad day."

"I'm not going to give Eric Gilet the satisfaction of thinking of him."

"Who is Eric?"

"The director for that show I auditioned for."

"Oh, that guy."

"Yeah. Sort of makes for a wasted trip."

"Except for today?" Finn sounded hopeful.

"Yes, except for today." Iris smiled.

They sat quietly for a moment, finishing the sandwiches. Finn crumpled the wrapping from hers and tossed it into the cooler as if it were a basketball aimed at a hoop.

"Three points." Finn imitated a sportscaster. "The crowd goes wild."

Iris found the whole display amusing.

"So, what's next for you? Given your job just ended."

"That's a nice way of saying I *got fired*." Finn grinned. She didn't seem that upset about it. "Maybe I should do what I've been wanting to do."

"What's that?"

"Take a stunt driving course. There are plenty of movies being shot in Atlanta. I think if I had some professional credentials I could get some work that pays better than driving a limo."

"Well, as someone who knows from firsthand experience, there are sometimes gaps between jobs."

"Really? Acting always seems like such a glamorous occupation."

"Not everything you see on Instagram is reality." Iris adjusted her position so that she could lie on her side, propped on her elbow, facing Finn.

"How does it work? Do you have some fancy agent?" Finn seemed genuinely interested.

"I have an agent and a manager. Two people to keep happy." Iris plucked a blade of grass and twirled it between her fingers.

"Tell me more."

"Okay, if you really want to know."

"I do." Finn mirrored Iris's position, propped on her elbow, with her head braced on her hand as if she were expecting to hear an exciting tale of adventure or something.

"The process isn't as interesting as you might imagine. The first level of audition breakdowns are sent out by casting agents to talent agents. Each project has a breakdown of who they are looking for."

"I'm not sure what that means."

"Think of it like a menu, where a casting agent asks for what they want—looking for thirty-year-old white female, quirky best friend. Or leading male, cop, six feet tall."

"Oh, I get it. Literally, like an actual menu." Finn frowned. "Weird."

"You get used to it."

"Does it ever work on your self-esteem? I mean, not that I would expect you to have any trouble with that, I mean, not with the way you look anyway…" Finn fumbled to dig herself out.

"I think I know what you're trying to say." Iris smiled and Finn relaxed. "Hollywood is tough. It can be very superficial. That part is hard to get used to. I try not to take that on, but sometimes you can't help it."

Iris thought of some of the comments she'd seen online after her breakup with Kent. Anonymously, people could be so cruel. Maybe they were always cruel and social media just offered them an amplified voice. The optimistic side of her nature told her that wasn't true. She redirected her thoughts back to their conversation.

"What's kept you from enrolling in a stunt driving school?"

"Home, probably." Finn rolled onto her back, folding her arms behind her head.

"Oh, do your parents need you to be here for some reason?"

"No, it's nothing like that." Finn was reflective, as if she were carefully choosing her words. "Few places are more stunting than home wouldn't you say? A place where you're safe, unchallenged, cared for, well fed…"

"I suppose that depends on how you define home." They were treading on dangerous ground now. Iris had feelings about home and not all of them were good. And she wasn't sure she was ready to share. This was serious get-to-know-you stuff. "I'm not so sure I ever considered home as a place as much as it is a feeling." That was a safe way to frame it.

"I think that can be true too." Finn regarded her with a serious expression. "Home can be something to long for, or something to return to, or something to be shared."

Finn's words, her soft drawl, were like a tender embrace. Her words made Iris's heart flutter. How was it possible that she could feel understood by someone she'd only just met the previous night? Finn acted as if she didn't take anything seriously, as if everything in her life was about having a good time, but her words gave her away. Beneath the bravado Iris suspected there resided a sensitive soul.

"It might take a little longer for this." Finn checked the status of her still damp shirt. "Hey, in a little while, after this dries and I find someone to rescue those canoes, would you like to go for a drive in the mountains?"

"Sure." Iris looked around at the lush wooded hills surrounding the lake. "But aren't we in the mountains?"

"These are the foothills. About an hour from here are some amazing overlooks." Finn settled back on her elbows. "Unless you have other things you wanted to do. I mean it is your birthday after all."

"No plans. I'm all yours."

Finn grinned broadly, and Iris couldn't help laughing at her unintended flirtatious word choice.

CHAPTER TWELVE

Finn's shorts were still damp in places, so after another hour or so at the lake, they stopped by her cabin for dry clothes. Iris waited in the car while she tugged on faded, button-fly jeans. Low-rise Chucks were best for driving so she ditched her flip-flops for a pair of red Converse sneakers. She glanced out the window as she pulled a fresh T-shirt over her head.

She paused to enjoy the view. Iris seated in her roadster was like something out of a classic movie. A beautiful combination that made Finn wish she had her phone to snap a photo through the open window. The scene was framed by the light fabric drapes shifting in the soft breeze. Iris tucked an errant strand of hair behind her ear and replaced Finn's cap. She let Iris keep it for the drive. Short hair worked much better in a convertible, but Finn was always attracted to women with long hair. Iris had gorgeous long hair that fell in silky waves halfway down her back. Finn imagined Iris leaning down from above, her hair trailing across Finn's bare chest. Her libido began to hum.

She squeezed her eyes shut and shook her head.

Snap out of it.

She grabbed a sweatshirt and a jacket and pulled the door closed. Depending on the drive it might get chilly as they climbed and the sun dipped. She wanted to have something warm to put on just in case. Iris must have been lost in thought because she seemed surprised by the sound of Finn closing the trunk.

"Sorry, I was throwing in a couple of jackets in case we need them."

"I was daydreaming and didn't know you were so close." Iris smiled as Finn settled into the driver's seat.

She wanted to get on the road before her mother caught sight of her and saddled her with chores. She'd already forgotten the groceries her mother had requested the day before, now Finn was out gallivanting when there was no doubt plenty to be done around the place. She'd have to make up for it tomorrow.

The day was perfect for a drive, not too hot or humid. Traffic was sparse as they headed northeast. One of Finn's favorite overlooks was Neel's Gap. It was about a forty-five-minute drive from Watt's Mountain, along a winding two-lane highway. Motorcyclists loved this particular route for all its hairpin curves. It was a fun road in a sports car too. The snaking road required constant footwork between the clutch, the accelerator, and the gearbox.

As she drove it was hard not to let her hand drift from the gear shift to Iris's shapely thigh, so tempting. Iris sat with her knees together, angled in Finn's direction. The view was distracting. She reminded herself to keep her eyes on the road.

There were a few other cars out front when they pulled alongside Mountain Crossings at Walasi-yi in Neel's Gap. The stone structure was built by the Civilian Conservation Corps in 1936. It originally functioned as an inn and restaurant for the few brave souls who ventured this far into the blue-ridged wilderness from Atlanta. Now the building was a hiker's paradise, with the Appalachian Trail cutting right through the building.

"What's with all the shoes?" Iris was standing beside the car, looking up.

A large tree near the parking lot was strewn with shoes and boots as if they were Christmas ornaments. The way people sometimes threw tennis shoes strung together over telephone wires, except these were all in a single tree.

"Hikers." Finn pointed toward a breezeway along the outside wall of the large stone building. "See that white blaze? The white rectangle of paint?"

"Yes."

"That's the Appalachian Trail which runs from Georgia all the way to Maine. This is the only building that actually sits right on the trail."

"I've heard of that trail. There was a movie, or a book, or both, right?"

"Yeah, I think it was called *A Walk in the Woods* or something. I haven't read it. But I've hiked sections of the trail here and in North Carolina, even a short bit in Virginia."

"Sounds like an adventure."

"It was." Finn started up the steps toward the overlook and Iris followed. "If you like sleeping on the ground and carrying all your own gear."

"Not your thing anymore?"

"Not so much. I'd rather experience the great outdoors from the comfort of a convertible."

The overlook was a flat patio made of the same gray stones as the building. There were a couple of picnic tables, but both were vacant. It was later in the afternoon, well past lunch. Finn sat at the edge of the short wall that bordered the patio that overlooked row upon row of blue-green mountain ridges.

"Wow." Iris stood beside her looking toward the vista. "This is really beautiful."

"Worth the trip?"

"Definitely. And I enjoyed the drive also. That's a great car. I can see why you love it."

They were quiet for a few minutes, enjoying the view.

"You know, this used to be a major intersection of Cherokee trading paths."

"Really?" Iris turned to look at Finn.

"Yeah, before it was the Appalachian Trail, like a hundred years ago, right through here was a Cherokee trail. The remains of the original Cherokee town are down there somewhere." Finn leaned over, glancing past the ledge.

"You're a good tour guide."

"Too much local history?" Finn rocked back, shoving her hands in her pockets.

"No, I'd say you're just right." Iris smiled.

There it was again, a hint of flirtation. Finn was sure she wasn't imagining it. They sat down on the top of a nearby picnic table, dangling their legs like little kids. Every time Iris's leg brushed Finn's she'd feel a little electrical surge. No matter how hard she tried to fight the attraction, it was no use. Iris was her type in almost every way. Iris was dream girl material.

Finn bought them a couple of sodas from the Mountain Crossings camp and supply store. The place was stacked with backpacking gear and clothing, but luckily also had a stocked drink cooler for thirsty hikers. They sat for another twenty minutes sipping the drinks and enjoying the view. Finn hoped Iris was having half as much fun as she was.

"I was thinking, there's only one thing wrong with this day so far." Finn tried to look serious but couldn't stop the smile.

"What?" Iris sounded concerned.

"Cake. This day needs cake."

Iris laughed, a magical, genuine laugh that hung a string of lights around Finn's heart.

"Well, who am I to say no to cake?"

"Excellent. A birthday requires cake, and I know just where we can get some." Finn jumped down and extended her hand to Iris. "Shall we?"

Iris accepted Finn's hand and allowed their fingers to entwine for the briefest of moments as they walked to the car. The warmth from Iris's touch shimmied all the way up Finn's arm and settled in her chest before dropping into her stomach. With or without cake, from Finn's perspective, this day couldn't be more perfect. Dessert for dinner? Well, that was just an added sprinkling of powdered sugar.

CHAPTER THIRTEEN

Iris couldn't help grinning. The whole day with Finn had been so easy. Not just easy, but truly fun. There was hardly ever a lull in interesting conversation, and when there were segments of silence she had no compulsion to fill them. Being quiet with Finn was just as pleasant as chatting with her.

Her feelings defied logic, but Finn made Iris feel calm. There was something solid about Finn. She had this way about her that made Iris think she was a person she could count on, that in a crisis, she'd be there for her. Of course, it was ridiculous to think this about someone Iris had known for only twenty-four hours, but there it was nonetheless. Iris had trusted people before and they'd let her down. Her father being chief among them. He'd been a huge, hurtful disappointment. She wondered if that's how she'd ended up dating a guy like Kent, cavalier and generally immature, just like her father. Those were qualities she didn't want to seek out in her next relationship. More than anything, Iris wanted to feel safe before she gave her heart away again. Safety would only come with trust.

Twenty or so minutes after leaving the overlook, they drove into a charming town called Blue Ridge. An historic railroad depot was the central focus of the quaint downtown, home of the Blue Ridge Scenic Railway.

Shops and eateries were in abundance up and down Main Street parallel to the train tracks. It seemed the little village was only a few blocks long and beyond that, everything quickly reverted back to a rural two-lane road.

Finn waited for someone in a pickup truck to back out and then parked in front of a Victorian building with a wide wraparound porch. The back of the truck had a patchwork of bumper stickers, but the one that caught her eye said "American by birth, Southern by the grace of God." There were several others in support of the NRA. She reminded herself that she wasn't in California, although, in the foothills of the Sierras they had their own sort of gun fans.

Sally's Sweets was painted on the large front window, and the smell of baked goods overwhelmed her senses when they entered the cozy bakery style café. A bell chimed as they crossed the threshold, and a woman smiled and waved them toward a table near the front window. A cozy little two-seater, with fresh cut wildflowers in a Mason jar.

Now that they were here and the smell of confectionary delights surrounded them, all Iris could think about was dessert.

"The coconut cake is really good, but so is the key lime pie." Finn was perusing the menu as she talked, not really looking at Iris. "I could go for pie or cake, I'm easy. I mean, only about cake." She looked up at Iris and grinned.

"Good to know." Iris was amused by Finn's playful flirtation. She pretended to read the menu.

"It's your birthday. You should pick."

"Maybe we should have a little of each." Iris glanced up.

"A woman after my own heart." Finn set the menu aside. "We order at the counter and then they bring it over. I'll go order. Do you want coffee too? Or tea?"

"A latte sounds good. Or just regular coffee if they don't do espresso."

"You've got it." Finn ambled toward the counter.

Iris made a mental note that Finn's ass looked very good in the jeans she was wearing. They fit just right, a little loose in the butt, low on her hips, and tapered through the legs. Finn made casual look good, effortless. People in LA probably paid hundreds of dollars to buy jeans pre-worn and distressed to perfection like the ones Finn was wearing. Iris had no doubt that all the custom wear on these jeans had been done by Finn personally.

Iris took a minute to look around the bakery. This place was an explosion of country cute. Funny sayings written in flowery hand-lettered fonts and then framed ornately, hung everywhere. The one closest to their table read, "We don't have Wi-Fi, pretend it's 1995, talk to each other." She was pretty sure she'd seen that one on Twitter, but it still amused her.

The framed quotes were mixed in with paintings of barns, cows, and other rural scenes. And shelves of vintage looking dishware ringed the room close to the ceiling. The decor was basically a well-groomed, higher-end flea market, with baked goods. Cluttered, cozy, and not altogether unappealing if country chic was your thing. Given the context of Blue Ridge, it seemed to Iris that the owner had struck just the right note.

Finn returned with two lattes and set one in front of Iris.

"They'll bring the cake and pie over in a minute. She's a little backed up with drink orders." Finn dropped one brown sugar cube into her coffee.

"Finn, thank you for today. Everything we've done has been really fun. I literally had no expectations for how I would spend my birthday other than possibly lounging and reading a good book. So thank you."

"I've had a really good time too. You made the day-after-getting-fired seriously okay."

The woman who seemed to be running the whole place delivered the desserts. Finn had been resting her elbows on the table. She rocked back in her chair to make room for the largest slice of coconut cake Iris had ever seen. There were four layers of cake, each separated by at least a quarter-inch of frosting.

"Wow." The pie was piled with whipped cream.

"We can take a few bites of each and then switch if you want."

"And then who drives us home when we pass out in a sugar coma?"

Finn laughed.

"Don't worry, I have a high tolerance for decadent behavior, and that includes sweets."

"Great. If I find myself in a confectionary crisis in the future, I know who to call."

The key lime pie was in front of Iris, so she started with that. The flavor was amazing, and the graham cracker crust was perfect, not too hard, not too crumbly. They each took two or three bites without talking. Iris felt the sugar rush almost immediately. She knew that in about half an hour all she'd want to do would be to take a nap.

"So, how long does it usually take after you read for a part? You know, to hear if you got it or not?"

"A few days." Iris scooped an entire spoonful of whipped cream and then licked the spoon. Finn was right, these desserts were decadently good.

Finn swallowed and took a sip of water. Watching Iris leisurely lick her spoon was doing nothing to temper her libido. She wondered if Iris truly had any idea how sexy she was. She must. She'd have to. People noticed Iris. It had started with her friend Ward, but all day long Finn couldn't help but note how much attention Iris garnered from every random person they encountered, male or female. She wondered what it was like to go through the world that way. Finn cleared her throat and tried to focus on the cake in front of her.

"But you said you're leaving tomorrow." Small talk. Finn was trying her best for neutral subjects, when what she really wanted to do was ask Iris to meet her at the car so they could make out.

"I'm supposed to fly out tomorrow. I suppose if I get the part I'll have to decide if I'm actually going to take it."

"What's your gut tell you?"

"My gut is currently experiencing a tsunami sized sugar rush." Iris shoved the half-eaten pie in Finn's direction. "Want to switch?"

"Sure." Finn slid the cake over to Iris.

"Can we not talk about the show?"

"Oh, sure. Sorry." Finn regretted bringing it up. She could tell it was a sore subject for Iris.

"It's okay. I just don't want to end the day talking about it. Especially since my gut has no idea how it feels about the situation."

"Let's change the subject."

"Thank you."

"What's your take on Crocs?"

"As in the rubber garden shoe?"

"Yes."

"Can't stand them." Iris laughed.

"Agreed. That's definitely a check in the *yes* column for you."

"Oh, how's my score so far?" The corner of Iris's mouth tilted up teasingly.

"High. Very high." The temperature in the room seemed to soar suddenly.

"Good." Iris held a forkful of cake near her tempting lips. "A girl likes to know where she stands."

Finn would give anything to know for sure where she stood. Did Iris even like girls, the way Finn liked girls? Women, she corrected herself. Did Iris like women? Finn was sure Iris was flirting with her, but was this simply friendly female flirtation or was this flirtation that might lead to other things? She just wasn't sure and it was beginning to drive her crazy. If Iris were planning to stay longer in Georgia then Finn would've just come right out and asked her. As it was, Iris was leaving tomorrow, so knowing or not knowing probably didn't matter.

"Can I ask how you got into acting?" Maybe that was a happier question than asking about the current show she'd read for.

"Hmm, okay, here's what happened." Iris set her fork down and Finn knew that despite efforts not to, she'd asked another heavy question. "In my senior year of high school I lost half my family in a bad divorce."

"I'm sorry." Finn felt terrible for asking. She sincerely thought she'd picked a safe topic.

"My dad was a philanderer, which didn't help, but he and my mom were mismatched from the beginning. When they divorced, his entire family turned against my mom and by extension, me."

"Wow." Finn felt sad for Iris. Her family by comparison was drama free, except for the usual meddling relatives.

"When I started applying for college I thought I'd go into science, or teaching. I'd really enjoyed biology in high school. I had to pay my own way so I ended up auditioning for the theater troupe that gave scholarships. That's how it started, and then I just fell in love with it."

Finn sipped her coffee and waited for Iris to continue. Iris looked out the window as if she were remembering something she was fond of.

"Acting, theater, gave me a family and sense of security when I felt like I had none." Iris turned toward Finn. Her direct eye contact was as tangible as if Iris had reached across the table and touched her. "And then I dated a woman in college, so when that news came out, no pun intended, I lost a few more people in my life. But my theater family didn't care who I slept with, they cared about me."

There it was, the answer to the question Finn hadn't been able to voice. Iris *had* dated women at some point. The flirtation she'd picked up on wasn't all wishful thinking.

"My theater friends became my chosen family. I think a lot of actors get into this because they're broken people somehow." Iris took a sip of water. "Of course, there are always people who want the fame and money. But I've met so many actors who were orphans of the world and that's why they found their way to it."

"Thank you for telling me." Finn sensed that this wasn't something Iris readily shared. Iris had allowed herself to be vulnerable and Finn didn't take that offering lightly.

Iris expected Finn to run for the door. She hadn't meant to speak so openly, but once she started talking it simply spilled out. She was afraid she'd made the conversation heavy. She couldn't read Finn's expression. Was that empathy or annoyance? Was Finn sorry she'd asked? Iris had two modes—avoidance or overly honest. She either didn't share at all, or she told the truth completely. Sometimes honesty worked against her.

"Sorry, that was probably more than you bargained for when you asked." Iris still couldn't quite read Finn's expression.

She wanted to give Finn an out. To her surprise, Finn covered Iris's hand with hers and let it rest there, despite the crowded café. Clearly, Finn wasn't worried about the small display of affectionate support.

"I'm glad you told me."

But Iris still wasn't sure she believed Finn.

"What about you?" Iris wanted to change the subject, lighten the mood.

"Me? Oh, I can't act. I'm terrible at it."

Iris laughed. Just like that, Finn had lightened her mood.

"Lean in. I'll take a photo of us before all the birthday cake is gone." Finn held her phone at arm's length.

"And birthday pie." Iris scooted forward.

Finn and Iris both leaned toward the center of the table, and Finn snapped a couple of shots.

"Will you send me the photo?"

"Sure, here, put your number into my phone." Finn handed Iris the phone. "I probably have some good shots from the lake too. You can scroll through and just put a heart on the ones you like."

"Hearts and cake and birthday wishes." Iris entered her number.

"Wishes. I knew I was forgetting something. We need a candle...for wishes we definitely need a candle..."

Iris laughed at Finn's faux display of urgency.

"Don't move. I'm going in search of fire."

Iris watched in amusement as Finn left her to search for a candle for the last third of the epic slice of coconut cake.

The return trip to Hideaway Haven seemed too short. Iris was grateful that Finn had thought to bring jackets for them. She'd gladly pulled on Finn's heavy hooded sweatshirt for the drive down the mountain after their yummy dessert dinner in Blue Ridge. She'd been wearing Finn's baseball cap most of the day. It was nice to loosely braid her hair and tuck it into the cozy hood for the drive back to the cabins.

Only briefly did she get a glimpse of the night sky as they wound their way through all the hairpin curves. The two-lane road was narrow and only occasionally did the thick canopy allow for a view of the moon. The air had cooled just enough as to be refreshing, but not chilling. And night sounds were all around them—tree frogs and cicadas.

They'd hardly talked the entire drive. Iris had been thinking that the whole day with Finn had been like a glorious vacation from reality, from her life in California. Maybe Finn was thinking something similar? Hard to tell from the expression on her face as she drove. Every now and then she'd glance over at Iris and smile. More than once, Iris thought of reaching over to rest her hand on Finn's thigh, but that would just be a tease for both of them. She was leaving tomorrow, and chances were she wouldn't be back. Better not to start something she might actually want more of.

Finn parked in the open-air garage, and after they took the towels and cooler out of the trunk she helped Finn replace the cover over the car. Finn left the cooler and towels piled on her porch and walked Iris to her cabin.

Suddenly, things were awkward. Iris remembered she was wearing Finn's sweatshirt and tried her best to tug it over her head gracefully. Not an easy task. The hem of her shirt slid up, exposing several inches of her stomach, and her hair feathered everywhere from a light dusting of static electricity. She righted her shirt and then smoothed her hair down with her hand as she held the sweatshirt out to Finn.

"Thanks for this. It made the ride home pleasantly warm."

"You sure you don't need it?"

"No, I'm just going to take a hot bath and probably curl up with my Kindle." Iris could tell Finn wanted to kiss her, but hesitated. "Thank you again for today."

"It was fun for me too. It always seems like you don't take time to enjoy where you live until someone visits." Finn draped the sweatshirt in the crook of her arm and shoved both hands in her pockets as if she needed somewhere to put them.

Finn considered kissing Iris. What did she have to lose? Iris was leaving so it wasn't as if she could totally screw something up. There was no *something* at this point. Unless she was completely crazy, during the day, Iris had definitely at times been flirtatious. She took a deep breath and looked around to see if anyone was about. *Just do it.* When she turned back Iris had stepped closer, invading her personal space.

Iris rested the palm of her hand against Finn's torso. She closed the space between them, almost in slow motion, and their lips lightly made contact. Iris sank into Finn and allowed her lips to linger on Finn's. Iris pulled back just a little and ran her tongue over her lower lip. Finn let her hands drift from her pockets to the curve of Iris's hips.

She gently drew Iris close and kissed her tenderly, letting the soft connection of their lips deepen. Iris broke the kiss, pulling away to study her. They stood looking at each other for a moment, their faces only inches apart, and she wondered if Iris was as surprised as she was by the kiss. Not just the kiss, but the unexpected intimacy of it.

She wanted to say something, anything to make the encounter last.

"Good night, Finn." Iris turned partially toward her cabin door. Words failed her.

"Good night, Iris."

There was nothing else to say as she watched Iris close the door. Her brisk pulse made her flesh tingle as she walked back to her cabin. Only a short walk that might as well have been two thousand miles, the distance from Georgia to California.

She splashed water on her face and undressed as if partially in a trance.

Finn wasn't sure how long she lay under the light covering. The night air had cooled and the window beside her bed was open. She wondered if Iris was awake also, despite the fact that the cabin lights were dark. Moonlight danced through the trees so that she could see the outline of Iris's cabin from her window. She closed her eyes and pictured Iris asleep, the way she'd slept that night in Finn's bed.

She was sorry now that they'd kissed.

If they hadn't kissed then Finn wouldn't know the taste of her lips, the scent of her skin. If they hadn't kissed then Finn wouldn't know how much she wanted Iris. Finn's heart hurt and there was nothing she could do about it.

CHAPTER FOURTEEN

Iris left early for the airport. Too early to say good-bye to Finn.

As she turned into the rental car return queue, that was all she could think of. She should have said good-bye. Maybe she didn't want to say good-bye. If she thought there was any way she could take the role she'd auditioned for, then she would be in Atlanta and maybe there'd be a chance to see Finn again. But that was a ridiculous thought. There was no way she could work with Eric and he was the director for the show. She was screwed.

A guy in a green vest signaled for her to follow a line of cars forward. She got out and retrieved her bag from the back seat. If she'd seriously planned to drive to California she'd have kept the rental, but she'd realized there was no way she could really do a road trip of that magnitude alone. That would have just been crazy. So here she was, back at the airport for another death-defying flight.

"How was your trip?" A woman handed her a receipt after checking the mileage on the car.

"It was great, thank you." Most of it was. Especially the parts in which Finn had a starring role.

"Have a nice day."

Iris followed other travelers with rolling luggage toward the train for the terminal. She texted Maggie to tell her she was at the airport. It was still too early on the West Coast so she was sure

Maggie wouldn't even look at her phone for a while. It was more of a compulsion to check in, to let someone know where she was.

She scrolled through photos on her phone, wishing she'd taken more while she was with Finn. She had one really great shot of Finn looking out at the mountains from the overlook they'd driven to. She'd snapped two in rapid succession, one when Finn didn't know she was being photographed and one when she turned to look at Iris. *Those eyes.* Iris enlarged the photo with her fingers for a closer look. She took a deep breath and exhaled slowly.

The train from the rental car center hissed to a stop and the doors opened. Time to begin the gauntlet of commercial air travel.

❖

Finn slept later than she'd meant to. After a fitful night she'd finally sunk into a deep sleep in the wee hours of the morning. There was slim hope that Iris might still be around. But when she strolled to the main house for coffee the rental car was gone, and linens piled on the front stoop of cabin number two confirmed that her mother had already started prepping for its next occupant.

She needed to take the limo into the city and drop it off. She texted her brother, Trey, to see if he could give her a ride home. He usually made an appearance for Sunday lunch so it shouldn't be too much of a hardship. One home cooked meal on Sunday kept him going all week at Georgia Tech. It also gave him a chance to do laundry for free, an opportunity not to be missed. Especially since their mother usually fussed over him to the point of doing it for him.

Traffic was sparse heading toward downtown.

She'd taken a to-go cup for coffee. She sipped and blared music as she headed toward the lot to drop off the car. She hoped Everett would still be at church when she arrived. Finn wasn't in the mood for a lecture or career advice from her former boss. He'd no doubt mean well, but she wasn't in the mood. She wanted to drop the limo off and get on with the rest of her life. She was getting plenty of advice from her mother anyway. A person could only tolerate so much self-reflection before noon.

The office was closed when she arrived. Finally, a little luck. She parked the limo next to a line of sleek, black cars and dropped the keys through the slot in the door. She doubted Everett would pay her for that last job, but who knows, maybe he'd consider it severance or a parting gift. Not likely.

She texted Trey to check his ETA and leaned against the side of the building while she waited. She scanned slowly, taking in the view. The parking lot was in an industrial area, surrounded by chain link fencing and nondescript concrete buildings. Was this where she wanted to be?

Fuck no.

She'd decided right then that it was time to quit screwing around. Stunt driving had been this holy grail that she kept telling everyone she was going in search of. It was time to stop talking about it and actually do it. She had enough money saved to get to LA and take the course. The question she hadn't quite answered for herself was if she'd stay in LA or come back to Atlanta. There were a lot of movies being shot in Atlanta, but there were probably more opportunities in Los Angeles. And now she actually knew someone on the West Coast, Iris. Someone she actually wanted a chance to see again.

A cross-country move was a little intimidating, but people did it all the time, right? And if she got out there and didn't like it she could always come back, no harm, no foul. At least she'd have tried it instead of just talking about it. Finn didn't want to be one of those people who was all talk and no action. Those kinds of people drove her crazy.

She saw Trey's truck turn into the lot and pushed off the wall and waited for him to pull up. Trey drove a 1974 Ford F-150. He'd gotten Ward's help to rebuild it from the ground up and it was a beauty. The truck was some shade of green that was only ever popular in the seventies, but he'd wanted to return it to its original color. They'd checked the VIN number, and sure enough, it had been green before some jackass who had no respect for history painted it gray.

"Hey." Trey handed her a coffee. "I thought you might need another one."

"Thank you, brother, you read my mind."

"So, you got fired?"

"Did Mom tell you?"

"Of course she did. You know she can't stand a secret until she shares it."

Finn sipped the coffee. Her mother had been in the kitchen when she'd grabbed a muffin for the road. She'd known right away that something wasn't right with Finn, and Finn was completely incapable of lying to her mother. She'd told her mother she was fired. Her mother assumed that's why Finn was just south of melancholy. Finn didn't share that Iris's departure was more likely the cause.

"Want to tell me what happened?" Trey merged into traffic. The road was packed with folks either headed home from church or to brunch or somewhere. Suddenly all of Atlanta seemed to be on the road.

"It's a short, sad story that ends with me punching out a client." Finn took her sunglasses from on top of her head and put them on. She wasn't about to share details about Iris.

"I knew I gave you boxing lessons for a reason."

Finn smiled. It was nice to have a good cup of coffee and a driver. She slouched on the bench seat, getting comfortable for the ride home.

Iris stared at the desk agent. Her uniform was pressed and her hair was perfect. For some reason, Iris had been totally distracted by the woman's excruciatingly pink nail polish as she'd handed over her ID.

"Wait, what?" Iris looked down, blinking at the card in her hand.

"I said, your driver's license has expired. Do you have another form of photo identification?"

Iris studied the card for a minute, looking for the renewal date. Damn. Her driver's license had expired on her birthday and she hadn't even noticed the expiration was looming. Didn't the state of California send out reminders about things like this? Thoughts zoomed through her brain as she tried to problem solve without giving up her spot in line.

"I said, do you have another form of identification? A passport would work." The agent at the counter was the epitome of neutral professionalism.

"Um, no, I don't have my passport with me."

"Maybe someone could bring it to you." A perfectly sane suggestion, but not at all helpful.

Was she serious? It wasn't like someone could just run it out to the airport in Atlanta from the West Coast. Especially not in the next hour and half before her flight left. Iris sensed the restless passengers queued up behind her waiting to check their bags.

"I'm afraid you'll need to sort this out before I can book you on this flight."

Iris turned to walk away, still holding her ID, in a bit of a daze.

"Miss, don't forget your bag."

Iris was about to wander off without her luggage. She'd left it on the scale so that it could be checked in. People scurried all around her as she stood near the kiosks trying to figure out her next move. She could call Maggie later. Maggie could FedEx her passport… somewhere, but that wasn't going to help her now. She texted Maggie, feeling the need to talk the problem through.

Getting ready for work. Can I call you later? Maggie responded.

Sure.

It wasn't like Maggie would be any help right this minute anyway.

Maybe she should stick with her original plan and drive back to California. No, wait, that wouldn't work either. She couldn't even rent a car without a valid driver's license. Iris stared at her phone, brainstorming.

And then a thought came to her.

There was one person who could help.

She texted the only person in Georgia she knew.

Hi, Finn. Is there any chance you're in Atlanta today? I'm stranded at the airport.

She remembered that Finn had said something about returning the limo. And luckily, she had Finn's number from when they'd shared photos at the bakery.

❖

Finn felt her phone vibrate in her pocket. Casually, she reached for it. The minute she read the screen she sat bolt upright.

"Is something wrong?" Trey was alarmed by her sudden shift in mood.

"Turn around."

"Why?"

"Just do it." Finn was texting as she talked. "We need to go to the airport."

"Seriously?"

"Come on, what else do you have to do today? I'll reimburse you for gas."

Trey sighed heavily, but did as she asked. As soon as he got a break in traffic, at the next light, he did a U-turn.

I am in town. I'll pick you up. What terminal? Which door? Finn responded.

Not sure, I'll find out and text you. Thank you!!

Finn's mood soared. She was getting a second chance to see Iris. She turned to Trey and smiled. He just shook his head.

It took a half hour, with the usual traffic along the connector through downtown, to reach the airport. The pickup lanes for the south terminal were congested, which made Finn antsy. As Trey wove in and around parked cars she scanned the curbside for Iris.

"There she is." Finn pointed.

"Where?"

"There...the blonde with the—"

"That's who we're picking up?" Trey's voice went up a notch.

"Yeah, that's Iris."

"Holy shit." Trey eased toward the curb. "You might have mentioned that she was smoking hot. I'd have agreed to do this airport run without the gas money."

"Shut up." Finn punched his arm.

"Ow."

She waved to Iris, who smiled and waved back. The truck had barely stopped rolling when Finn jumped out.

"I'm so glad to see you." Iris did seem genuinely happy, maybe even relieved.

"I'm glad to see you too." Finn reached for Iris's bag and stowed it behind the cab of the truck.

Trey smiled from the driver's seat.

"Iris, this is my brother, Trey. Don't believe anything he says." Finn let Iris slide onto the bench seat first, then followed.

"Hey! I haven't even said anything." Trey playfully scowled. "Nice to meet you, by the way."

The minute they pulled away from the curbside lane, Iris felt the tension ease from her shoulders. Finn had come to her rescue; all she'd had to do was ask. At least now she'd have a few hours to figure out a plan for getting back to California. She hadn't wanted to spend the money for an Uber if she was going to need to pay for a couple more nights at a hotel while she waited for Maggie to FedEx her passport. That's assuming she remembered where she'd put it. Hopefully in her top dresser drawer, but it had been a while since she'd needed it, so she wasn't sure.

She took a moment to settle.

Finn's brother, Trey, was good-looking. Like a scruffy, guy version of Finn. He had a thin growth of beard, more of a fashion statement than a beard. And shaggy brown hair. The first thought she had was that he looked as if he belonged in Portland or Seattle. He had that sort of look—faded plaid shirt, rolled to his elbows, boots, and dark jeans.

"Thank you so much for coming to get me. Seriously, you don't know how grateful I am."

"What happened?" Finn's arm was across the back of the seat. Her arm brushed Iris's shoulder as she partially turned toward Iris.

"I mean, not that I'm not excited to see you, but I thought your flight was this morning."

"My ID expired yesterday."

"On your birthday." Finn made the connection.

"Yes, and I guess I wasn't paying attention to the renewal date. I don't have my passport so I'm going to have to reschedule my flight. I mean, I can't even rent a car without a valid driver's license."

"What a pain. Plus, you really have the criminal element look about you." Trey grinned.

Iris laughed, feeling more at ease. She was among friends. New friends.

Trey merged onto the freeway heading back toward Atlanta.

"So, where are we going?" he asked.

Oh, no, Iris hadn't really sorted that out.

"Why don't you come back for another night at the cabins? I'm sure the black bear is long gone by now." Finn sounded hopeful.

"Sure, that sounds good." Given that she had no plan of her own in mind.

Why not stick with what she knew? Plus, this way Trey and Finn wouldn't have to go out of their way to deliver her somewhere else. She assumed Finn was heading back to Watts Mountain.

"Did you return the limo? Is that why you're in the city so early on a Sunday?" She wondered if the drop-off had been awkward.

"Yeah, I was trying to beat my boss to the office. Plus, I knew if I was early enough I'd catch a ride with Trey. He always tries to mooch a free meal while Mom does his laundry."

"Hey, don't give away all my secrets." He scowled at Finn.

"Such a big baby, making Mom do his laundry still." There was playfulness in Finn's words.

"Trey and Taylor." Iris looked from one to the other. "Cute."

"Except no one calls her Taylor."

"Yes, why *does* everyone call you Finn? I was curious about that." Iris had wondered but hadn't asked. Taylor was such an unusual name for a woman. She liked it.

"Oh, she didn't tell you?" Trey sounded conspiratorial, as if he were about to reveal some deep dark secret. "Because she couldn't spell in grammar school. And she couldn't pronounce t's. But for some reason she could say and spell Finn."

"Thank you for sharing." Finn reached across Iris and punched him in the shoulder.

"Ow. Sibling abuse!" He rolled his shoulder as if Finn's light punch actually hurt.

It was obvious that Finn and Trey were close. It was nice to be around siblings who cared about each other. Watching them interact made her a little lonely. She was an only child and had always wished for a brother.

CHAPTER FIFTEEN

Iris was relieved to be back at the quaint Hideaway Haven. Even if the reprieve from life was only going to be brief. Trey dropped them off and then drove over to park nearer the main building.

"Why don't you put your stuff in my cabin and come have lunch. We'll get you the key to your cabin after." Finn was about to reach for Iris's bag, but hesitated, waiting for confirmation.

"Are you sure I'm not imposing?" Lunch sounded good. She'd meant to grab something at the airport for breakfast, but after the ID debacle, it had slipped her mind. Her stomach had growled earlier reminding her of the oversight.

"Please do. My mom loves to meet new people, especially when she gets a chance to feed them. Sunday lunch is a time-honored southern tradition meant to be shared."

"All right, if you think it's really okay for me to crash."

"Absolutely." Finn started walking and Iris followed.

The main house was a large, two-story, home. The entry hall was set up for guest registration, and the sitting room had been converted into a dining area where they served a continental breakfast and coffee all day. Iris hadn't really sampled the breakfast display because Finn had delivered coffee and biscuits right to her door.

She followed Finn through the dining room. They passed through double swinging doors that ushered them into a large, eat-in kitchen. They were greeted by a flurry of activity—food being placed on the table in large plates, glasses being filled with ice, a pitcher of tea almost sliding off the counter. In other words, homespun chaos.

"Taylor, pour the tea before your father spills it all over the floor." Finn's mother looked up from the serving dish, visibly surprised to see a stranger in her kitchen. But she rallied quickly. "Well, well, hello. Taylor Elizabeth Finn, where are your manners? Introduce your guest."

"Mom, you remember Iris from when she checked in? And this is my dad."

"Hi." She tucked away the amusing knowledge that Finn's middle name was Elizabeth for a later date. "It's nice to meet you, Mrs. F—"

"Call me Betty and Taylor's father is Michael. We're on a strictly first name basis around here…Betty and Mike." Betty fussed with arranging the food in the center of the table, adding serving spoons as she talked.

"Thank you for letting me join your family lunch."

"Now, now, we all have to eat and it's so much more pleasant to eat together." Betty surveyed the table. She seemed satisfied. "All right now, everyone take a seat before everything gets cold."

Trey was quick to find a chair. He started to reach for a piece of fried chicken but slowly withdrew his hand due to Betty's scowling glare.

"Sorry, Mama."

"Honey, will you say grace?" Betty looked at Mike, seated at the head of the table. Betty was on one end and Mike was on the other.

Finn held out her hand to Iris. A tiny rush of adrenaline traveled through her bloodstream as she accepted. Finn's hand was warm and strong as her fingers lightly curled around Iris's. Betty held Iris's other hand. It had been a long time since she'd been at a table where anyone said grace before a meal. This act of thanks was oddly touching in a way she hadn't expected.

"Dear Lord, we thank you for this fine meal and we're grateful to those who prepared it. Bless this food to the nourishment of our bodies and our bodies to your service. In Christ's name we pray, amen." Everyone softly echoed *amen*.

"I like how he always says them, when the Lord knows I'm the only one in the kitchen." Betty passed the chicken to Finn, quirking an eyebrow playfully at her husband.

Finn held the plate of chicken out for Iris to take a piece. Then served herself. Next came mashed potatoes, green beans, carrots, and more of those amazing biscuits. Within mere moments, Iris had a plate piled high with food.

"Now, Iris, you're not from Georgia are you?" Betty sipped her iced tea.

Iris swallowed her mouthful of food and then dabbed at her lips with the napkin.

"No, I'm from California. I live in Santa Monica."

"She's an actor, Mama. She came to Atlanta to read for a part." Finn smothered the bottom half of her biscuit with butter.

"An actor." Betty entwined her fingers in a little triangle above her plate. There was a twinkle in her eyes. "Do you know George Clooney?"

"Mama, not everyone in the LA area knows George Clooney." Finn shook her head.

"I'm sorry, no, I don't know him." Iris was amused by the idea of it.

"He's a mighty good-looking man, yessir, mighty fine looking," Betty crooned.

"I'm sittin' right here." Mike frowned and then returned his attention to his meal, shaking his head.

Iris tried not to laugh.

"That's why you look so familiar." Trey set down his fork. "I've seen you in something. What was it?"

"*Law and Order*? I played the wife of a murder victim in one of the show's last season." Iris threw out a suggestion.

"No, it wasn't that." Trey's brow furrowed as if he were focusing on something intently.

"A Doritos commercial?" It was unfortunate that her stint as a barmaid during the Super Bowl was what most people seemed to remember.

"That's it! Oh, man, you were so h—"

"Don't say it." Finn threatened her brother with her dinner knife.

"I was gonna say talented." Trey cleared his throat.

"Yeah, that's what I thought you were going to say." Finn winked at Iris and resumed her meal.

"Has George Clooney ever done a Super Bowl commercial?" Betty was hopeful.

Everyone laughed.

Finn's family was a pleasure to be around and the meal was delicious. Mostly the conversation was light and friendly. Once it had been settled that Iris and George Clooney were not acquainted then Betty moved on to other topics. Some of which included chores she wanted Mike to do, or Trey, while he was there for the afternoon.

"I told Dad that we need bear lockers too." Finn served herself a second helping of mashed potatoes. "Did he tell you there was a bear out behind cabin two getting into the trash?"

"No, he neglected that detail." Betty worked at the chicken on her plate with a fork.

Iris was never sure if it was acceptable to eat fried chicken with your fingers or if she should use a fork. Perhaps either method was okay.

"I'll figure something out." Mike reached for another piece of chicken. "They're just hungry is all. They don't mean no harm."

Finn watched Iris daintily hold a piece of chicken between her slender fingers. She seemed to be taking the Finn clan in stride. Luckily, nothing too embarrassing had happened so far, except her mother's reveal of her middle name. That was unfortunate. Finn liked to keep those sorts of details to herself.

"Is cabin two still open?" Finn asked her mother.

"Yes. I swapped out the sheets and towels this morning." Her mother settled her fork across her plate.

"Good. I'll get Iris the key after lunch." Her phone buzzed in her pocket. She checked the screen. She had a text message from Ward. "Say, after we get you checked in, do you want to ride over to Ward's place with me?"

"Sure." Iris sipped her tea. Her plate was nearly empty.

"I forgot that I told him I'd stop by when we saw him at the store yesterday."

She didn't miss the fact that her mother perked up at the news she'd been with Iris the previous day. But she wasn't in the mood to get into all of it now. She was sure her mother would pelt her with questions later.

"Mama, do you want me to stay and help with the dishes first?"

"No, Trey can help. You girls go ahead. You can get Iris's things settled too." Her mother seemed as pleased as a meddling matchmaker.

"Hey, why do I have to do dishes?" Trey on the other hand, was less than pleased, although he was clearly joking.

"He who eats free helps with dishes." Her father settled back in his chair and held out his cup. "Is there coffee made?"

"Good Lord, you'd think a grown man could get his own coffee. I swear I have to do every little thing around this kitchen." Her mother touched her dad's shoulder affectionately as she served him coffee. "Does anyone else want coffee?"

"No, thanks, Mama." Finn took one last swig of her iced tea. "Lunch was great, thank you."

"Thank you, Betty. That was a terrific meal." Iris stood and slid her chair back in place. "Are you sure I can't help with the dishes?"

"No, no, you're our guest. You just get yourself settled in. Taylor can help you with your bags." She started to shift the leftovers to containers on the counter. She obviously only called Finn by her first name. "You girls have fun."

She followed Finn to the front office to find the keys for cabin two. They stopped off at Finn's cabin to retrieve Iris's suitcase.

"Thank you for inviting me to join your family for lunch. That was really fun." Iris stood back while Finn unlocked the door. "Your mother is a great cook."

"I'm just thankful they didn't say anything too over-the-top." She stepped aside to allow Iris to enter. "I mean, the George Clooney question was bad enough. My mom is fifty and still as boy crazy as ever."

"She's sweet. And so is your dad." Iris took the bag from Finn and rolled it into the bedroom. "Even your brother is charming."

Hmm, Iris obviously liked her brother. Should she be jealous?

"He's almost as charming as you are." It was as if Iris had read her mind.

"Nice save." Finn leaned against the frame of the open door. "So, are you still up for going for a drive over to Ward's?"

"Sure, just let me take a few minutes here and then I'll meet you at your car?"

"Sounds good." She turned to leave but stopped before she closed the door. "Hey, Iris?"

"Yes."

"I'm really glad you're here." She hoped Iris knew how sincerely she meant that.

"Me too."

CHAPTER SIXTEEN

Ward's garage and repair shop was a long building, like a small warehouse, constructed mostly of corrugated metal. Large sections looked as if they were on the brink of rusting through. There were two bay openings, and cars in various stages of reconstruction or deterioration were scattered all over out front. Frankly, the whole place was so perfectly disheveled that it struck Iris as if she were stepping into a location for a film.

Ward stepped from the shadows, wiping his hands on a red cloth. He shoved the rag in his pocket as they approached.

"Hey, thanks for coming by. I needed a break." Ward smiled.

"You remember Iris?" Finn lightly touched Iris's shoulder.

"Hello." Iris nodded. She was a little out of her natural habitat. A bit out of her element.

"Of course. Nice to see you again." He motioned toward the truck parked inside the bay. It was up on some sort of lift. "I was attempting to fix a spongy brake pedal in that ninety-three GMC Sierra. I bought a new master cylinder and it was crap."

"Fascinating." Finn studied him with her hands at her hips.

"And before that it was a power steering pump. The replacement pump had a faulty bypass valve. It was as if there was no assist at all. The pump made a bunch of noise and fluid churned about in the reservoir, and…"

"He babbles when he's around beautiful women," Finn half-whispered to Iris.

She appreciated that Finn was able to jokingly harass her friend while simultaneously paying her a compliment. This wasn't the first time she'd thought Finn was gifted at flirtation.

Ward continued to relay all the details about his current repair project, as if anyone was actually listening. Finally, Finn cut in.

"You see, this is why I don't drive a GMC." Finn grinned at Iris. "One of many reasons."

"Not all of us get to drive our dream car." Ward scowled.

"I hear ya, brother." Finn patted him on the shoulder. "So, what do you need?"

"There's a race this weekend in Dawsonville, and I wanted you to take the car for a few turns." Ward started walking toward an older model, two-door seventies era Ford Mustang.

"Who's driving?" Finn asked.

"Ned Ames."

"He's such a dick." Finn walked around the car, inspecting it. "Why do you keep fixing cars for him?"

"That ancient evil known as money." Ward shrugged. "He's got more money than sense."

"He's got more money than skill." Finn crossed her arms.

"That too. Let me just hit pause on this and I'll grab the keys." Ward turned to walk back into the darkened garage and they followed.

There was an elegant vintage Lincoln parked in one of the bays. Mostly it was black, except for a few large organic shapes of gray primer. The hood was up. It looked like another project in process.

"That's a 1964 Lincoln Continental. It has suicide doors." Finn opened the back driver's side door so that Iris could see the red leather interior.

"The door is backward." Iris didn't know anything about cars, but even she could see that the hinges were at the rear rather than the front of the door.

"That's why they call them suicide doors. Because they're generally considered to be unsafe." Finn grinned. "Unsafe but unquestionably cool."

"Whose car is this?" Iris would have described the car as sexy, over cool.

"Mine." Finn closed the door. "Apparently, cars from the late fifties, early sixties are my ideal vintage."

"So, you have the smallest car and the longest car?" The Lincoln was huge compared to the roadster.

"Well, I always figured we'd restore the Lincoln, and if things didn't work out, I could always live in it."

Iris laughed.

Ward rejoined them. He and Finn started back toward the front of the garage, where the stock car was parked. Iris followed several feet behind, taking in the shelf along the back wall filled with motorsport trophies.

It took a moment for Iris's eyes to adjust to the brightness after the dark interior. She shielded her eyes.

"So, what do you say? Will you take it around a few times and let me know how it feels?" Ward held a helmet out in Finn's direction.

"Sure." Finn put the helmet on. She looked at Iris as she adjusted the chin strap. "This won't take long."

The door was welded shut, so Finn slid into the seat through the window using something like a gymnastics move. The engine roared to life. Iris watched as Finn steered the car toward the pasture near the shop. Although, as she walked closer she could see that a dirt road circled the tall grass and shrubs of the open field. Finn turned onto the road and hit the gas. Dirt and dust billowed behind the wide tires as the car spun out and then lurched forward, fishtailing just a little before stabilizing. Finn was going so fast so quickly that it made Iris's pulse quicken. The whole setup seemed sort of wild and rough. There were no guardrails unless bales of hay along the side of the dirt track counted.

"Do you like cars?"

Iris had almost forgotten Ward was standing next to her until he spoke. She'd been completely distracted watching Finn.

"Oh, um, well, I own a car. But it's more about simple transportation than anything else." Iris didn't really care what model she drove as long as it was safe and dependable.

"Lucky you."

"Why do you say that?" Was he being sarcastic?

"It's an expensive hobby once the bug bites."

"What bug?"

"Car fever." He smiled.

"Does Finn ever drive in races?" She was reminded of her time with Kent. How she'd worried about his reckless weekend racing.

"She used to race a lot. We've got a shelf full of trophies in the garage to show for it. But she hasn't been racing lately." Ward sounded like maybe he didn't agree with Finn's choice to stop.

"Did the other racers give her a hard time?" Iris wondered if Finn had stopped racing for some particular reason. Racing had to be a hard career choice for a woman.

"Sometimes. Guys can be assholes." Ward smiled. "Especially when a girl kicks their ass on the track."

The Ford roared past, sliding a little through the curve, and then gained speed in the straightaway. Iris could feel the sound reverberate in her chest. She took a few steps back.

❖

Finn gripped the wheel aiming for balance through the curve. Then she upshifted and hit the accelerator as she came out of the curve. Controlling the V8 beast gave her an adrenaline boost, a thrilling injection that pulsed through her entire system. The car was tight. Ward had made some good modifications that Ned should be pleased with. She was almost jealous that it wasn't hers to drive, but she needed to stay focused on a different path. Especially now.

She'd done the dirt track circuit for a few summers. There was no doubt it was fun, and sometimes you won and actually made some cash. But the culture that surrounded the races just wasn't where she wanted to be any more. Plus, there were too many redneck amateurs signing up to race which made the whole endeavor unsafe for everyone.

She downshifted heading into the next curve. In rapid succession, she worked the clutch and the accelerator. The goal was to avoid using the brake to slow the car and manage the turns while maintaining as much speed as possible. The right rear wheel hit the grass on the outside of the curve. She'd overshot and had to course correct. The steering wheel shimmied as she fought the car back onto the rutted dirt road.

She did two more laps and then turned the Ford toward the driveway in front of the garage. Iris was holding herself with her arms crossed as if she were chilled, but the air was plenty warm. Finn couldn't be sure, but Iris almost looked annoyed. Maybe she'd taken too long. Maybe she shouldn't have suggested that Iris come with her. Usually women liked the whole racing vibe. It was a turn-on for some. And if Finn were being honest, she'd admit that she'd wanted to show off just a little for Iris. She still couldn't quite figure out if Iris was into her or not. If her expression in this moment was an indication then the answer was no.

Finn tossed the helmet on the passenger seat and climbed out of the car. She was sure she had dust in her hair. She could see it on her jeans. She dusted them off.

Iris could almost taste the adrenaline pulsing off Finn. It was obvious she loved driving. Like, loved it as in it might be an obsession. She could never get serious again with someone who so carelessly put themselves at risk for thrills. This little trip to the track had been a needed reminder for Iris of who Finn really was. Beneath all the easygoing charm was a thrill junkie, just like Kent. She knew the adrenaline rush was addictive. Kent had said as much. As if it wasn't his fault, as if he couldn't help his need for it.

"Hope I didn't keep you waiting for too long." Finn handed the car keys to Ward.

"Not at all." Iris shook her head, but Finn didn't really believe her.

"Well, how'd she drive?" Ward was anxious to hear Finn's feedback.

Iris stood a few feet away as Finn and Ward talked. It was as if she were eavesdropping on two people speaking a foreign tongue. Talk of torque, tension, steering, balance, and other things she knew related to the car, but made no sense to her.

Finn swept her fingers through her hair. There was a smudge of dust on her cheek. Once again, she couldn't help but notice how good Finn looked in Levi's. In the white crew neck T-shirt, cuffed jeans, and Converse, Finn looked like some extra from a fifties-era movie. Cute, sexy even, because of the way her biceps filled out her shirtsleeves, her well-defined muscles pulling the sleeve snug around her upper arm.

Finn glanced over, making direct eye contact. She'd caught Iris looking. Iris let the connection linger for a moment before she forced herself to look away. Earlier, she'd constructed a list of why she should not have any interest in Finn. Five minutes later, she was editing that list and replacing everything on it with all the ways in which she found Finn attractive.

Get serious.

The only reason she was even entertaining an attraction at all was because all of this was a short-term layover. A distraction from LA and the stress of figuring out how she was going to get home.

CHAPTER SEVENTEEN

Finn sensed that Iris's mood had shifted. It was almost as if a dark cloud hovered over her head, despite the bright blue of the summer sky. In an attempt to cheer Iris up she suggested they go to Turner's Corner for ice cream.

Iris waited at one of the outdoor picnic tables near the creek while Finn fetched the ice cream. There were limited flavors in the case near the deli, but the ice cream was locally made and organic. Chocolate for Finn and strawberry for Iris, who preferred a cup to a cone. That made sense. Cups were tidy and manageable. Cones could be messy and hard to control. Finn sensed that Iris liked to keep things under control.

"Here ya go." Finn handed Iris a heaping cup of strawberry.

"Oh, wow. Is that really a single scoop?"

"Yeah, they don't skimp on serving size." Finn swung her leg over the bench seat and settled in across from Iris.

They sat quietly for a few minutes, listening to the soothing sound of the babbling creek nearby. A bluebird landed at the far end of the table and cocked his head to one side. The bird probably hoped for a nibble of Finn's cone, but she wasn't ready to give any of it up just yet.

"So, what are you going to do about getting the whole ID thing straightened out?" Finn took a bite, mixing ice cream and cone together. The oversized waffle cone was homemade too and delicious. She'd almost be willing to just eat the cone all by itself.

"I was going to try to have my roommate FedEx my passport, if I can remember where I left it." Iris sighed. "Letting my driver's license expire was so stupid."

"And out of character."

"Why do you say that?" Iris looked so serious.

"I just meant that you seem pretty organized...you know, and professional. I'll bet that sort of thing doesn't happen to you very often."

"Yes, I suppose it is a bit out of character." Iris relaxed and returned her attention to the last of her ice cream.

Finn watched Iris and listened to the stream bubbling behind her. The bluebird took flight. A white jet trail cut across the sky. A Jeep drove by with the top down. The radio blared Lynyrd Skynyrd. The southern anthem, "Free Bird," trailed off as the Jeep turned right and sped away. And in that instant, clarity struck. Everything seemed to slow down and almost come to a stop. Finn held her cone in both hands as if it were an offering.

"What's wrong?" Iris must have sensed her sudden jolt of inspiration.

"I have an idea."

Iris set her cup down and focused on Finn.

"What's the idea?"

"What if I drove you back to California?" Finn held her breath for a few seconds.

"Are you serious?"

"Yeah, why not?" The more Finn rolled the idea around in her head the more she liked it. "I'm done here."

"You've only eaten half your ice cream."

"No, not that. I mean, I'm done *here*. Done with postponing what I really want to do. All the best stunt driving schools are in LA, and you need to get back to California. Why don't we go together? It'll be an epic road trip. What do you say?"

Iris studied Finn. Was Finn serious? She seemed serious. Finn had an almost giddy, excited expression. Her eyes sparkled and she was grinning broadly.

"You're really serious." Envisioning a cross-country road trip with Finn made her skin tingle. Was that nerves or excitement or a risk response? She wasn't sure.

"Yes, I'm serious." Finn took a bite of her cone.

"Have you even registered for a course yet?"

"No, but I could do that tonight or when we get there. That's what I've been saving up for. It would take us at least a week to get there, so chances are a spot would open up by then." Finn took a deep breath. "And if I had a friend near LA who would let me sleep on their sofa for a couple of nights, then I'm sure I could figure things out even if I had to wait a week or two for the course to start."

"A friend, huh?" Iris wondered what Maggie would think of Finn sleeping on their couch.

"What do you say?"

"Well..." Iris wasn't sure what to say. Should she think it over? Maybe she should sleep on it. But why? She needed to get home and Finn was offering to drive. She'd considered driving by herself, although she hadn't shared that idea. "You know, I had such a terrible flight into Atlanta that I actually considered driving all the way back to Santa Monica myself."

"Really?"

"Yes, really. But I wasn't sure doing that trip alone would be a good idea. Of course, without a driver's license that option was off the table anyway."

"So, this bad flight was in addition to your *very bad day*?" Finn was sympathetic.

"Yes. The plane dropped, as if it hit a wind shear or something. It was seriously scary."

"Wow." Finn shifted forward, leaning on the edge of the table, and then her expression grew serious. "That settles it. We should definitely drive to California. What do you say?"

Iris had never done a cross-country road trip. It wasn't as if she needed to get back in a hurry. What did she have to lose?

Finn waited expectantly for her answer.

"Okay."

"Okay, you're up for a road trip?" Finn sounded hopeful.

"Yes, okay. Why not?" Iris couldn't help smiling.

This might be the craziest idea she'd agreed to in a long time, maybe ever. Driving two thousand miles with someone she hardly knew but couldn't stop thinking about. Things could get complicated in all sorts of ways.

❖

Iris kicked off her shoes and waited for Maggie to answer. Finn had dropped her off and taken the car to Ward's for a quick once-over before they took it on the extended drive to California. Iris tucked her feet under her and angled in the overstuffed chair so that she could look out the window.

"Hey, are you back?" Background noise on Maggie's end suggested she was not at home.

"No, I'm still in Georgia."

"I thought you were flying back today...hey, listen, sorry I didn't return your call. Work was crazy and then, you know..." Laughter and music in the background made it hard to hear.

"Where are you?"

"Sorry, it's loud. I'll step outside." Maggie said something to someone, Iris couldn't make out what she'd said, and then a few seconds later she came back. "I'm out for coffee with some work friends. So, why are you still in Georgia? Did you get the part?"

"I don't know yet, but my driver's license expired so they wouldn't let me board the plane."

"Oh, no, are you serious?"

"I was going to ask you to send me my passport, but now I'm just going to drive back."

"You're going to drive...all the way to California...by yourself?" Maggie's voice pitched up at the end. "Isn't that like four thousand miles?"

Iris laughed. "More like two thousand."

"Either way, still a long effing drive to manage alone."

"I'm driving with a friend."

"Hmm, he must be cute," Maggie said.

"Yes, *she* is."

"Oh…she, huh? She, as in, we like to wear the same kind of heels? Or she, as in, I think she's hot?"

Iris laughed again. "Yeah, the second option."

"Sounds like a blast, Iris. You've been needing a vacation. I think this is a great idea."

"You do?"

"Yes, absolutely. Cute girl, road trip, summertime. Have fun. Just text me every now and then to let me know your progress. And text me a photo. I need to see a picture of…what's her name?"

"Finn." Iris took a deep breath. "Taylor Finn."

"Sexy name. She must be hot."

"She's cute."

That's as much as Iris would reveal, but there was no denying that Finn was hot, and sexy. What was she getting herself into?

❖

Finn spent two hours with Ward going over the MG with a fine-tooth comb. The car was in excellent shape to make the trip. That is, excellent shape for a decades-old roadster. Was she crazy to put this much mileage on an antique car? No. The roadster was never meant to be a show car. It was always her intention to drive it and enjoy it, rather than save it for some auto show reveal. She topped off the tank and headed back to her cabin to pack.

Why was she suddenly a giant knot of nerves?

It wasn't like she'd committed to moving to California forever. She was simply going for a couple of weeks to gain some credentials. But what if she didn't have what it took to be a stunt driver? It was easy to mouth off about some pie in the sky career while she was cooling her heels at a safe distance. It was going to be another thing to put it all on the line for real. No more stalling.

And she'd offered to take Iris with her.

What the hell was she thinking?

Or a better question, what was she thinking with?

Yeah, this trip was going to be tough any way she looked at it. She'd have to do all the driving in a two-seater with a woman she was completely crushed out on. There were so many ways this whole excursion could go sideways. Too many to count.

She parked in front of her cabin instead of in the garage. Finn stood beside the car deciding what to do first. She needed to pack, obviously, but she also needed to go online and actually register for the driving school. If she had to wing it for more than a week after arriving in LA she'd run out of funds. She also needed to break the news to her parents that she was going to take off and try to make her dream a reality. Probably a week to drive out, five days for the class, and another week back if the whole plan turned out to be a disaster. That was barring any other unforeseen speed bumps. It was hard to anticipate what those might be ahead of time.

She decided to pack and check out openings for the class. Her mother would be tired this late in the evening and inevitably wouldn't take the news as well. She'd talk to her tomorrow over breakfast.

The cabin was a bit of a mess. Maybe her folks would hold off renting it for a month in case she needed to skulk home with her tail between her legs.

Luckily, she'd restocked the mini fridge. She grabbed a beer and booted up her laptop. Rick Crenshaw's Stunt Driving School was the place she'd been stalking. The course was held at the Willow Springs Raceway in Rosamond, California, just north of Los Angeles. The price was steep—twelve hundred dollars for one day, multiply that times five for the entire course. She had almost fifteen thousand in the bank. Following this dream might take all of it.

No gamble, no gain.

There were a few openings on the schedule. She reserved a spot for a week and a half out. That would give her a few extra days in case the drive took longer than she thought. For now, she'd just book the first two days. She could always add days once she got there. What if she hated stunt driving?

That seemed unlikely.

Finn sank back in her chair taking a long swig of her beer. She glanced out the window. Iris's lights were still on. She wondered if Iris was having any second thoughts. Maybe she should text her just to make sure.

Checked over the whole car with Ward. All good. She's ready to head west.

Finn waited for a reply. It only took a couple of minutes for Iris to respond.

Great. What time should we leave?

Finn did some math about distances. It would take probably three hours over back roads to get to Columbus. From there, how far was it to Meridian? She decided to do some figuring quickly using Google Maps. It was about three hundred and fifty miles from Watts Mountain to Meridian, Mississippi. They could easily do that in a day. Couldn't they?

Want to leave around 9:00 tomorrow? There was no point leaving during rush hour. If they left at nine they'd be behind Atlanta commuter traffic.

Sounds good. There was a break in the thread and then a second text came through from Iris. *Can I borrow that sweatshirt again for the drive? I didn't really pack a jacket for this trip?*

Sure.

Finn checked the time. It wasn't that late. Maybe she should try to talk to her parents now. Better to get the drama over with. Otherwise she wouldn't be able to sleep very well. Plus, that'd be one less thing to deal with in the morning.

CHAPTER EIGHTEEN

The trunk of the MG was so small that Finn ended up strapping Iris's small suitcase to the luggage rack. If they found themselves in a downpour they'd have to find cover anyway. The cloth convertible top was only marginally weatherproof. She decided not to share that detail with Iris just yet. It was early in the trip. Might as well let her think the best of Scarlett in the beginning.

As it turned out, the conversation with her parents hadn't been as drama-filled as she'd expected. Finn actually thought her mother was happy that she was finally going to *do something* with her life. Even if it wasn't the *something* she'd hoped for. Finn suspected her mother's positive attitude had something to do with the fact that Iris was traveling with her and that Iris seemed like a responsible grown up. Apparently, her parents thought Finn still required adult supervision.

They left Hideaway Haven with a thermos of coffee and biscuits for the road.

The first hour of the drive, the conversation was sparse. By nature, Finn wasn't really chatty in the morning, and Iris seemed distracted by thoughts of her own.

Iris held up the thermos, an offer to pour coffee for Finn.

"Thanks, that'd be great."

But as soon as Finn had the cup she realized Iris would have to hold it for her so that she could shift gears.

"We can both drink it." Finn was happy to share with Iris. And the coffee was a nice icebreaker. Finn took a sip and handed the cup to Iris. "So, what do you think so far?"

"Georgia is very green." Iris held the cup close to her lips. "Living in California you forget how green summers can be. It's so dry in Southern California that all the grass turns golden by late spring."

"I look forward to seeing that for myself."

For Finn, having a vintage car meant avoiding four-lane freeways whenever possible. She'd plotted a course along old Highway 80 as far as Texas, then they'd turn north and pick up old Route 66 in Amarillo.

Highway 80 took in miles of rolling countryside as it cut across Georgia. The two-lane blacktop was peppered with dozens of small towns. The road wound through thick hardwood and pine forests. They passed white-columned farmhouses with wide lawns along the way and an equal number of rundown tin-roofed dwellings that looked as if a strong wind could blow them over. Most of those places had yards full of rusting appliances and old cars on blocks, partway covered with kudzu.

They'd only stopped once for a restroom break before they reached Columbus. It was midday and they were making good time. It had been a long time since Finn had driven through Columbus. Downtown offered a range of eateries from down-home to high-end. Country's on Broad served classic homestyle cooking. If Finn was remembering correctly, their barbeque was excellent. The restaurant was located in a remodeled 1930s bus depot, complete with an old bus for a dining area.

The place reminded Finn a little of the diner where she and Iris first met. As she got out of the car and stretched, she couldn't help smiling.

"What's funny?" Iris had a curious expression.

"I was just remembering how the first time we met we were in that diner and you threw water in my face." She held the door for Iris as they entered the bustling restaurant.

"Maybe you should keep beverages out of reach this time."

"I'll take that under advisement."

It was hard to believe where they'd started and where they'd ended up. They'd only known each other for a little more than forty-eight hours, and now they were on an epic adventure. One thing was for sure, five days from now they'd know each other a lot better. Finn couldn't help wondering exactly what that might mean.

She'd been on pins and needles since they left Watts Mountain. A bundle of nerves. Everything about Iris made Finn's skin all tingly, other parts too. Thank goodness she was driving. Keeping her focus on driving gave her something to do with her head and her hands.

❖

Lunch was a leisurely affair. Iris felt as if she'd consumed her weight in French fries, but battered and dipped in ketchup, they were hard to resist. They left Columbus and started across the bridge. She looked north as they crossed the Chattahoochee River that separated Georgia from Alabama. The water was brown and churned beneath them, making its way to the Gulf of Mexico.

The car had no air conditioning, but luckily, the day was overcast. Cloud cover and wind from the open windows saved them from the summer heat. They stopped for a break just outside Montgomery to use the restroom and stretch their legs. The car was fun but small, and as Finn had explained to her, it had a tight suspension. Iris soon realized that was "car talk" for a stiff ride. She could tell this was going to be a trip with frequent stops, which she was actually happy about. While they were parked at the convenience store, Finn decided to put the convertible top down for the rest of the afternoon.

It was nice to be in the open air, although Iris had to pull her hair back with a couple of hair ties to keep it from creating a driving hazard.

"Have you ever been to Montgomery?" Finn accelerated onto the highway.

"No, I haven't."

"We should take a little detour then." Finn turned toward her and smiled. She was wearing old school Ray-Bans, and her dark hair fluffed in the breeze of the open-air roadster. "There's a lot of history in Montgomery."

Iris was intrigued. And besides, why not take some detours along the way. That was the whole point of a road trip, right? They drove for a few minutes before Finn began to point out landmarks.

"That's the state capitol building, and right across the street is the first White House of the Confederacy. That's where Jefferson Davis and his family lived before they moved from Montgomery to Richmond." Finn slowed as they passed. They'd only driven one block when she pointed to another building. "And this is where Martin Luther King Jr. preached. The Dexter Avenue King Memorial Baptist Church."

"Only a block from the house where Jefferson Davis lived?" The red brick church was right on the corner with white steps leading up to the front entrance from two sides.

"Crazy, huh? A single block isn't much distance considering the huge gulf, historically, between whites and blacks in Alabama." Finn slowed as they passed the church. Then made a turn to take them back to Highway 80. "Like I said, the South is complicated."

Just around the corner from the church Finn slowed again.

"That's the Civil Rights Memorial." Finn pointed.

As they slowly rolled past, Iris got the chills. This had been a community that had endured much and come through the other side. Although, sadly, images in the news sometimes made it seem as if the country was right back where it had started.

Montgomery had been the largest city they'd driven through since leaving Columbus, and it felt like a sleepy small town. Route 80 cut through the rural midsection of Alabama. The road alternated between old-style two-lane and sections of newer, four-lane freeway. It was much more pleasant than driving on an interstate. Iris tried to picture Finn on the 405 in LA. She couldn't quite see it. Los Angeles probably used to be a fun city to drive in. In modern LA the traffic was so bad every freeway just ended up resembling a parking lot.

They stopped for gas about an hour outside Montgomery, just after crossing the Tombigbee River. Another slow moving, wide, muddy waterway. Darker clouds in the distance signaled that maybe a summer storm had stirred up the water. The air smelled damp, like rain.

"We'll be in Meridian soon." Finn was checking her phone.

Iris was glad. The day of driving had been fun, but her back was stiff, and after riding for a few hours in the humid climate, she was ready for a shower. She was sure her hair was expanding by the minute from the humidity. They were parked in the shade, at the side of the gas station, standing near the car.

"Um, I was wondering..." Finn sounded unsure.

Iris removed the elastic ties and ran her fingers through her hair, swinging it from side to side to allow air to reach the back of her neck.

Finn froze. Iris was doing the sexiest thing with her hair and Finn couldn't help but stare. She swallowed and tried to remember what she'd been about to say.

"Yes?" Iris pulled her hair up into a knot, away from the elegant curve of her neck, and stayed it with the ties again.

"Huh?" Finn realized she was still staring.

"You said you were wondering about something." Iris was clueless about her effect on Finn. Or maybe not.

"Um..." Finn swallowed again and stowed her phone in her pocket. "I was just thinking that maybe we should talk about where we're gonna stay tonight."

"I thought we decided to stop at that place in Meridian?"

"Yeah." Was she going to have to spell it out? "What I meant was, are we going to get one room or two?"

"Oh." Iris's expression was hard to decipher.

"I mean, obviously if we get one room we can get two beds...I was just thinking we'd stretch our money further if we shared the cost and only got one room." Now that she'd seen Iris's whole display with her hair, maybe Finn was asking for trouble by suggesting they share a room.

"I'm okay with it if you are?"

What did Iris mean by that? Was she saying that it wasn't a complication for her to share a room? That there was no attraction she'd have to ignore if they slept in the same room? Well, if it was fine for Iris then it was fine for Finn.

"Yeah, I'm okay with it." Finn replaced her sunglasses and opened the car door, a signal that she was ready to get back on the road.

They'd kissed once, but neither of them had mentioned it again. Maybe it was a fluke. Maybe it had been nothing more than a *thank you*, friendly kiss in return for Finn taking Iris out for her birthday. It hadn't seemed like a thank you kiss. But Finn had been wrong before, and she was prepared to deal with being wrong again.

Iris's indifference annoyed her. Maybe she was simply tired and it was time to call it a day. She'd been doing all the driving, and handling the roadster was almost like an all-day sporting event. Driving the MG required active driving. It wasn't as if you could just engage cruise control and relax at the wheel.

Iris glanced at Finn who seemed extremely focused on the road. Every now and then the muscle along Finn's jaw clenched, as if she were tense, or annoyed, or possibly fighting the urge to say something. Iris couldn't help feeling she'd said something to upset Finn, but she couldn't figure out exactly what. Was it about sharing the hotel room?

She reached over and put her hand on Finn's thigh. Finn visibly flinched and Iris felt the muscle beneath her palm tighten. Finn looked over at her and then down at Iris's hand on her leg. Iris held her position.

"Is something wrong?" She gave Finn's thigh the slightest squeeze.

"Um, no, why?" Finn didn't sound very convincing.

"You just seemed…I don't know, you just seemed bothered by something." Iris moved her hand back to her own lap.

"No, I'm fine." Finn smiled thinly. "Really."

Iris didn't believe her. She was sure it had something to do with the shared room conversation, but she wasn't sure what. She turned to watch the landscape sweep past. Her attention was redirected when Finn touched her hand. Finn had reached over and covered Iris's hand with hers. Iris rotated her hand so that she could entwine her fingers with Finn's. She sensed that whatever had disturbed Finn, it had passed.

She looked down at their joined hands. The connection sent a little jolt up her arm.

Finn was holding her hand. Iris couldn't help smiling.

CHAPTER NINETEEN

The quality of the roadway, the smoothness of the pavement, seemed to shift when they crossed the state line into Mississippi. Much of old US 80 had been replaced by I-20, which was probably considered a freeway by the locals, but barely. The pavement was rough and the roadster registered every imperfection and pockmark on the surface. The blacktop wasn't really black either, but rather a pebbled brown color, sometimes in sections as if it had been laid down one giant rectangle at a time.

It was late afternoon when they neared Meridian, their planned stop for the first night. As they drove through the leafy and clean downtown area, Iris was struck by the many Victorian and art deco buildings in varying stages of repair. She wasn't sure what she'd expected, but the style of the architecture surprised her.

They'd checked prices, and while there were nicer hotels in the area, they decided on the America's Best Value Inn. They were on a bit of a budget so saving whenever possible was the plan. The hotel looked clean and well kept. It reminded Iris of an old roadside motel from the 1970s and it had the color scheme to match. It was two-story with doors facing outward toward parking all along the front.

Iris waited in the car while Finn got the room. They'd agreed to take turns each night and then refund any cost imbalance at the end of the trip. The whole arrangement was all business. Maybe too much so from Iris's perspective. This road trip was supposed to be fun. It would be more fun if she got the chance to know Finn a little better. The glimpses she'd gotten so far only made her want to know a little more.

Finn flashed card keys as she walked from the office back to the car.

"We're on the first floor." Finn drove to the far end of the parking area.

They carried their bags inside. The room was clean but certainly nothing fancy. Two queen beds and a flat screen TV on a long cabinet along one wall. There was a round table and two chairs beside a large window facing the parking lot. Finn was happy that she could easily keep an eye on the car from the room.

The air in the room was a little stuffy. Iris adjusted the thermostat down a few degrees.

"Are you hungry?" Finn was leafing through some fliers on the nightstand between the beds. "It looks like we can order a pizza and have it delivered."

"That sounds great to me." Iris tossed her suitcase on the bed and unzipped it.

"How does pepperoni and mushroom sound?"

"Yummy."

"Extra cheese?"

"Sure."

"I'll get a couple of sodas too." Finn reached for the phone.

"Do you mind if I shower? I'll be done by the time it arrives."

"Go for it." Finn was dialing and didn't look up.

Iris let the hot water run for several minutes, long after the soap was gone. She toweled off and then realized she'd gotten a shirt and shorts from her bag but had forgotten underwear. She wrapped the towel around her body. She tucked the corner of it under her arm so that it covered her breasts and hung to about mid thigh. Her hair was damp. She swept it to one side. She peeked out of the bathroom. Finn was lounging on the bed nearer the window, channel surfing.

"The pizza will be here in about ten minutes." Finn held the remote, punching channels, looking at the TV rather than Iris.

"Okay, I just need to dry my hair a little." Iris riffled in her suitcase for undergarments.

Finn glanced over when Iris spoke. *Good Lord Almighty.* Finn almost tossed the remote across the room from surprise. Iris was half naked, wearing only a towel. What part of Finn being clearly gay had Iris not understood? Was she trying to get Finn's attention? Well, she'd succeeded.

"Forgot underwear." Iris smiled. She waggled a very tiny purple thong in the air with one hand and held her towel in place with the other.

"Yeah…um…" Finn didn't know what to say and couldn't help but enjoy the view.

There was a knock at the door. Saved by pizza.

That was either the shortest ten minutes, or she'd miscalculated. Or possibly seeing Iris fresh from the shower in only a towel had somehow managed to bend time, or speed it up, or both.

"My wallet is in my purse if you want to get some cash," Iris yelled from the bathroom.

"I got this one." Finn wasn't about to go searching through Iris's stuff. Who knows what she'd discover.

"D'you order a medium pepperoni and mushroom?" A skinny guy in a Pizza Hut shirt held a receipt up to the light trying to read the name.

"Yeah, that's us." Finn was about to hand him cash. "We ordered a couple of drinks, too."

"Oh, sorry." He left the pizza box with Finn and jogged back to his car for the sodas.

"Um, I'm a little short." Finn was looking at the receipt when he came back with the drinks. "Hang on."

She turned to get her credit card and almost bumped into Iris.

"How much do you need?" She was dressed now and was pulling cash from her wallet.

"Do you have a five?" Finn was standing in the open door, between Iris and the pizza dude.

"Doritos!" Pizza guy's face lit up.

"What? We didn't order Doritos." What was he shouting about?

"No, not the chips, her…you look just like that girl from the Doritos commercial." He was talking to Iris and was about a minute away from going total fanboy. He took a step closer.

"Yeah, but what would she be doing here, right?" Finn stepped forward, partially blocking his view. She and the guy shared a laugh as Finn handed him the additional money. "Keep the change."

The door swooshed closed when Finn stopped holding it open with her foot.

"Thank you." Iris gave her a sideways glance as she retrieved plastic wrapped cups from near the coffee maker.

"I figured you'd rather not be stalked by your fans, when all you wanted was a little pizza for dinner."

"You know, I've done a lot of work I'm proud of, and it seems I'm only going to be remembered for that stupid commercial."

Finn was kicking herself for not looking it up already on YouTube. It seemed to be a fanboy favorite. First her brother and now this guy.

They ate slices right out of the box. Finn sprinkled some hot peppers on her half; Iris only added a packet of parmesan cheese to hers. Finn inhaled the first slice, barely taking a breath. She was hungrier than she'd realized. A shower was next on her agenda, but she needed food first. Halfway through the second slice, Iris was giving her a look. Not an intense look, more of an *I'm trying to puzzle you out* sort of look.

"What?" Finn took another bite and chewed, waiting for a response.

"Nothing."

"You're giving me a look?"

"Am I? I didn't mean to."

"If you want to ask me something just ask." Maybe the hot peppers were going to her head. Finn was feeling brave. "Go ahead."

"Do you think I'm pretty?"

Finn coughed. Maybe almost choked was more like it. She blamed the peppers. She took a swig of her soda.

"Yes." Her response came out raspy. Was that a trick question?

"But I'm not your type, am I?"

"Why would you assume that?" Iris was definitely her type.

"Because you haven't once tried anything." Iris nursed her soda, keeping the cup close to her lips. "And when we kissed…that one time we kissed, I kissed you."

"And I kissed you back." Finn set her half-eaten third slice in the box. She wanted Iris to have her full attention.

"Yes, but would you have kissed me if I hadn't kissed you first?"

"I thought about it." How honest should she be right now? "But you had talked about your ex-boyfriend and I wasn't sure if you were into…"

"Women?"

"Yeah."

"So, even though I said I'd dated a woman before, you assumed I was straight? You've never made out with a straight woman?"

"I have." There were a few curious straight girls in her dating history. Those were enjoyable, but mostly short-lived. "But you're not straight."

"I guess I consider myself bi, although labels really annoy me. I wish people could just be people and love who they love without having to be put into some category." Iris took a bite and chewed, letting her declaration hang in the air. "Does it make you uncomfortable that I've dated men and women?"

"No, why would it?" There were reasons to find Iris intimidating, but the fact that she had an ex-boyfriend wasn't at the top of Finn's list.

"I don't know…because we're sharing a room…and because we kissed."

"I can control myself if that's what you're asking." Finn took a wild guess.

"What if I don't want you to?"

Whoa, she did *not* see that coming. Finn expected there to be tons of subtle flirtation, just like now with the towel scene, and possibly another kiss or two. She thought maybe something would happen between them on this road trip; she'd hoped it might. But Iris was just full-on putting it out there. Performance anxiety set in with a vengeance. She adjusted her position. Her chair was suddenly uncomfortable.

"If…if you wanted me to, I mean if you didn't want me to, just say so." Finn's voice cracked. She wasn't making sense. She cleared her throat and took a sip of her soda. She rubbed her palm on her thigh. Why was she so nervous? They'd spent all day together in a small, confined space. And now they were going to sleep in the same room. No big deal. They'd slept in the same room before.

"I know you're probably tired tonight and you just want to take a shower, I was simply curious…you know, about how you feel." Iris held a piece of crust in her fingers and nibbled at the end of it.

"I feel fine." Was Iris trying to be confusing or alluring? Or was she more tired than she realized, because she'd sort of lost her way along the path of this conversation. Did Iris want Finn to make a pass or not?

"Okay, well, I'm glad we talked."

"Me too." But for the life of her, Finn had no idea what they'd decided, if anything.

Finn finished off the last slice, still unsure.

"I can clean this up if you want to jump in the shower." Iris started throwing discarded napkins into the empty box.

"Okay, thanks." Finn grabbed a T-shirt and boxers and headed for the bathroom.

CHAPTER TWENTY

After standing in hot water for a few minutes, Finn turned the knob to cool. She was completely off balance and needed something to jolt her back to normal. The cold water was a welcomed shock. She took two, three deep breaths and then switched the warm water back on.

Wasn't she the *player* in this scenario? How had she let Iris turn the tables on her so quickly? She hadn't even seen it coming. She was going to have to up her game or be on her guard or some other sports metaphor she couldn't think of at the moment. She was tired and practically in a pizza coma. Yeah, that's it. She blamed the extra cheese for slowing down her brain.

She pulled on a T-shirt and boxers and was still towel drying her hair when she leaned around the doorframe to see what Iris was doing. Only one lamp in the room was on and it was low-wattage, which made the glow from the TV seem bright. It cast a blue highlight along the curve of Iris's shapely legs as she casually lounged on the bed. Iris was completely engrossed in a rerun of *Friends* and twirling her hair around her finger.

Was the laugh track mocking Finn? *Go ahead, laugh. The joke's on me.*

Finn covered her face with the towel and took a deep breath. This was either going to end up being the greatest week of her life or the worst. It was too soon to tell.

She hung the towel on the back of the door, giving herself a pep talk.

You've got this. There's a totally hot woman sleeping in the same room with you. And she just told you she's into women. So what? You've been with beautiful women before. You know what women like. Be cool. Ice cool.

Finn shuffled out of the bathroom, raking her fingers through her damp hair. She concentrated on looking at the TV rather than Iris. *She wants you to notice her legs. Don't.*

Finn didn't want to be such an easy mark. If something did happen between them and it was all on Iris's terms, then Finn would be in serious trouble. She needed to adjust the balance of power back in her favor.

Iris laughed and Finn glanced over, but not fast enough for Iris not to make eye contact. Busted.

They watched back-to-back episodes of *Friends* and then the beginning of some other nineties movie that Finn had seen part of before. She was bored and despite concerted effort not to be, was completely distracted by the curvaceous body lounging on the neighboring bed. Finn calculated that there was probably three feet of open air between them, maybe four, and still, the proximity of Iris made her skin warm.

At some point, they agreed to turn the TV off and go to sleep. But Finn wasn't really sleepy, her entire system was idling fast. She lay on her back staring up at the ceiling. Every rustling sound from the other side of the room caught her attention. She had this fantasy that Iris would simply slip into her bed. That Iris would decide she could no longer fight the attraction and she'd let Finn know by crawling under the covers during the night.

Oh, who was she kidding?

As quietly as she could, Finn tugged her laptop from her bag and tiptoed into the bathroom. Now was as good a time as any to search for that Doritos commercial on YouTube that everyone but her had seen.

Iris heard the soft squeak of bedsprings. She opened her eyes just in time to catch a glimpse of Finn slipping into the bathroom. She rolled onto her back and exhaled. Why was she so restless?

Maybe because she'd eaten half a pizza. That was more gluten and dairy than she'd allowed herself in months. Oh, and it was delicious, by the way.

Or possibly their dinner conversation was keeping her up.

What had she been thinking? She'd blurted out what she'd suspected was unsaid, hanging in the air between them. But talking about it hadn't solved anything. She still had no idea if Finn was truly attracted to her.

Iris had a habit of being too honest. And in Hollywood, that was a flaw. She knew this from her friends. Sometimes people wanted to ignore the truth. They didn't want to have it served up to them during dinner. They wanted to enjoy their pizza in peace and denial. She knew all about denial, firsthand.

She sighed and turned onto her side, facing the window. The streetlight was doing its best imitation of the full moon. A strand of light cut across the blanket. Iris got up to close the drapes. She heard a familiar sound and tiptoed to the bathroom door to investigate.

With her ear to the door, she heard the faint jingle from the Doritos commercial. Finn was checking out her work online. This discovery made Iris smile. She hurried back to bed before she was discovered. Iris tugged the covers up over her shoulder and rolled onto her side with her back to the bathroom door.

Finn easily found the commercial. All the Super Bowl ads were online. The Doritos commercial was funny and sexy. It was no mystery now why everyone seemed to remember Iris from her starring role as a buxom barmaid. Damn, she looked sizzling hot.

She decided to poke around and see what else she could find. She checked IMDB for Iris's film credits and then started doing other searches on YouTube for excerpts of various shows. Cross-references came up for Kent Kenny. For another fifteen minutes, she got totally lost watching videos of some of Kent's stunt driving moves. There were links to his Instagram account and she couldn't help herself, she clicked over and started to scroll through pics.

Kent was too good-looking, and Finn wasn't even into guys. If Captain America took up surfing and became a stunt driver, he'd look exactly like Kent. Finn closed her laptop and exhaled.

How could she ever compete with that?

Iris's ex was a superhero hottie. The worst sort of ex. She'd never measure up.

Now she was feeling more tired, and deflated. Sluggishly, she got to her feet and switched off the light.

❖

Iris heard Finn sink onto her bed; the noisy springs gave her away. She pretended to be asleep. Finn was interested. Or at least curious enough to spend a good half hour with her laptop to investigate Iris online.

As much as it annoyed her to have a life captured on video and now easily accessible online, sometimes it worked in her favor. They had a few days of quality time together to figure things out, and maybe they'd have some fun along the way. Not that things had to evolve into something sexual between them, but if they were both attracted to each other and didn't eventually act on it then this was going to be a very tense drive.

Finn was fun and easy. Getting out from under Kent's ego, she could finally breathe, and she could also see how wrong they'd been for each other. His ego was so out of bounds that there was almost no space for her. She should have ended it long before she caught him in bed with someone else. Catching him cheating simply forced her to deal with the problem she already knew existed. First, Kent only really cared about himself. Second, she didn't love him. She liked him, they'd had a good time together in the beginning, but she could never fully trust him. Without trust there was no way she could fall in love with him.

Yeah, she should have ended it sooner.

Happy thoughts floated through her sleepy brain—the canoe outing on the lake, the picnic with Finn, their drive into the mountains to the overlook. Sleep seeped in from the edges and she gave in to it. She was smiling as she drifted off.

CHAPTER TWENTY-ONE

Iris squinted into the glare. A slip of bright light cut across the room from the edge of the drapes. Iris had forgotten to set an alarm. She wondered if Finn was awake. Not that she was hung up on specific roles or anything, but at this moment she hoped Finn was one of those chivalrous butches who would bring a woman coffee in the morning. Finn had delivered coffee to her cabin that one day, but it was possible that was just a happy accident. Or a peace offering to make up for the bear encounter.

She went to the bathroom to brush her teeth and wash her face. Her hair was a bit of a mess from taking a shower the night before and going to bed while it was still damp. About a hundred strokes with a wide-toothed comb later, Iris tamed it into a loose braid. That seemed like the most sensible solution to all the wind from the car's open cockpit. That's assuming they drove with the top down for part of the day. And even if they didn't, the windows would be open.

Iris was dressed and gathering up her things from the bathroom when she heard the door open. She walked out with her makeup bag and various skin care items to see Finn holding a paper plate piled with food and a cardboard tray with drinks.

"You're my hero." Iris dropped her toiletries into her suitcase.

"It's a lot easier to be this sort of hero." Finn grinned. She balanced the tray with one hand and slid her sunglasses to the top of her head.

"Oh, wait, I forgot you're not so good with trays. Should I take that?" She couldn't help teasing Finn about the strawberry jam disaster.

"Ha ha, very funny. She's a comedian *and* an actor." Finn set the tray on the table. She had piled one paper plate with a bunch of things from the free continental breakfast. There were two empty plates under the top plate. She set one in front of Iris. "I wasn't sure what you'd want so I just got a little of everything."

There was a cheese Danish, a boiled egg, a biscuit, pats of butter, a few slices of cantaloupe, and one giant strawberry.

"Oh, and this…I forgot I put these in my pocket." Finn produced two tiny containers of blueberry yogurt from her jacket pockets.

"Wow. Thank you." Iris impulsively kissed Finn on the cheek.

They both froze for an instant.

"Sorry, I…thank you." She'd kissed Finn without thinking. The gesture seemed so…normal.

"No worries." Finn blushed.

Iris touched Finn's shoulder lightly as she sat down. What she needed most was coffee. She took a sip and smiled. Finn had remembered that she liked only cream. Damn, she was good.

Finn sat down. She'd left while Iris was asleep, and in the half hour she'd been gone had forgotten how gorgeous she was. Her appetite waned, butterflies swarmed. She waited for Iris to choose what she liked, but it seemed Iris was enjoying her coffee too much to care about food at the moment.

"Please, take what you like. I'm not a big breakfast person anyway." Iris sipped her coffee. "Plus, I had way too much pizza last night."

Finn was pretty sure she'd eaten most of that pizza. Iris had teasingly nibbled on one piece forever and then only eaten half of a second slice.

"So, what's our plan for today?" Iris opened one of the yogurts and sampled it.

Finn had gone over the route with Iris before they left Georgia, but it seemed like roads and maps weren't really Iris's thing. Finn loved maps. Even as a kid, before she could drive, she'd thought maps were beautiful. They were like treasure maps for discovery. Her parents were amused by how she could sit for an hour and study the road atlas. She'd kept a journal for many years of all the places she'd go when she got her first car. But she hadn't visited most of them, or hardly any of them. Once she was old enough to drive she'd realized you also need funds to travel. Gas wasn't cheap. Part-time jobs took up any free time, and then she started rebuilding cars and doing races with Ward at different regional tracks on the weekend.

Man, while you're doing other things, life just kept speeding by. She was way overdue for this trip to LA. It was time to figure out the next phase of her professional life. Hell, her life in general.

"I was thinking we'd drive all the way to Dallas today." Finn had already eaten the cheese Danish. She sat back and sipped her coffee. "It'll take us two days to get across Texas."

"I guess I didn't realize Texas was that big."

"It's huge." Finn checked the time. "We should probably get going soon so we can stop and take a break midday. I think it might get hot today. We'll need a rest and so will the car."

"I'm ready. I just need to use the restroom once more and zip up my bag." Iris shoved the plate of remaining food toward Finn. "You'll be driving. You'll need your strength."

❖

There wasn't much to see as they cut across Mississippi from Meridian. Miles and miles of flatland and trees, lots of trees. Iris didn't say much; she was reading news alerts on her phone. Finn was happy to have the quiet, the only noise was from the engine and the wind from the windows. Iris casually propped her bare foot on the dashboard. Finn tensed and shot Iris a look, which she didn't see because she was staring at her phone.

"Hey, not to be a jerk, but do you mind?" She motioned toward Iris's foot.

"Oh, I'm sorry. I wasn't thinking." Iris removed her foot and dusted the dash with her fingers. "I think I'm much more casual about cars than you are."

"Yeah, I know I'm a pain. Just think of it like expensive furniture, which you probably wouldn't put your feet on." Finn cringed a little. She knew she was pickier than most about how her car was treated. It made her nervous every time they drank coffee in the car, but it would be silly not to allow any drinks given the extreme length of each day's drive.

"You're not being a pain." Iris smiled at her. She didn't seem bothered in the least. "Asking for what you want is a good thing."

Finn nodded. She had a feeling Iris wasn't just talking about car etiquette.

"Thanks for understanding."

Jackson came and went in the middle of the state. They stopped in Vicksburg for more coffee. Vicksburg was kind of a cool old river town. It might have been fun to walk around a little, but not much was open except the coffee shop. Things seemed to open late down by the river. They crossed the Mississippi River three times. Iris didn't take her seriously when she'd first suggested they cross the bridge again. Finn just grinned and turned the car around. This was a milestone, one of the big landmarks along the way. Finn intended to savor it. They were now west of the Mississippi. For Finn, that was a big deal. She'd only been west of the Mississippi once before. Her church youth group had gone to the Grand Canyon when she was a senior, but they'd flown to Arizona. Crossing the big river in the roadster was an entirely different experience. She felt like an explorer and an adventurer.

Iris didn't quite share her same level of enthusiasm for crossing a wide muddy waterway three times, but she also didn't give Finn a hard time about it.

They drove for an hour across bayous after leaving Vicksburg before reaching Monroe, which felt strangely abandoned. There were some photo-worthy old buildings and a slew of faded roadside signs, but otherwise, not much to see.

The low country transitioned to forested, rolling hills. This part of Louisiana was a far cry from the Cajun fun of the southern half of the state. This was Baptist country, part of the Bible Belt heartland. Having been raised Southern Baptist, Finn was well acquainted with these sorts of communities. Louisiana ended up being the transition between the agricultural Deep South and the oil industry of Texas.

They stopped in Shreveport, near the state line, but only for gas. Finn wanted to take a longer break in Jefferson, Texas. It was a small side trip, only about four miles north of Marshall.

Jefferson was an almost perfectly preserved bayou town that looked as if it were stuck in time somewhere in the late 1800s. According to the historical marker near where they parked, Jefferson during the 1870s had been one of the busiest inland ports west of the Mississippi. They left Scarlett to cool off under a moss-filled shade tree and began to explore. It looked as if there were plenty of antiques shops and cafés to choose from.

They meandered through the Jefferson General Store. It was full of the usual stuff—old school candies, replicas of tin signs, and about a million other kitschy items that no one really needed but probably remembered fondly from their childhood. Finn purchased a small bag of assorted candy. Sugary treats might come in handy for the drive. She picked hard candies that wouldn't melt if they forgot and left them in the car. Finn was very particular about not eating food in the roadster. Drinks with lids were nerve-racking, but tolerable. They'd eaten what her mom had packed for them the first morning, and Finn had been finding crumbs in the carpet ever since. She'd been known to let laundry pile up in her cabin, along with dishes in the sink. Tidiness in other areas of her life weren't as high a priority as the pristine condition of her car.

"I think we should try that place for lunch." A little way from the store, Finn stopped on the corner and pointed. Across the street was Kitt's Kornbread Sandwich and Pie Bar.

"That sounds…scary." Iris quirked an eyebrow.

"Come on. I'm a sucker for cornbread." She started across the street toward the red brick building. "And if the cornbread sucks, at least we know they have pie."

The place was packed and it wasn't even a Saturday. A waitress was bussing a booth about halfway up the wall, and Finn tugged Iris toward it. Kitt's was a country style diner, with booths all along one wall, a long counter with stool seating, and tables in the middle. Overhead was peppered with slow moving ceiling fans.

"Thank you." Finn accepted a menu from the woman who'd cleaned their table.

"I'll give you a few minutes to look it over. Would you like a drink?" The waitress lingered, looking back and forth between Iris and Finn.

"I'll take a sweet tea." Finn spoke first.

"Just water for me, thanks."

Iris was continually surprised by how much she didn't know about the South. In a restaurant where they spelled cornbread with a K she'd expected to be called "hon" by a full-figured, big-haired matronly waitress. Instead, the young woman who brought their drinks was probably in her twenties with a sleeve of tattoos up one arm. In LA, she would have blended right in, until she spoke. Her accent would have given her away.

"Are you ready to order?" The waitress returned while Iris was still looking things over.

"You can go first. I'm still thinking." Iris deferred to Finn so that she could give the menu one more glance.

"I'll take the Kornbread cheeseburger with chips." Finn was too fast.

"And for you, miss?"

"Okay, I think I'll try the Kornbread club sandwich. No chips." Iris could tell this was not going to be a low carb trip. She needed to start cutting out things where she could.

"Can we get a piece of pecan pie to split too?" Finn folded her menu and grinned.

So much for saving calories.

The food came pretty fast, despite how crowded the café was. And as advertised, the cornbread was delicious.

"So, how did you sleep last night?" Iris asked.

"Fine...you?" Finn took a big gulp of tea.

"Fine. I only asked because I heard you get up for a while."

"Oh, that. Yeah, I remembered that I needed to respond to some email, so I went in the bathroom with my laptop. I didn't want to wake you up."

Finn wasn't going to admit she'd googled Iris's commercial. Should she give Finn a hint that she knew? No, she'd give Finn a break. It was sufficient to know that Finn cared enough to look her up.

"How's your sandwich?" Finn changed the subject.

"Great. I love cornbread, who knew?" Iris finished the last bite just as the waitress returned with a piece of pecan pie piled high with whipped cream. "Go ahead and start on that. I'm not sure how much I'm going to have."

"Well, I'll take the first bite, but you have to try it too, okay?" Finn sampled the pie. Her expression told Iris that it was delicious.

"Okay, the look on your face compels me to try it."

Finn grinned around her second mouthful. Iris dipped her fork into the dessert, trying to get an even ratio of pie filling and pecans. The sweetness of the first bite gave Iris a head rush. She started to giggle and covered her mouth with her hand.

"What's so funny?" Finn held a forkful of dessert in midair. "Are you okay?"

Iris couldn't speak until she swallowed, and she couldn't swallow because she was about to laugh, and trying not to laugh with a mouthful of pie was difficult. She fanned herself with her hand and looked away, trying to focus on swallowing.

"Here, take this. Drink it, don't throw it." Finn offered up Iris's water glass. Her expression was a mixture of concern and amusement.

"Don't make me laugh." Iris's voice was raspy. She took another few sips of water.

"Sorry." Finn grinned.

"That was like a glucose bomb. It went straight to my funny bone." Iris shook her head and took another long drink of water.

"I've never seen pie have that effect on someone before."

Iris carefully slid the pie across the table toward Finn. "This stuff is dangerous. I think you should finish it."

"Can't handle it?" Finn pulled the dessert plate closer.

"How do you eat like this all the time and stay so fit?"

"Hmm, you think I'm in shape, huh?" Finn waggled her fork in the air.

"Yes, I mean, you know you're in like really good shape, right?" Iris knew she was busted. But it wasn't her fault for noticing. Finn had taken her shirt off the very first day they'd hung out at the lake.

"And you're not?" Finn arched an eyebrow.

"Not like you. I have to watch what I eat for sure." Iris took another sip of water to dilute the sugar rush still zooming through her system. "No one eats like this in LA, at least, no one I know."

Finn noticed just the slightest shift in Iris's mood. Like a small cloud passing in front of the sun before it brightens again. She wondered what it was like to have a career so focused on looks. It must get tiresome. To Iris's credit she hadn't once avoided eating anything that Finn had suggested. Finn appreciated women who liked food. Women who weren't afraid to indulge.

"Come on, let's blow this town." Finn grabbed the check and slid out of the booth.

"Are you sure you don't need something sweet to chase that pie?" Iris was quick with the sarcasm.

"Don't be jealous just because I have a higher dessert tolerance, *shugah.*"

Iris laughed. That magical, *string of lights* laugh that Finn was beginning to crave.

CHAPTER TWENTY-TWO

Dallas and Fort Worth, two cities that shared one huge patch of urban sprawl in the middle of a whole bunch of open space. Finn had mostly avoided freeways thus far, but heading into Fort Worth, there was no other option. The Stockyards Hotel had been made famous by Bonnie and Clyde. It had been restored and redecorated based on western themes. It also had a really fun bar downstairs with barstools made of saddles.

Finn studied the lobby while Iris checked them in. The walls around the registration desk were a dark reddish color, and there was a random assortment of upholstered chairs, no two the same. All the furniture looked like a mixture of special finds at estate sales. Somehow, even though nothing really matched it all worked. Finn decided she liked the decor.

This was an old hotel; it had character. The on-site restaurant was a steak house, of course. They took the bags to the room first. The room wasn't anything fancy, but it was comfortable. Whoever had remodeled the place had definitely stayed with a Wild West, Texas feel. The only thing the room lacked was an old wagon wheel mounted on the wall.

Dinner was casual. Finn had a steak even though she'd had a burger for lunch. She figured, when in Rome, or when in Texas, eat beef. Iris opted for salad. This time, Finn passed on dessert.

Once back in the room, Finn spread the road atlas out on the bed while Iris showered. She knew where they were and where they were headed, but she couldn't help studying the route.

"You love to look at that, don't you?" Iris squeezed handfuls of her hair with the towel.

"Yeah, I've always loved maps." Finn closed the frayed cover and launched off the bed. "I've had this one for a couple of years, but this is the farthest I've traveled with it."

She dug out a clean T-shirt and boxers and started toward the bathroom. After all day in the roadster she felt as if she'd run a track event. She was sweaty, stiff, and tired. In another day or so she'd need to do some laundry. The MG didn't exactly allow for extra stuff or abundant packing. She'd brought just enough to get by.

Iris watched Finn from across the room as she gathered her things and disappeared into the bathroom. Finn seemed just the least bit shy, especially as bedtime approached. She was afraid she made Finn nervous but wasn't sure what to do about it. And then an idea started to germinate while she listened to the water run.

Iris was seated cross-legged on the bed when Finn emerged from the bathroom. She hung the towel on the back of the door and finger-combed her hair.

"Why don't you come lie down and I'll give you a back rub?" Iris tried to sound neutral.

It was an offer of kindness, but based on Finn's expression, you'd have thought Iris fired a gun in the room. There was an awkward pause, and then finally Finn spoke.

"That's okay." Finn shook her head, but otherwise, seemed rooted in place.

"No, really, I feel bad that you're having to do all the driving. Let me at least give you a shoulder rub." Iris patted the bed next to where she was seated. "We still have a few more days of travel. And you have a copilot who can't drive a stick shift. This back rub will be as much for my benefit as yours. It's in my best interest to keep the driver in good condition."

The offer was definitely also for her benefit. It wasn't simply the tension in Finn's shoulders she wanted to relieve, but also the unease between them, especially as nighttime neared. The air seemed to almost crackle around Iris from all the free-floating charged particles of attraction. And she sensed the same from Finn.

It didn't seem as if Finn was going to make the first move, so she'd left Iris no choice. Iris felt some sort of physical contact, even the most platonic connection, would alleviate some of the escalating pressure.

That was only a theory, of course. She was prepared to be wrong, but at this point, after spending two days with Finn, Iris had the strongest urge to touch her. A back rub was the most innocent way to make that happen. She realized a back rub was a bit of a lesbian seduction cliché, but why fight convention.

"We can watch something on TV while I massage your shoulders and back."

Finn still seemed unsure, although Iris sensed that she was seriously considering the offer. After another minute that seemed as if it lasted ten, Finn followed Iris's direction and stretched out on the bed. They were oriented so that they could both see the TV. Finn lay on her stomach, with her arms crossed and just barely dropping over the edge of the mattress at the foot of the bed. Iris sat next to her with her legs folded beneath her.

Iris had channel surfed until she found an old movie on AMC. She thought the laugh track from a sitcom set the wrong mood, and an action flick was too loud. It seemed as if watching classic movies in bed was going to be their thing. That was how the first night had gone, and it made Iris smile just thinking of it.

At first, she lightly rubbed Finn's back through her T-shirt, but that wasn't working so well. After a few minutes, she got up and retrieved some oil from her suitcase.

"I think you should take your shirt off so I can do this properly." She didn't look at Finn, but rather poured some of the oil in her palm and rubbed it between her hands. She was afraid if she looked at Finn she would chicken out, or give something away in her expression. She was attracted to Finn. It was impossible to ignore that fact, whether Finn shared the attraction or not.

Finn hesitated, but then tugged her shirt over her head. She'd barely raised up when she'd done it, so she didn't really give Iris any sort of view. Except now that she was shirtless and lying on the bed, Iris could see the smooth skin over her ribs, the sculpted muscles of her back, and the outer curve of Finn's breast. Iris took a deep breath and climbed back on the bed using only her legs. She didn't want to use her hands and end up wiping the oil all over the bedspread. This time, instead of sitting beside Finn, she straddled her waist, so that she had a much better angle.

Finn tried to relax, but Iris's soft caress only revved her heartbeat into high gear. Not to mention the brush of Iris's inner thighs along the exposed skin where her boxers ended just above her waist. She pretended to watch TV, but if anyone had asked, she'd have had no idea what she was even watching.

"That smells good." The oil warmed her skin.

"It has rosemary, which makes it great for sore muscles."

She made slow circles on Finn's back. Iris worked the muscles along the edge of her shoulder blades and then the tight muscles across the top of her shoulders. Iris also paused to knead the tight little knots in her neck and then slid her fingers up into the short hair at the back of Finn's head.

Finn was feeling intoxicated by Iris's touch, lightheaded even. She forgot that this wasn't really a date. She forgot that she was trying not to let things move too fast. Dizzy from her humming libido, Finn hazily rolled over and drew Iris down until their lips met.

She kissed Iris tenderly at first, and then deeper. Iris was still straddling her waist. Finn slipped her hand up the back of Iris's skintight top. She slowly caressed Iris's back with her fingertips.

"Hey, I thought I was giving the back rub."

"You did, and it was amazing."

Iris slipped her shirt off. She'd been wearing a form-fitting tank top with thin straps and no bra, along with some silky girl's boxer shorts. She looked sexy as hell.

After Iris's shirt was gone, she sank into Finn. The skin on skin contact gave Finn the chills. She shivered.

"Are you cold? I could turn the AC up." Iris sounded so sincerely worried about Finn's comfort.

"No, I'm warm. It's not the room temperature."

"Oh." Iris met Finn's gaze.

Iris's breasts were soft against her chest. Finn wanted to pull away just enough to be able to see Iris's body but couldn't bring herself to let go. She'd wanted Iris close since that first kiss on the doorstep of cabin two.

Finn had suspected that a back rub would lead to other things. And she definitely didn't regret that it had. She was totally crushed out on Iris and she was sure Iris knew it.

Iris stopped kissing Finn for a minute so that she could see Finn's face. She liked what she saw in Finn's eyes—vulnerability, attraction, and honesty. She held Finn's face in her hands and kissed her again. Finn's fingers trailed up her back and then drifted down along the outside curve of her breasts. One of Finn's hands slid down her side so that she cupped Iris's ass, pulling her more firmly against Finn's body.

Iris pulled away and reached to switch off the glaring bedside lamp, leaving only ambient light from the TV.

"Too bright?" Finn rested her hands on Iris's thighs.

"Yes." Iris flipped her hair to one side and then over her shoulder as she looked down at Finn. God, she was gorgeous. "Are you okay with this?"

"I'm very okay with this." Finn tugged Iris back down on top of her.

Finn tipped Iris over, rolling her onto her side so that they faced each other. Then she began to explore with her lips along Iris's jaw, down her neck, past her collarbone, until she captured one of Iris's nipples gently. Finn stayed there for a moment, caressing and teasing with her tongue. Iris pressed her palm against Finn's small, firm breast and then pinched the hard tip of her nipple lightly. Finn inhaled sharply against Iris's chest.

They were lying on top of the bedspread, upside down on the bed. Finn rotated, tugging Iris along with her so that their heads were now on the pillows. Iris tossed the covers back so that they could slip under.

"I feel like that wasn't a very satisfying back massage for you."

"Hmm, I'm actually feeling pretty good about it." Finn drew her close and nuzzled into her neck.

Iris couldn't decide if this was too much too fast, or just enough. Was this going to make things more uncomfortable or less? They had more days of driving together in a very small car. What if this turned out to be a mistake?

If Finn was having any doubts, she wasn't voicing them. As she kissed Iris again, deeply, Iris felt Finn's fingers slide up the sensitive skin along her inner thigh. She teased at the bottom of Iris's boxers. The warmth of Finn's hand seeped through the thin silky fabric and the edge of Finn's hand brushed the highly sensitive place between her legs.

Iris simultaneously wanted to pull away and grind against Finn's hand. They were swiftly approaching the point of no return, and uncertainty swarmed in Iris's head. Finn applied pressure with her fingers. Iris touched Finn's arm.

"Should I stop?" Finn's mouth was on Iris's so the the question was more of a murmured whisper.

"Maybe." Iris still wasn't sure, but for some reason she was scared to let things move too fast. Even though she was the one who'd started this whole make out session in the first place.

"We can stop." Finn brushed an errant strand of hair off Iris's cheek. She kissed the tip of Iris's nose. "There's no hurry, right?"

"It's nice to be in your arms." Iris snuggled close, tucking her head under Finn's chin. Finn's strong arms tightened around her. She felt grounded and safe. She felt cared for.

She rotated in Finn's embrace, spooning against her. Finn propped up a little more on the pillow, and they held each other. The TV was still on and Iris stared at it, but her focus was somewhere else. It was impossible to think of anything except Finn's fingertips caressing her stomach as they relaxed into each other. Iris was turned on, but for the moment, relieved that they hadn't gone further. She needed to allow her brain to catch up.

Finn woke suddenly. She had no memory of falling asleep. The TV was dark, so at some point, Iris must have turned it off. It was late. Iris's back was snuggled close against her chest. Moonlight seeped through a small opening in the drapes to highlight the edge of Iris's exposed shoulder. They were both still shirtless, and Finn wondered if Iris was as turned on as she was. She fought the urge to rub her crotch. She didn't have to touch herself to know she was wet.

Iris moaned softly and shifted her ass more firmly against Finn. Was she awake? Did Iris have any idea the effect she was having on Finn?

She placed her palm on the soft curve of Iris's stomach and leaned over just enough to whisper in her ear.

"Are you awake?"

Iris mumbled something and rolled over so that she was facing Finn. She kissed Finn, draped her arm over Finn's shoulder, and pressed her breasts against Finn's.

She was still unsure of whether Iris knew what she was doing.

"Iris, are you dreaming?"

"I don't know...am I?" She sensed Iris's lips curl into a smile against hers.

Finn pressed Iris onto her back and rolled on top of her. Her thigh was between Iris's legs. She caressed Iris's breasts with her hand and then with her tongue. Iris moaned softly again and arched against her mouth.

She returned to kiss Iris's lips, and without breaking the kiss, slid her boxers down underneath the covers with one hand. She kicked them off. Finn wanted to feel Iris, all of Iris. Iris's hands were on her ass now. Finn took this as a sign. She trailed kisses down the middle of Iris's chest, across her stomach, and then hovered there as she eased the silky boxers over the curve of Iris's hips. She kissed Iris's skin every time an inch or so was revealed. Finally, she rocked back on her knees, and slipped the undergarments all the way off.

Finn lingered, looking down at Iris, who was now wide-awake. She could see, even in the darkness of the room, that Iris regarded her with an expression of vulnerability. Iris moved to cover her breasts with her arm, but Finn stopped her.

"Don't. I just wanted to look at you for a minute." Finn hesitated, hovered above Iris, and then lowered herself to cover Iris's body with hers. "You're so beautiful."

"So are you." Iris brushed her fingers across the top of Finn's shoulders tenderly.

Finn covered Iris's mouth with hers, kissing her deeply. She caressed Iris's arm and then trailed her fingertips lightly over Iris's ribs. She backtracked to tease Iris's nipple, bringing it to a hard point.

She rocked Iris gently, moving on top of her, using her thigh to apply pressure.

Finn changed her position, slipped her hand between them, and stroked Iris's sex. Iris opened her legs for Finn. She kissed Iris, their tongues danced together, as she teased farther with her fingers, circling but not slipping inside. Iris moved beneath her as if signaling she wanted more, that she was ready for more.

Gently, tentatively, Finn slid one finger inside. Testing, gauging, she pulled out and then used two fingers.

"Is that okay?" she whispered.

"Yes." Iris was breathless, her eyes were closed. Iris dug her fingers into Finn's back, riding her hand. "Go slow."

Finn tried to match the rhythm of her breathing to Iris's. She wanted more than anything to please Iris. She wanted to make Iris want more of her, more of this. She tried to heed Iris's request, but as Iris's climax gained altitude she urged Finn to increase her speed.

"Faster...yes...yes...you feel so..." Iris cried out, sinking her nails into Finn's ass.

Finn moved so that her thigh was braced against her hand to increase the pressure. Iris was grinding against her palm as she climaxed.

"Oh, Finn." Iris tightly wrapped her arms around Finn's neck. She trembled, cried out once more, and then dropped to the pillow.

Finn sank on top of her. She kissed Iris languorously, pressing her body into Iris's. Finn's thigh was still between Iris's legs, which meant that Iris's thigh was between hers. She shifted when she sensed Iris's hand slipping between them. Iris's fingers found the sensitive, very wet, place between her legs.

Fuck, if Iris touched her she was going to come so fast. Iris seemed unsure, so Finn guided Iris's fingers until Iris slid inside.

"Like this?" Iris's lips brushed the outside edge of her ear.

One of Iris's hands was at the small of her back as she rode Iris's other hand against her thigh.

"Yes..." But she could hardly speak.

She was coming hard. She squeezed her eyes shut and tried not to lose herself. She'd been so turned on that the climax came with blinding speed, like a bolt of lightning in darkness, it seared through Finn's body, cutting a jagged path of light. And then as she sank against Iris, she held Iris's hand in place as shock waves from the orgasm rippled through her system.

Breathless, Finn rolled onto her back, pulling Iris with her. She sank into the pillow and Iris settled her cheek into the hollow space in Finn's shoulder. Iris draped her arm across Finn's stomach and snuggled against her. After a minute, after Finn stopped seeing stars, she rotated and pressed her lips to Iris's forehead.

This was all unexpected, but inevitable at the same time.

She'd wanted to be close to Iris from the first moment she'd seen her. Well, maybe not the first moment. Not at the diner, but later, when they'd talked in her cabin and she'd extracted the sharp leaf shard from Iris's delicate foot. Definitely since then.

She exhaled slowly. Her arm was around Iris, and she let her fingertips caress in small circles on Iris's arm.

"What are you thinking about?" Iris kissed her jaw.

"How I wanted to be with you like this...since...since that night in my cabin."

Iris raised up on her elbow so that her face was just above Finn's. She pressed her lips to Finn's and lingered. Finn savored the contact. Iris was so fucking sexy, and the way she kissed Finn, the way she touched Finn, it felt so...intimate. As if there was nothing between them, no barriers, physical or imagined.

Her emotions were right on the surface, like sensitive skin after a rug burn. She swallowed them down. The last thing she wanted was to get all emotional the very first time they made love. Iris made her feel things, and she wasn't ready to broadcast that to the world, and especially not to Iris.

Finn lay there with Iris in her arms, looking at shadow patterns on the ceiling for some time. She wasn't sure how long. She sensed that Iris had fallen asleep. At some point, her lids began to droop and the heaviness of exhaustion pulled her under. She drifted off to the soft scent of vanilla and the warm comfort of Iris's body pressed against hers.

CHAPTER TWENTY-THREE

Iris woke first. Finn was on her side with her back toward Iris. The blanket and sheet were rumpled and askew, as if there'd been a tug-of-war during the night and Iris had won. The majority of the covering was on her side of the bed. Finn's shoulder, arm, and one toned leg were exposed. Iris sat up. She reached for her phone to check the time. It was almost eight.

As quietly as possible, Iris slipped from the bed. In the bathroom she freshened up and put on clothes to go in search of coffee. She figured it was her turn to forage for the breakfast offering.

When she returned to the bedside, Finn hadn't moved. She was reminded of that first night when she'd woken early and gone back to her cabin. She'd watched Finn sleep and considered waking her. It was hard to believe it had been less than a week since their first encounter. So much could happen in a week.

Iris leaned down and tenderly kissed Finn's shoulder.

As she mingled with other travelers near the coffee dispensers, she felt as if she were on vacation, on some grand adventure. She was relaxed and happy. Good sex and sunshine agreed with her.

Iris stirred in cream and took a few sips before pouring a cup of coffee to take back to the room for Finn.

Part of her couldn't believe they'd slept together, and the other part wondered why it had taken so long. Iris couldn't remember the last time she was so immediately drawn to someone. And it wasn't simply that she'd wanted to have sex with Finn, she'd wanted to be close. For Iris, closeness didn't always equal sex, but in this case, she couldn't stop herself. Once Finn's skin touched hers, once their bodies were pressed together, she surrendered to her desires. Her desire for closeness, her desire to be touched, and Finn had not disappointed.

It seemed that Finn somehow knew exactly how she wanted to be touched.

A sense memory caused Iris to shiver. She closed her eyes and savored the sensation rippling through her system. She exhaled slowly and tried to focus on gathering a small plate of food from the continental buffet.

When she returned to the room, Finn had changed positions but was still asleep. The door clicked shut and Finn stirred. Sleepily, she rolled onto her back and rubbed her eyes. Her hair was adorably tousled.

"Good morning." Iris sat on the edge of the bed and set Finn's coffee on the bedside table.

The drapes were partially open, flooding the room with light.

"Good morning." Finn squinted, her greeting was gravelly from sleep.

She kissed Finn lightly on the lips.

"I brought you some coffee and a sampling of food from downstairs."

"Hmm, thank you." Finn stretched and yawned. "What time is it? Did we oversleep?"

"It's a little after eight."

Finn sat up and the blanket dropped to her waist. She reached for the coffee and took a swig. Iris sipped her coffee and tried not to stare at Finn's body, but it was impossible. Finn didn't seem aware of the effect she was having on Iris, or if she did, she didn't show it. Iris held onto her coffee with both hands, fighting the urge to push Finn onto her back and make love to her.

After a few sips of coffee Finn seemed to realize she wasn't wearing any clothes and reached for her discarded T-shirt. Once she put her shirt on, Iris was able to relax and consider taking a few bites of food. She carried the plate of fruit and muffins over to the bed and let Finn balance it on her lap.

"We should probably get going soon." Finn polished off the last bit of a small blueberry muffin. "At this rate, it'll be three before we make it to Amarillo."

"I'm pretty much ready." Iris folded her clothing into her suitcase.

Finn watched Iris zip her suitcase as she felt around under the covers, near the foot of the bed, for her missing boxer shorts. Yes, they'd slept together, but she was feeling shy about traipsing across the room in only a T-shirt.

"Give me a minute to get dressed and I'll be ready." Finn tossed the covers back and launched into the bathroom to freshen up.

Was she feeling awkward about last night? She wasn't sure just yet. Iris seemed totally fine. If she had any uncertainty about the previous night's sexcapades, she hid it well.

Within a half hour or so they were in the car and on the road. The drive northwest to pick up Route 66 in Amarillo was going to take almost six hours. Hours of sameness as they drove through Wichita Falls, cutting a diagonal across the Lone Star State. The scenery wasn't going to be much of a distraction, which meant only one thing—conversation.

This was the part that Finn usually checked out for. This was the part where *stay* made her simply want to leave. The irony was that she was leaving, and Iris was leaving with her. Maybe she should have thought her impulses through a bit more before she took her hands off the wheel and allowed her libido to drive.

What if things had gone badly? What if she'd read the signals completely wrong, then where would she be? In the middle of Texas with more days of driving before they could part ways.

But things hadn't gone badly. In fact, sex with Iris had been incredible. They'd only spent a few days together, and yet, when they made love it was as if they really knew each other. How do you casually sit next to someone and talk about that without sounding like a lovesick teenager? She had no idea.

Iris's cell buzzed and she searched in her bag for it.

Saved by the phone.

"It's my agent, Judith." Iris read the screen but didn't answer. "I think there's too much wind noise for me to hear her. Can we pull over so that I can call her back?"

"Sure. Let me find us a good spot." Finn scanned the horizon.

A mile or so in the distance, she saw some sort of building. As they got closer she could see that it was a long-closed gas station. The concrete island where the pumps had been was weathered but intact. The overhang that extended from the front of the building to posts anchored in the island offered shade. The air was hot and dry. Finn parked in front of the vintage service station. She got out and peered through the broken front windows while Iris returned Judith's call.

Iris walked away from the car out of earshot. She paced in a small circle as she held the phone to her ear. Judith was doing most of the talking, and Iris's expression gave Finn no clues about how the call was going.

Iris glanced back at Finn. She was nervous about calling Judith, but she couldn't avoid the inevitable. If she'd gotten the part then she was going to have to tell Judith she wasn't taking it. She hadn't quite decided whether to explain the reason for declining the offer. But she was getting ahead of herself. For all she knew, Judith was calling to tell her she hadn't gotten the part.

"Hi, Iris, I thought I should give you a quick call and an update."

"Thanks, I appreciate the call."

"Well, don't get too excited, because I don't know anything about the casting for the show yet."

"Really?" That seemed odd.

"There's been some sort of delay." Judith took a breath. "My guess is that legal has put this on hold to sort out something with the author. You know, this whole series is based on a novel."

"I think I knew that." She did know the show was based on a book, although she hadn't had a chance to read it yet.

"Anyway, I'll let you know as soon as I hear something, okay?"

"Sure. Thanks for letting me know the status, Judith."

"Talk soon." Judith clicked off.

Iris stood looking at her phone for a moment. She'd gotten a reprieve from making a decision, one way or the other. She walked toward where Finn was casually leaning against the side of the car in the shade. God, she was sexy.

"Everything okay?" Finn's arms were across her chest as she lounged against the car.

"Yes. Judith was letting me know there's been some delay with the show." Iris tossed her phone past Finn onto the passenger seat. "So, no news yet."

"I'm sorry. I mean, if that's the right thing to say."

Iris nudged Finn's arms apart so that she could settle against her chest. Despite the heat, she wanted to be close. She wanted, no, needed, a hug. Finn seemed surprised by Iris's sudden need for affection.

"Is this okay?" Iris kissed Finn's cheek.

"Yes...I mean, of course." Finn stroked her back as she held her gently.

Iris slipped her fingers inside Finn's shirt and across her stomach. Finn's legs were braced, and Iris had insinuated herself between them so that she was leaning against Finn, applying pressure to her crotch. Finn took a deep breath and adjusted her stance. Then she clasped Iris's face in her hands and kissed her, softly at first, then with more force. Finn's hand was at the back of Iris's neck, her fingers were in Iris's hair. Finn's other hand was at the small of her back, drawing her closer.

Iris wanted to slip her fingers down the front of Finn's jeans. She wondered if that would be too much. She slid her hand up the inside of Finn's T-shirt and teased her nipple through the thin fabric of her sports bra.

Why not take this to the next level? No one was around on this two-lane back road in the middle of nowhere. Iris tugged the top button of Finn's jeans free and then the next one and then the next one, and Finn didn't stop her. The kiss intensified. Finn wanted her and Iris was happy to be wanted.

Finn moaned against her mouth as her fingertips made contact. Finn was so wet. She adjusted her stance to give Iris better access.

"Iris—"

An eighteen-wheeler, a beat-up flatbed drove past at a fast clip. The sound of the truck caused Finn to break the kiss for an instant, but Iris didn't stop. She was stroking faster now. Finn's focus returned. She kissed Iris again but then stopped, clutching Iris tighter as she came. Iris loved that she could have such power over Finn. Not that she was on some power trip, but the ability to make Finn feel something, especially this, was intoxicating.

"I can't believe we just did that." Finn was breathing hard. Her forehead rested against Iris's.

"I can." Iris's hand was still in the front of Finn's jeans. She slowly withdrew her fingers and then pressed her body against Finn's.

After a minute, Iris stepped back, and Finn refastened the buttons of her Levi's. Then she reached for Finn's hand and pulled her to a standing position, away from the car.

"Come on, we should get to Amarillo before it gets too late."

"I'm not sure I can drive." Finn swept her fingers through her hair and took a deep breath.

"I know we were going to drive farther today, but I'm thinking we should just find a hotel in Amarillo." Iris grinned.

"Yeah, I'm liking this revised plan." Finn circled the car and opened the door. "I'm liking this new plan a lot."

CHAPTER TWENTY-FOUR

Iris looked for hotel options on her phone while Finn drove. The Quality Inn seemed the best option for their budget. Especially since they'd splurged a little in Fort Worth. This place was conveniently located to the highway and had the highest rating for a lower price. And most importantly, it had a bed. Which is where Finn wanted to be, with Iris, as soon as possible.

The check-in was painfully slow. The couple in front of Finn asked a million questions, all of which could have been asked *after* check-in or by looking at a phone or laptop. While Finn waited to get a room, some older guy was chatting Iris up. Iris was standing across the lobby with their luggage. She'd stepped away to return a call from her roommate, Maggie, but the minute she'd left Iris alone, the man had walked up. Iris was like a guy magnet.

Finally, the clueless couple left and Finn was able to get a room. When asked whether she wanted a single king bed or two queen beds she hesitated, but then realized it didn't matter. Butterflies swarmed in her stomach at the thought of sharing a bed with Iris again.

She walked in Iris's direction. The gentleman was still talking. Iris glanced in Finn's direction, her expression said *save me*.

"Well, nice to meet you. I should get going." Iris reached for the handle of her rolling bag and started to walk away to join Finn.

Finn had to give Iris points for being polite.

"You and your boyfriend have a nice trip." He called after them as they headed toward the elevator.

"Does that happen a lot to you?" Iris asked as they stepped into the lift.

"What?" Finn hit the button for their floor.

"People thinking you're a man."

"Oh, that. Yeah…pretty much all the time." Finn shrugged.

"Does it bother you?"

"When I was a kid it made me feel a little weird to get called a boy in the girls' bathroom, and that still happens, but now I don't really care." And she meant it. "I'm comfortable with who I am. And this is me."

"I like that about you." Iris stepped closer and kissed her lightly on the cheek.

The doors swished open and Iris exited. Finn was giddy and a little lightheaded. She followed Iris as a woman and her kid got into the elevator. Finn's phone buzzed just as she dropped her bag on the floor.

"I should take this. It's my mom." Finn held the phone but didn't answer right away.

"Go ahead, I'll take a quick shower."

Finn wanted to join Iris but answered her mother's call instead. If she didn't answer now, her mother would inevitably worry and keep calling until she answered.

"Hi, Mama."

"Hello, Taylor. I just wanted to check in with you girls and see how the trip was going."

"It's going well. We just stopped for the night in Amarillo."

"Well, I hope you're sharing a room. It's not safe for young women to travel alone in this day and age." She could hear the TV in the background. Her mother was addicted to CNN and the Weather Channel. It sounded as if she was watching the Weather Channel at the moment.

"It's supposed to be hot tomorrow, chance of isolated thunderstorms in central Texas."

Bingo, the Weather Channel.

"We didn't have any thunderstorms today. And tomorrow we'll be in New Mexico." She'd ignored her mother's comment about sharing a room. She was fairly sure her mother hadn't meant *share* in the Biblical sense of the word.

"How are you and Iris getting along?"

"Fine…good." Or maybe she had no idea what her mother meant. She wasn't sure exactly how to answer.

"I like her. I think she'd be good for you."

Was her mother actually suggesting that Finn should date Iris? Finn started to sweat and her mother was four states away.

"I like her too." Finn's throat was dry, making her sound unsure. She cleared her throat. "I like Iris. A lot."

"You know, it would be good if you found someone who was your equal, so that they could support you as much as you support them…I mean, emotionally support, you know…I just worry that you're always getting mixed up with people that, well, that aren't going to be a real partner for you."

Finn's heart was thumping in her chest. She and her mother never, as in *never*, talked about Finn's social life or who she was dating. She'd have sworn her mother didn't have a clue of what she was up to, but she could see now that'd she'd been wrong.

"It means a lot to hear you say that." She didn't want to leave her mother's comment hanging out there. She'd clearly taken a chance by saying something to Finn about Iris.

"I just want you to be happy." She was silent for a few seconds. "That's what every parent wants for their child." She heard her father's voice in the background but couldn't make out what he'd said. "And once I get you settled I can start focusing on Trey."

"Thank you, Mama." Finn smiled. Trey would not be happy about that. But hey, that's the price of doing your laundry at home.

It was emotional for Finn to hear her mother talk so openly about Iris. They'd come a long way since Finn was in high school and had first come out to her parents. That was one of the toughest conversations she'd ever had to initiate. At first, her parents had given her the silent treatment, probably unsure of how to respond. But gradually, they'd come around. These days, things were almost normal. And now her mom was comfortable enough with her gayness to give her dating advice.

She heard the shower cut off.

"Well, Mama, I should hang up. We're going to go get some dinner." She hoped they were eating in, but that was more information than she was willing to share.

"All right then. You tell Iris we said hello and tell her to come back and visit soon."

Finn clicked off at the same moment that Iris appeared, wrapped in a large bath towel.

"I feel so much better." Iris hadn't washed her hair. She'd pulled it up into a knot. She released it and let it tumble to her shoulders.

So. Fucking. Sexy.

"My turn." Finn kicked off her shoes. "Mom said to tell you hello."

"That's sweet."

"She wanted to make sure we're getting along." Finn slipped past.

"Oh, I'd say we're getting along very well." Iris grinned. "Would you agree?"

"Absolutely," Finn yelled from the bathroom.

She waited for the water to get hot and stepped into the spray. Finn was anxious to freshen up and rejoin Iris, for dinner, or whatever, so she didn't linger. She tugged on a T-shirt and slipped her jeans on again. She had the button fly almost all the way closed when she stepped out of the bathroom. She stopped dead in her tracks, her toes digging into the carpet to keep her from toppling.

The lights were off, except for the glow from the bathroom seeping into the room. But there was plenty of light to see Iris, naked, reclined. Iris had tossed the covers back and she was lounging on crisp white sheets, which were pale and otherworldly in the low light.

"I don't think you'll need those jeans."

Finn jerked the fly, which pulled all the buttons free, and shucked her pants in record time. The T-shirt was next. She threw it onto a nearby chair. She crawled slowly up the bed, feathering kisses up Iris's legs as she progressed.

Iris could only see the top of Finn's head and her broad shoulders as she crept up the bed. Finn's butterfly kisses made her skin tingle. She shivered.

"Are you cold?"

"No." Iris brushed her fingers through Finn's hair.

Finn kissed Iris's stomach before working her way to Iris's lips. She lingered there for some time, all the while applying pressure with her muscled thigh between Iris's legs. She was getting so turned on. Ever since she'd come back to the room that morning to find Finn still naked and in bed. She'd literally been turned on all day, and if Finn didn't make love to her soon, she was afraid she might burst into flames.

Her face felt hot. She licked her lips as Finn left them to move back down her body. Finn used the tip of her tongue to trace every contour as she slid southward. Finn settled between Iris's legs, she lifted Iris's ass up, tilting it for a better angle. At first, Finn kissed the sensitive area around her sex. Finn would come so close to her clit, but at the last instant move away to kiss her inner thigh. Finn was driving her crazy.

"Finn, please..." She had a fistful of Finn's hair.

She exhaled sharply when Finn's tongue stroked her clit. Skillful and confident, Finn knew exactly what she was doing, and Iris wasn't sure she'd survive it. She writhed beneath Finn, arching against her mouth, but Finn held on. It was as if she was riding the wave of Iris's orgasm along with her.

"Oh, yes, I'm coming..." In addition to Finn's mouth, Finn's fingers were pumping inside her now. "Finn, fuck me...faster... yes..." She had both hands in Finn's hair. She felt the need to hang on for fear she might fly apart.

The sensation started slow and then exploded. Her climax undulated through her core. Her legs trembled. Her arms were suddenly weak. She braced her hands against Finn's shoulders.

Everything was still as she strained against it, every muscle taut before her nervous system took flight, letting go. Was she floating now? Her skin felt raw and soothed at the same time, as if she were lying in the silted shallows of a warm, slow river. She trailed her trembling fingers across Finn's shoulder as if it were a delicate thing she was trying to tease closer.

Finn captured her hand and kissed her palm. She braced for an instant above Iris, then gently covered Iris's body with hers.

"You're so beautiful," Finn whispered.

She looked up at Finn. She knew tears had gathered, and when she blinked, a heavy drop rolled down her cheek. She draped her arms around Finn and pressed her damp cheek against Finn's neck.

"Hey, are you crying? Don't cry. Did I hurt you?" Finn's words were laden with concern. Iris could hear the worry in her question.

"No, baby, you didn't hurt me." She kissed Finn.

The truth was she'd never had such an intense orgasm. She'd never felt like this during sex. In fact, everything before this night felt like sex. But this, being with Finn, this felt like making love. How could she explain it? It was too soon to say those things.

"All I want is to make you feel good." Finn brushed the back of her fingers across Iris's cheek.

"Trust me when I say, I feel good...extremely good." Iris smiled and kissed Finn again.

She wanted to roll Finn onto her back and return the favor, but she needed a moment to regroup. Her body was spent. Her sex throbbed in step with her heart. She took a deep breath and exhaled slowly. She pressed Finn's head to her shoulder so that she could stroke her hair.

"I want to make you come," she whispered into Finn's hair.

Finn shifted and kissed Iris's neck. She adjusted so that her thigh was between Finn's legs and Finn was fully on top of her again. She slipped her hand between them and touched Finn. She was wet and swollen, and Iris's fingers easily slid inside. Finn was braced above her with closed eyes. She moaned softly and began to move on top of Iris, grinding against her hand. She was close. Iris studied Finn's expression. She drew Finn's face toward hers so that she could kiss her, deeply, tasting herself on Finn's tongue.

Finn was riding her hard now, her body tensed. Finn increased the pressure, the friction, between them. Finn's mouth was open, but she was holding her breath.

"Ahhhh…" It was more of a sound than a word.

Finn's body was rigid, rock hard, and then her muscles released. Finn's biceps tensed, trembled for an instant, and then she lowered herself. Iris relished the weight of Finn on top of her. She was anchored and safe. She held Finn and kissed her damp forehead.

"God, Finn, you are so sexy."

She felt Finn's lips curl into a smile against her shoulder.

CHAPTER TWENTY-FIVE

As they left Amarillo, there was one place Finn had to visit. She'd seen photos and she'd heard about it for years. For those who loved cars, it was a *must see*.

Cadillac Ranch was visible from the highway. And even though it was located on private land they were able to drive to it by using the frontage road. Finn pulled over and they walked through an unlocked gate so that Finn could get a closer look at the row of vintage Cadillacs buried nose first into the ground.

The cars, which had long since lost their original color, were vividly spray-painted with graffiti. Finn wrapped one arm around Iris and took a selfie with the artistic auto installation in the background.

A few others had stopped to investigate the odd, planted autos. Finn felt exposed. She wondered for a moment if it was obvious to anyone who saw them that they'd spent the previous night having amazing sex. No one gave them a second glance. It was probably all in her head.

She had to fight the impulse to shout that Iris was the most amazing woman she'd ever met. She wanted the world to know her joy. Instead of shouting, she simply smiled and took Iris's hand as they strolled back to the parked roadster.

After a few minutes, they were back on the road, heading west on old Route 66.

The previous night had been filled with the fierce necessity of sharp desire. Her skin still tingled from the fresh memory of Iris next to her and beneath her.

Finn's thoughts drifted and a sense memory cascaded through her chest—the taste of Iris, the smell of her skin, the intensity of emotion. Overcome by the need to be together, they'd skipped dinner altogether and stayed in bed. Around midnight, Finn ventured out to raid the snack machine down the hall. They'd taken time for a huge breakfast before leaving Amarillo, which more than made up for the previous night's missed meal.

For all that there was to remember about Texas, Finn would forever only connect the Lone Star State with one thing: Iris.

Three days ago, maybe only two days ago, Finn had wondered if the entire trip would turn out to be a huge mistake. Now she never wanted it to end. She was in a magical bubble with Iris and she'd be happy to stay there indefinitely. But *Destination Reality* was just ahead on the horizon. Los Angeles was less than two days by car from their current location, maybe three if they wanted to actually enjoy the drive. Finn had considered ways to slow the journey, to make it last. She was afraid when Iris returned to LA and her friends and her glamorous life that things between them would change. They had to change, right? At some point Finn would go back to Georgia and Iris would stay in California.

It would take them six and a half hours to reach Gallup, New Mexico. Finn was cautious about driving too much farther. The last leg of the journey would be the hottest for the roadster. Not only did she want the drive to last so she'd have more time with Iris, but she wanted Scarlett to survive the journey. Also, without air conditioning the heat was as exhausting for the passengers as it was for the car.

As they traveled west, Finn was hyper aware of even the tiniest contact between them. Iris rested her palm on Finn's thigh and heat radiated from her touch. The entire day was like a lovely, fevered dream.

Shortly after leaving Amarillo, Finn had to abandon the vintage roadways for I-40. She could see the dirt path of Route 66 to the south, and she knew they would cross the old alignment again as they continued west.

Gallup was situated in the northwest corner of New Mexico, near the Four Corners region, and was bisected by the original route of Highway 66. The town offered a diverse collection of galleries and shops. All of which were a blend of Native American and Southwest Hispanic arts and crafts. But that wasn't what captured Finn's attention. The landscape had begun to transition. There were red mesas to the north and east. The mountains and painted deserts of Arizona lay ahead of them to the west.

For about five minutes she considered picking up a piece of jewelry for her mother, but quickly dismissed the idea. Turquoise wasn't really her mom's style.

They decided on the Route 66 Railway Café for dinner. Vintage diners were the theme for this trip, and this place was a classic. Red vinyl bench seats accented the booths along the wall. There were a few tables with chair seating. The decor was vintage Route 66 memorabilia, and nothing on the menu was low cal.

It was early for dinner, so the crowd was thin. A waitress waved them to one of the booths and Finn waited for Iris to be seated before she slid into the other seat. The vinyl was cool against her back. Today's drive had been a hot one, literally and figuratively. Despite the heat, Finn was in the mood for comfort food, something heavy. Sex always made her hungry. She opted for chicken fried steak with mashed potatoes and green beans. Whatever vegetable content had existed in the beans had long been cooked out of them. They were soft and savory, having been simmered in a pot with chunks of ham.

"Even the vegetables aren't vegetarian." Iris examined the small side dish of green beans.

"My favorite kind of vegetables." Finn smiled. "How's that grilled chicken sandwich?"

"Not fried." It was one of the few things on the menu not battered.

"You're missing out. Wanna bite?" Finn cut a generous piece of chicken fried steak and held it out to Iris.

Iris shook her head and focused on her sandwich.

"I can't keep eating everything in sight or I'm going to be in real trouble when I get back to work." Iris took a few sips of water.

"Do you really have to watch what you eat that closely? I mean, you have an amazing body." Now that Finn had gotten the opportunity to study it intimately, she could speak with some authority on the subject.

"Thank you. You're sweet to say that."

"I'm not being sweet, I'm being honest." Finn set her fork down and tried to convey the sincerity she felt. "You, Iris Fleming, are beautiful."

Iris smiled and shook her head. "Eat…and stop saying things like that. You're going to make me blush."

By the time they reached the Best Western, Finn was beat. Two nights in a row of not much sleep and then days of driving had taken their toll. The heavy meal at the diner put her over the edge, and all she wanted was to cuddle up with Iris and go to sleep. That's assuming sleep was possible to attain while cuddled up next to Iris's intoxicating body.

After quick showers they crawled into bed. It was barely twilight, but Finn didn't think she could keep her eyes open for one more minute. The thick drapes blocked what was left of the vanishing daylight, casting the room in darkness. Sleep would come quickly.

Finn was lying on her back when Iris snuggled against her shoulder. She adjusted, slipping her arm under Iris's neck and around her shoulders. The now familiar scent of her vanilla lotion deliciously invaded Finn's air space. She was sure she'd drift off to slumber land smiling.

"This is nice." Iris draped her arm across Finn's stomach.

"Yeah, it is." Finn exhaled and rested her cheek against the top of Iris's head.

"Good night." The words were barely audible. As if Iris was already talking in her sleep.

"Good night."

Her limbs felt heavy and carried a deep vibration as if her body was still in motion, as if they were still driving. She relaxed into the warmth of Iris against her. She figured her arm beneath Iris's head would go to sleep, she could already feel the pins and needles, but Iris was asleep and Finn didn't want to disturb her. She thought of ways to reposition without waking Iris, but in the end, she was otherwise so comfortable that she simply drifted off.

❖

Finn heard a siren in the distance. She reached for her phone on the bedside table and squinted at the time. It was three thirty. She was hot and thirsty. Iris was sound asleep and Finn attempted her best stealth move to roll away to sit at the edge of the bed. The fog of sleep took a moment to clear.

She groped around on the dresser in the dark for the bottle of water they'd brought in from the car. Finally, she had to use the light from her phone to locate it. She took several long gulps before she felt quenched.

For a minute, Finn wondered if the siren sound had only been in her head. She took a few deep breaths and tried to gauge her level of stress. For some reason, it felt higher than it should be coming out of sleep. Maybe she'd had a bad dream and simply couldn't remember it.

There was a chair near the window; she decided to sit down.

Right before she woke up, or right when she'd woken up, she had been thinking something. Finn had panicked slightly when she'd thought of actually reaching for her dream. It was all well and good to aspire to stunt driving when it was only an idea, a practically unattainable thing out there on the horizon. But the closer they got to Southern California, the more real things would become.

Were these just late-night fears of unworthiness?

Yes, absolutely.

Iris already had a career. She'd attained at least some level of success in her chosen field. What had Finn done? Nothing. She'd driven a limo and won a few races at a dirt track, big deal. Those achievements were going to seem like a whole lot of nothing in Los Angeles.

Watching Iris sleep wasn't easing her mind. Did Iris see this as a road trip fling and nothing more? Did she even take Finn seriously? Or was Finn simply a ride back to California?

Finn was tired and her thoughts were spinning. She shook her head to try to settle her brain. After another few moments, she eased back onto the bed, trying her best not to wake Iris. At least one of them should get some sleep.

She lay on her back, watching headlights from the highway seep around the edge of the drapes and flash across the ceiling. A siren wailed in the distance. Maybe the first one hadn't been in her head either.

Beside her, Iris stirred, rolling onto her side.

Finn tenderly caressed Iris's face and then settled back and waited to fall asleep.

CHAPTER TWENTY-SIX

Crossing Arizona via I-40 gave Finn quick access to the best surviving stretches of the original Route 66 anywhere. Between the red rock mesas of New Mexico and the arid desert along the Colorado River, the route ran past dozens of old highway towns along some of the oldest and longest still-drivable sections of the Mother Road. The drive was truly spectacular, running at the foot of red rock cliffs, which towered above them.

Before the temperature climbed she'd put the top down so they could get the most from the vista that surrounded them. Once you'd experienced a scenic drive in the three hundred sixty degrees of a convertible there was no going back. The landscape was almost too expansive to take in. And the sky somehow looked bigger than it did back east. Maybe it was the lack of humidity that allowed you to see farther into the distance.

Finn couldn't quite shake her mood from the night before. She'd hoped exposure to open spaces and the warm air might lighten her thoughts, but so far that hadn't worked. She was sure Iris could tell something was troubling her. In fact, Iris had come right out and asked her. But she didn't feel like sharing her insecurities. How unattractive was that?

To Iris's credit, she hadn't pressed Finn to share. She'd allowed Finn to sit with her thoughts and drive in silence.

Midway across the state, the route climbed the forested Kaibab Plateau. A short drive north would take them to the Grand Canyon, but they opted to keep driving. They'd both visited the Canyon before. Finn remembered mostly how crowded the south rim was, these days so much so that you could no longer drive the rim road.

Just east of Flagstaff, the old road was submerged beneath the freeway. The last sixty-mile stretch of I-40 across Arizona was little more than one long speedway. Sustained highway speeds would no doubt cause the roadster to run hot. Finn started searching for a place to get off the freeway.

The only town for miles in any direction was Kingman, Arizona. It was really the only option for services between Flagstaff and Needles. The town felt more like a way station than a destination, surrounded by open space and high desert air.

Iris stood near the car as Finn raised the hood. Finn had suggested earlier that they might make it farther, but they'd only gotten as far as Kingman when the car started to run hot. The interior of the car was also very warm, bordering on uncomfortable. Finn called it a "cabin heat soak issue." Iris wasn't sure what that meant exactly, but the car was definitely unpleasantly hot. Finn had put the top up before midday to shield the cockpit from the sun, but the outside air was ninety-seven degrees. There wasn't a cloud in the sky to temper the sun's intensity. Iris shielded her eyes with her hand.

"How is the car? Do we need to stay here for the night?" Iris wasn't really in a rush to get back to California. One additional night in a hotel with Finn sounded very appealing. Especially if they cranked the air conditioning in the room.

"Running at a continual high speed in this summer climate is causing her to run hot." Iris couldn't help noticing the well-defined muscles in Finn's arms as she braced over the engine, under the open hood. "Ward and I installed a more efficient radiator, but today it's not completely solving the problem. I think we should find a hotel and let her cool down for the night."

"I like the sound of cooling down." Iris checked her phone for local hotels. "I wouldn't mind some cooling down myself."

"What's nearby?"

"There's a Super Eight just over there. The price looks good and they have a decent rating." Iris pointed in the opposite direction to the exit ramp.

They were parked at a convenience store where Finn had topped off the tank with gas. The map also showed a few food options along this exit off I-40.

"Let's do it." Finn closed the bonnet. "Maybe if we're lucky we can even park Scarlett in the shade."

"Why don't we just pick up some food and take it with us so we don't have to go out again."

"Sounds good to me." But Finn didn't seem happy.

It wasn't that Finn was unhappy. She seemed...preoccupied.

Finn had been distracted, bothered by something all day. Every time Iris asked if she was worried or upset, Finn shrugged and said nothing was wrong. But Iris wasn't convinced. She looked forward to being parked for the night, then Finn couldn't use the distraction of driving as an excuse not to talk.

After a brief discussion of restaurant options, they agreed on Chinese food and got a few different things to share. The salty food tasted especially good for some reason.

"Can you pass me one of those soy sauce packets?" Finn squirted soy sauce on her fried rice and stirred it with her chopsticks.

The room had initially felt almost as warm as the outside air, but ten minutes with the wall-mounted AC on high and things were beginning to feel a whole lot better. Iris pulled her hair up into a knot, away from her neck. Long hair was like wearing a blanket in this heat.

Iris wouldn't describe herself as chatty, but she definitely wasn't as quiet as Finn. She took a few bites of food as she considered what a safe topic for dinner conversation might be. Something to get Finn to open up a little. It took a moment to agree with herself on a topic to bridge the silence. And then it came to her.

"What is it about cars that you love so much?" Iris asked the question as if cars were the most interesting thing on the planet to her, which of course, they weren't.

"Freedom, I guess."

That was not the answer Iris expected.

Finn looked at something on the wall, above Iris's head, as if she were reading a sign.

"Yeah. Definitely freedom." Finn returned her attention to her fried rice.

"But why racing, why stunt driving? You could love cars without the risk." That was the thing Iris couldn't understand. It was one thing to find yourself in a risky situation by accident, but another thing to seek risk out.

"There's something about being in control of a machine with that much horsepower...controlling the beast...you feel alive." Finn looked at Iris. "It gives you a sense of exhilaration."

Her words made Iris warm, but not from the heat.

If Kent had talked this way, she'd have probably understood more. He could never articulate why he did the things he did. Possibly, he didn't even know. She'd always assumed he was simply a thrill junkie. Maybe there was more to it than that.

"When you're racing, are you ever afraid?"

"Not really. I mean, there's an adrenaline rush for sure, but it's not really fear in the purest sense of the word." Finn leaned her elbows on the table. "I read something once, about the guys who broke the land speed records back in the sixties. I can't remember who said this, but one of them said something like he wanted to see how far he could lean out the window without falling out. There's something invigorating about pushing your limits. About putting everything on the line. It makes you feel alive."

Listening to Finn talk, she realized the terrible truth. That Finn was wonderful and wild and dangerous, and Iris liked the way she felt when she was with her. She liked it a lot. She also wasn't ready for it to end.

"You're really not one for small talk, are you?" Finn's question surprised her.

"What do you mean?"

"You never ask me casual questions, like what's your favorite color or what's your favorite movie. It's always something big, you know, *meaning of life* stuff."

Iris smiled. "Because I asked you why you like cars?"

"Yeah."

"For most people, cars wouldn't be connected with the meaning of life."

"For a driver it is." Finn shrugged and captured a clump of rice with her chopsticks. "I like that our conversations are always interesting."

Iris was happy to hear that Finn thought their conversations were engaging because she'd hardly said two complete sentences to Iris all day.

"Have I done something that bothers you?" Now that she'd broken the ice she might as well ask.

"No, why?" Finn was genuinely surprised.

"Because you've been unusually quiet today." Iris hesitated. "And I thought maybe I'd done something, or said something, that upset you."

"I'm sorry." Finn set the food container on the table, with the chopsticks protruding from what was left of the rice. "I just had a weird dream last night. I think it put me in an odd mood all day."

"Do you want to talk about it?"

"Not really." Finn smiled. "I'm not one of those people who shares dreams."

"What are those people like?"

"You know, all woo-woo and touchy-feely. People who think dreams are real."

"Hmm, I see." Iris sipped her drink. "And yet, this dream that isn't real obviously had an impact on your entire day."

"Yeah, but—"

"It seems as if something with that much power bears examination." Iris watched Finn squirm.

"Yeah, well, regardless, I don't really want to talk about it." Finn kicked her shoes off and stretched her legs out in front of her. "It's not a big deal, and I don't want it to be a buzzkill for our big night in Kingman, Arizona."

Finn's gaze was sharp. Whatever had been a distraction earlier did seem to have dissipated. She was laser focused on Iris. It was her turn to squirm. And then she had an idea.

"Hey, I was thinking of taking a bubble bath. Want to join me?" Iris gathered the mostly empty food containers and put them back in the paper bag.

"You brought bubble bath?"

"I have a small bottle of a lemon bath. I checked the tub earlier and it's a little on the shallow side, but I still think we could make it work."

"Okay."

"You say that as if I'm forcing you to do some grueling task. Soaking in a hot bath is one of life's great pleasures, you know."

Finn grinned. "I'm more excited for the time with you than the bubbles."

Iris sensed that Finn's mood had lightened a bit. Maybe it had been nothing more than fatigue from driving or possibly the food had reenergized her, but Finn seemed more herself. Whatever dark cloud had been hanging over her head all day had cleared.

Finn waited for Iris to fill the tub and get settled before she joined her.

Iris catalogued all the sexy details of Finn's tall frame—her broad shoulders, her long legs, her leanly-muscled thighs, her well-defined abs, and her arms. Finn had gorgeous, sculpted arms. If she minded that Iris studied her nude body she gave no indication of it. Finn slipped into the sudsy warm water at the opposite end of the bath so that they faced each other. Iris slid her legs over Finn's, her knees broke through the poofs of suds like mountain peaks breaking through low-lying clouds. Finn swept her palm slowly up the outside of Iris's leg. Finn's eyes were closed and her head was tipped back against the tile. The light in the bathroom was off. Soft light from the lamp near the bed filtered in from the other room. Iris preferred candles, but this was the best mood lighting she could manage under the circumstances.

She rubbed her hands across her partially submerged breasts, lightly splashing warm soapy water across her skin. Finn's eyes were still closed. The seductive display had gone unnoticed. She liked that Finn wasn't too easy. The perfect balance for Iris was someone that found her attractive without going all fanboy crazy. She enjoyed the challenge of having to work for it a little.

Iris shifted her foot, resting it lightly against Finn's stomach and then slowly sliding it downward. As she neared the stiff patch of curls at the apex of her thighs, Finn opened one eye. She smiled and covered Iris's foot with her hand.

"Are you trying to help me relax?"

"I don't know, is it working?" Iris bit her lower lip.

"Does that help you focus?"

"What?"

"Biting your lip." Finn slipped lower into the water. "You do that sometimes when you're concentrating. It's pretty damn cute."

"Well, as long as it's cute." She applied teasing pressure with her foot and Finn moaned softly.

"Have we soaked long enough?" Finn's words were low and husky.

"I think I feel clean enough to get dirty, if that's what you mean."

Finn laughed. "Yeah, that's exactly what I mean."

Iris stood up. She sloshed water as she stepped out; suds slid down her legs as she reached for a towel. Finn followed her with her eyes, then slowly climbed out. She got a towel and draped it around her shoulders like a cape. She drew Iris into her arms and kissed her. Whatever darkness there'd been in Finn's head, it had receded. Iris wrapped her arms around Finn's neck. She was still dripping from the bath but let the towel pool at her feet. She pressed her body against Finn's and kissed her unhurriedly, passionately, as if they had all the time in the world and nowhere they had to be.

CHAPTER TWENTY-SEVEN

It was hard to believe that they had just set out on the last day of their journey. Kingman was only five hours from Santa Monica. They decided to leave as early as possible. Not because Iris was in a rush to get out of bed with Finn, but because this would be the hottest part of the drive west. The pink of the sun had just breached the horizon behind them as they rejoined I-40.

The roadster carried them across the Colorado River where it separated Arizona from California. Finn pointed and Iris looked downstream from the freeway to see the arching silver steel bridge that had carried Route 66 up until the sixties. It was still in use, but not for highway traffic. It supported a natural gas pipeline; beyond it, the red rock spires of Needles rose sharply out of the desert plain. Needles was one of the hottest places in the country. The temp was supposed to hit one hundred by two o'clock. Finn had said she wanted to be past Needles and the Mojave before the temperature climbed.

The Mojave Desert was an arid region that covered parts of southeastern California and portions of Nevada, Arizona, and Utah. For all the time that Iris had lived in Southern California, she'd never spent much time in the desert. Truthfully, the terrain scared her a little. Harsh, dry, and unforgiving.

She braced her arm on the windowsill and held her hair to tame it in this wind. After a minute, she decided to braid it loosely so that it wouldn't keep blowing into her face. Iris reclined against the seat to watch the landscape sweep past. Subtle variations of brown and gray with punctuations of dry grass or cactus were all that was visible for miles.

At first glance, the desert was empty. There was something cleansing about its nothingness. This was a place where everything was stripped away, leaving only the most essential elements—sand, salt, and air.

Maybe it was her changed perspective from time spent with Finn. Maybe it was simply the act of slowing down and actually seeing. But Iris decided the desert and its desolation was beautiful. She turned to look at Finn. Her dark hair and sunglasses contrasted against the pale, arid landscape. Iris committed the image to memory so that she could return to it later.

Finn's realness made her question herself. She often complained about the shallowness, the superficiality of Hollywood. The longer she ran in those circles wouldn't she have to become just as superficial to survive?

She needed to work harder to retain her sense of self.

Finn sensed Iris looking at her. She returned Iris's gaze and smiled. She captured Iris's hand and brought her fingers to her lips. Iris sighed and resumed her study out the window. She was happy.

The desert extended as far as Finn could see. There were large sections of what looked like nothingness. As they reached the desert's edge, Joshua trees began to appear. The trees looked otherworldly. In fact, the entire desolate landscape made Finn feel as if they'd missed a turn somewhere and ended up on Mars. This was a harsh landscape of volcanic cinder cones and sand dunes and prickly cactus.

As she scanned the horizon she couldn't help wondering what had gone through the minds of the first settlers who'd traveled west in wagons. How had they not given up and turned back at the desert's edge?

It was right about then that Finn began to question the whole plan. She might as well be on Mars, or some other distant planet. She was about to drive into the sunset and she had no idea what to expect from there.

As they continued west toward the coast, they passed through every type of Southern California landscape. Desert, over mountains, and through lush inland valleys and finally, to the beach town of Santa Monica, where Iris lived. California was like the land of insistent brightness. It had the feel of a place where it was always sunny.

There were quite a few locals on the sidewalks as they drove toward the beach. Quaint outdoor cafés peppered both sides of the street. People lounged at sidewalk tables or walked their dogs. A shirtless guy holding a surfboard with one arm rode past them on a cruiser bike headed toward the boardwalk. This place had the same vibe as a bunch of the beach towns in Florida except that everyone here was a bit more fashionable, a bit cooler, and Finn got the impression they had more disposable income than anyone she knew. Finn wasn't exactly sure why she thought that. Maybe it was the high concentration of expensive European cars and Teslas that surrounded them on the street.

"How does it feel to be home?" Finn shifted into a lower gear. Traffic had slowed to a crawl the closer they got to the pier.

"Weird."

"How so?" She glanced over at Iris.

"Driving is a completely different experience. When you fly, somehow, you don't realize how big the country is. You don't realize how far you've traveled." Iris paused and then pointed. "Just up there, take a right where that white car just turned."

The street Iris lived on was two blocks off the main drag. Most of the houses looked as if they were from the thirties or forties with well-groomed, mature landscaping. Iris directed her to park in front of a single-level, butter colored stucco house with a red tile roof.

"This is your place?" Finn thought the house looked like something from a classic movie set in old Hollywood.

"Well, technically it's Maggie's house and I just live here." Iris got out of the car and fished in her purse for her keys. "Her grandparents were the original owners, and when they passed away she moved in to take care of the place. That was about six years ago."

"It's a great house." Finn flexed her back. She was stiff from driving.

"Wait until you see the inside."

Finn followed Iris up the path of paving stones to the arched front entry. The wooden door looked as if it had seen a lot of action. There was a small inset window of stained glass in the pattern of a rose.

"Maggie's grandmother loved roses." Iris anticipated her question.

That seemed evident from the lawn, lushly edged with rose bushes.

They'd hardly gotten in the door with the bags when someone squealed from the kitchen.

"You're home!" A very attractive, dark-haired woman bounded from the kitchen and embraced Iris. Her hair was straight but not as long as Iris's. It barely brushed her shoulders. She had a slim build, elegant features, and brown eyes. And based on this first encounter, a bubbly demeanor. "I'm so glad. It's so boring here without you."

"Maggie, this is Finn." Iris made introductions.

"Hi." Finn was still holding the bags, but Maggie hugged her anyway. It seemed Californians liked to hug.

"Regina and I were just texting about a belated birthday party for you. I think we should do it tomorrow. What do you think?"

"Sure, why not." Iris smiled and then looked at Finn for confirmation. "Is that okay with you?"

"Absolutely. Your thirtieth birthday deserves serious recognition."

"I like her already." Maggie hooked her arm through Finn's. "Here, let me take one of those bags." She started to walk down the hallway from the entry, tugging Finn along. "We have a spare room, or are you two sharing a room?" There was playfulness in her question.

"We can put all the bags in my room." Iris looked over her shoulder at Finn.

Finn smiled. She was more than happy to share Iris's room. Her classes at the track would start Monday, so she really only had what was left of Saturday and Sunday to bask in Iris's company.

As expected, the decor of Iris's room had much more of a girlie flair than Finn's rustic cabin. Colorful cushions were piled onto a very cozy looking four-post bed. The floors were hardwood, but soft sectional rugs were scattered about the room in strategic locations. There was a bathroom adjoining her room also. The tile was a colorful mix with a Spanish flavor.

"You two settle in for a minute and then come sit on the patio with me. I picked up wine and some beer on my way home hoping we'd be having a party tomorrow." Maggie looked back from the doorway. "Super nice to meet you, Finn."

Yes, definitely bubbly, but sweet.

"We made it." Iris put her arms around Finn's waist.

"It feels sort of surreal to be here...in your house...in your room." Finn wrapped her arms around Iris.

"I think I know what you mean." Iris kissed her lightly on the lips. "Want to join Maggie out back?"

"Sure. Let me change into shorts and I'll come find you guys." Finn wore jeans while driving because the leather seats got uncomfortable in the heat without long pants.

"I'll get a drink for you. Do you want a beer?"

"Yeah, that'd be great."

Iris shut the door, leaving Finn alone to change. For a minute, she just stood in the center of the room letting everything sink in. She was feeling out of her element and nervous for some reason. She had no reason to feel unnerved. Maggie had been perfectly welcoming, and Iris had invited her to share her bedroom. What was she worried about? Oh, yeah, that's what it was. Everything was too perfect. She was getting everything she wanted, and that always made her a little nervous.

CHAPTER TWENTY-EIGHT

They hung out for a while with Maggie, but then she had to do a shift at the restaurant where she worked part-time. She was a painter by trade. The garage was her studio. But it was hard to have enough income from selling her paintings, so she picked up hours at a local restaurant. Finn hadn't gotten a tour of the garage yet, but she was curious to know what sort of art Maggie did.

After days spent in the car, Iris suggested they walk somewhere for dinner. There were several casual spots for tacos or California cuisine or sushi. They ended up deciding on tacos and enjoyed the cooling night air by eating outside.

After dinner, Iris was inspired to play tour guide so she steered them toward the Santa Monica pier, a local landmark. The pier boasted a small amusement park and the vintage Looff Hippodrome carousel, a national historic landmark. Iris seemed mesmerized by the carousel. Finn decided it would be easy to stand and watch for a half hour and completely lose track of time.

"So how did you and Maggie meet?" Finn stood beside Iris as they watched the colorful horses rise and sink.

"When I moved to Los Angeles, before I got my first acting job, Maggie and I waited tables at the same restaurant."

"She seems nice."

"Maggie is great. We became instant friends. And then when her roommate moved out she asked me to move in. That was a little more than four years ago." Iris turned to face Finn. "Should we keep going?"

"Sure."

A beachfront walkway headed south of the pier to Venice and the heart of Bohemian LA. Near where Santa Monica Boulevard dead-ended at Ocean Avenue, a brass plaque marked the official end of Route 66. "Main Street of America," read the plaque.

"I was sixteen when I first heard about Route 66." Finn stood looking at the inscription. "It only took me ten years to get here."

"Was it everything you hoped it would be?" Iris reached for Finn's hand.

"Everything and more." Finn smiled at Iris as they turned back, walking hand in hand.

There were lots of people out along the beach. They had to keep an eye out for joggers and cyclists.

"Is this okay?"

"What?"

"This, holding hands." Finn glanced down at their entwined fingers.

"Oh, you mean two women holding hands?"

"Yeah." Finn hesitated. "I mean, you can be openly gay in Midtown Atlanta, but other places in Georgia it's wise to be more mindful of where you are."

"It's totally fine here. Trust me, no one cares." She squeezed Finn's hand for emphasis.

"It does feel kinda…normal." Finn nodded and quirked an eyebrow. "I like it."

"Hey, want to get some ice cream before we walk home?"

"I never say no to ice cream."

They'd hatched this crazy trip plan over ice cream; it was only fitting that the epic drive should end with ice cream.

It was after nine by the time they got back to Iris's place. Finn was feeling the fatigue of their early morning departure and a day of adjusting to new surroundings, Iris's surroundings. This wasn't the first night Finn had shared a room with Iris, but this felt different.

This wasn't some hotel room on neutral territory, this was Iris's house, Iris's bedroom. Finn wanted to relax but was a little on edge, not wanting to assume too much or appear to make herself at home in Iris's space.

She stood in the center of the room, waiting for some cue from Iris.

Iris was tossing cushions from the bed to a nearby armchair. She must have realized Finn was watching. She straightened and looked at Finn.

"Is something wrong?"

"No, I was just waiting..." She let her words trail off as Iris approached. The look Iris gave her churned her insides.

"What are you waiting for?" Iris tugged at the hem of her T-shirt.

"This is your space. I just..."

"Finn, I want you here. I invited you, remember?"

"Actually, I'm pretty sure I invited myself. That day at the corner store when I suggested we drive to California."

"Well, however it happened, I'm inviting you now. Come to bed." Iris started to undress as she walked backward.

Finn shucked out of her clothes and followed Iris. She slipped under the light comforter. Iris's skin was smooth and warm and electric. Everywhere her flesh brushed across Iris's her skin tingled. Iris rolled onto her back and drew Finn along with her, pulling her on top.

Iris, what are we going to do about this? About Us? Those were the questions Finn wanted to ask but didn't. Instead, she brushed a strand of hair away from Iris's cheek and kissed the spot where it had lain. How could she ask those questions without seeming needy? Too needy, too soon. If Iris had any of the same questions about what the future held, she didn't voice them. So, neither did Finn. She stuffed those thoughts down and focused on Iris.

Iris rotated in her arms so that her back was against Finn's chest. Iris spooned in Finn's arms, pressing her ass against Finn. Iris had the most splendid ass. Finn swept her palm down the outside curve of Iris's hip, over her thigh and then back to rest on the soft curve at the lowest part of her stomach. Finn was tired, but snuggled against Iris's body like this made it hard to imagine falling asleep.

She brushed Iris's hair aside and tenderly kissed her neck. Iris moaned softly and shifted more firmly against her. Finn had one arm beneath Iris's neck, with just enough reach to cover Iris's breast. She teased Iris's nipple with her fingertips. Iris covered Finn's hand with hers, stroking her forearm lightly.

Finn was getting so turned on. She slid her other hand down farther and began to stroke slowly between Iris's legs. Iris turned a little, put her hand at the back of Finn's head and pulled her down until their lips met. Their tongues danced as the kiss deepened. Iris opened her legs for Finn. She was still partially spooned against Finn so that Finn could touch her, but Iris couldn't really reach Finn.

"Don't roll over. Just let me have you…like this." Finn rubbed faster and every few strokes, slid inside. Iris arched against her hand, matching Finn's rhythm.

Iris wanted to touch Finn, but her position had her at such an angle that she couldn't. She was at Finn's mercy. Finn squeezed her nipple teasingly as she increased the friction with her other hand over Iris's sex. She'd thought they might be too tired to make love, but the minute she'd snuggled next to Finn's body she'd been instantly awake. Finn's skin was like a match strike against hers. She gripped Finn's forearm.

"Let me…" She was breathless and could hardly get the words out. "Let me roll over. I want you to come with me."

She rotated in Finn's arms and then pulled Finn on top so that her thigh was between Finn's legs. She gripped Finn's hips and applied pressure. She wanted Finn to grind against her. Finn kissed her deeply and slid back inside. The cadence of their movements was perfect. Iris was going to come and she felt sure Finn was right there with her. Above her, Finn's entire body was rigid for an instant. She opened her eyes and looked at Iris with the most soulful expression. Iris felt Finn's gaze deep in her chest. The connection surprised her and she almost lost herself, but Finn was thrusting inside her now, and sucking her breast, and she was cresting the wave of her orgasm. It built and built and swelled until…she crashed. Her limbs trembled and she clung to Finn.

"Don't let go," she whispered. Her lips brushed against Finn's neck.

"I won't let go."

And Iris believed her.

She believed in Finn so much that she'd let go. She'd allowed Finn to slip past her carefully guarded emotional wall of safety. She'd let Finn come in, all the way in. Finn slowly moved her fingers, she was pulling away, but Iris touched her arm.

"Don't move." She pressed her lips to Finn's. "Stay."

Finn's heart was pounding in her chest and in her ears. She could feel Iris's heartbeat through her fingertips. She relaxed on top of Iris. Something had shifted between them just now. The intensity of their lovemaking had ratcheted up exponentially. She felt exposed, as if her chest cavity were open to the air and Iris had reached in and taken her heart into her hands.

Iris had asked her to stay. Stay. The word that always triggered her flight response. But when Iris had asked her to stay, for the first time in her life, that was exactly what she wanted to do. But how could she?

❖

The next morning, Iris woke before Finn.

She was home, but home felt different somehow. As if the air had changed, or the temperature of the room, or the angle of the sun. She couldn't quite put her finger on what exactly she was sensing. Beside her, Finn slept on her stomach. Her left arm, bent at the elbow, hung off the edge of the bed. Iris rolled over and kissed Finn's back. She fought the urge to slip her hand beneath the sheet and caress Finn until she was awake.

She propped on her elbow for a moment and watched Finn sleep. She checked her phone. It was only seven thirty. Why was she so awake?

Last night things had been different with Finn. She'd felt the shift like a small seismic aftershock. Up to this point she'd been having fun. They'd both been having fun, keeping things casual and light. But last night, things moved beyond that for her. She wondered if Finn sensed it too. She'd felt safe enough with Finn to be vulnerable.

The temptation was too great.

She feathered her fingertips along Finn's shoulder, then beneath the covers, down the curve of her spine to her waist. She slid her palm slowly across Finn's firm ass. She moved closer, so that she could lightly kiss Finn's shoulders while she explored with her fingers.

Finn was still wet. Knowing she made Finn this turned on made her smile.

Iris moved partially on top of Finn so that she could trace the outside curve of her ear with the tip of her tongue. Slowly, and very deliberately, she caressed Finn from behind. Finn moaned softly into her pillow and shifted her legs farther apart. Iris took this as a sign to continue. She was on top of Finn now, pressing her into the mattress as she teased Finn's sex and ground her own against Finn's ass. She was going to make herself come simply by touching Finn and rubbing against her.

Finn fisted the sheet as Iris slid her fingers inside from behind. She'd been sound asleep when she'd hazily realized Iris was caressing her. Like some erotic dream she wasn't sure if she'd imagined or was actually real.

Iris's hot mouth was on her neck. Her hair tickled her shoulder blades as she moved on top of Finn. And every time Iris rocked against her ass she teasingly brushed the hard points of her nipples across Finn's back. Finn had never been with anyone the way she was with Iris. She'd never allowed anyone to do the things Iris was doing right now, but she trusted Iris, she was in love with Iris.

Wait.

Full stop.

She was in love with Iris?

Iris was fucking her and she was about to completely lose control.

She reached around, filled her fingers with Iris's hair, and tugged Iris firmly against her back. She rocked into Iris as Iris pumped inside her.

"Oh God..." She was coming hard and she was completely at Iris's mercy.

"I've got you," Iris whispered urgently, breathlessly. "I'm coming with you...don't stop."

She arched her back, lifting off the bed a few inches as the orgasm raged through her body. Every muscle was taut. Every fiber strained to the point of snapping, and then, finally, release. Finn dropped to the pillow. Iris clung to her and trembled.

She rolled over in one strong move, throwing Iris onto her back. She kissed Iris hard, she fed on her mouth as if she'd been starved and Iris was the only thing to satisfy her hunger. She pressed her sex against Iris as one last tremor rippled through her body.

"Iris..." She didn't know what she wanted to say.

"Finn, last night was incredible." Iris held Finn's face in her hands. "I couldn't help myself...when I saw you sleeping there...so handsome. Your back, your arms—"

Finn kissed her, swallowing the words.

Iris, I'm falling in love with you. And that scares the shit out of me.

"What is it?" Iris broke the kiss and looked up at Finn with a searching expression.

"You're beautiful." Was all she could say.

She snuggled into Iris's neck and drew her close.

CHAPTER TWENTY-NINE

The afternoon sun was casting long shadows when Finn stepped through the French doors. She searched for Iris and finally spotted her on the far side of the deck talking to a friend. With a beer in her hand, she snaked her way through people gathered around the back yard. True to her word, Maggie had organized a party in honor of Iris's birthday and it was a casually festive affair.

The California crowd took some getting used to. Fashion was different here for sure. Attire choices were a weird mix of super casual but, Finn suspected, very expensive clothing. At a garden party in the South, you'd see mostly flip-flops and preppy shorts and shirts in primary colors. Everyone at this party looked like an extra from the Sundance catalog. Willowy women who could be models, maybe they were, lounged around the patio in long, flowing caftans and floppy Bohemian style hats. Finn felt underdressed in her hand-me-down Georgia Tech T-shirt and cargo shorts. But in her defense, she hadn't brought many clothing options with her.

As she wove between people, she heard a woman wearing a pocket romper over a bikini talk about days at Burning Man as if she'd experienced some altered state of being. Her companion was contrasting the desert revelry of Burning Man with his weekend at Coachella. Finn had attended neither event, but she'd at least heard of them.

The woman Iris was chatting with wore a skimpy bikini top that showed off her perfectly tanned skin and a sarong. Her hair was in long dreads that transitioned from blond to lavender, and her wrist was loaded with bangles that jingle-jangled like wind chimes every time she moved her arm. The whole outfit was self-consciously constructed to send a particular message, but Finn wasn't sure exactly what that message was unless it was, *I'm not trying too hard to be cool, but I kinda am.*

"There you are." Iris smiled as she walked up. "Finn, have you gotten to meet Regina yet?"

"Hi." Finn tipped her beer in Regina's direction. "Nice to meet you."

"Oh, I love your accent." Regina smiled flirtatiously, giving Finn her full attention.

"Do you need a drink or anything?" Finn asked Iris.

"And sweet too." Regina touched Finn's arm. "So, what do you do?"

"Finn's a driver." Iris answered for her.

"Hmm, like Kent?" Regina quirked an eyebrow. "Iris, you obviously have a type." She playfully swatted Iris's shoulder.

Kent Kenny. Finn had almost gone forty-eight hours without thinking of him. Was she Iris's type? Or was Kent? This whole scene was probably more up Kent's alley.

"You're so lucky you two met." Regina turned to Iris with a mockingly serious expression. "Dating in LA is a nightmare. Everyone is either stuck in traffic, looking for parking, or trying to network. It's impossible to hook up."

Iris laughed. She reached for Finn's hand. Finn shifted her stance, basking in this moment of closeness. She didn't want to rain on the whole idea of a big party, but ever since this morning, all Finn wanted was to have Iris all to herself. A gathering where she knew no one and had the distinct impression that about half the people weren't deep enough to wade into the shallow end of a pool was frustrating. She summoned patience and took a long swig of her beer. These were Iris's friends; she needed to give them a chance to prove her wrong.

Her mind drifted as Regina and Iris talked. Regina had various food allergies, and it was apparently very complicated to eat out.

Someone within earshot behind her was talking about a tattoo they'd just gotten and needed to keep out of the sun. It was supposedly the Japanese kanji character for abundance. Finn glanced over. She was fairly sure she'd seen the same character design on a packet of soy sauce. How could you ever be sure you were getting what you intended unless you could actually read Japanese? Abundance or soy sauce. At the end of the day, both were good, so she figured it was sort of a win either way.

Finn had never seriously considered a tattoo. Too much commitment.

Someone, a wisp of a guy with blond hair, grabbed Iris's other hand and tugged her away from Finn.

"I'll be right back." Iris waved to Finn as she was swallowed by the small crowd near the thatched overhang of the tiki bar.

Finn wanted desperately to leave. She felt lonely, like an outsider. She was used to being in a place where she'd known everyone since grammar school. This was a strange land inhabited by beautiful strangers.

She meandered through the kitchen for a second beer, then wandered back outside. She took a seat along a low rock wall, far enough from the party that she couldn't make out any one conversation, but close enough to keep an eye on Iris. She sighed and tipped the chilled brown bottle to her lips.

"Did I miss much?"

A guy had taken a seat next to her while she'd been lost in thought. She glanced over and almost snorted her beer through her nose when she saw who it was.

"I wasn't gonna show, but Regina texted me." Kent Kenny was even better looking in person, if that was possible.

"Yeah, it's a rager." Finn said the first lame thing that came to mind.

"She's something though, isn't she?" Kent took a long pull on his beer. He was wearing board shorts and flip-flops. His biceps strained against the sleeves of his T-shirt.

"Who?" But Finn was afraid she already knew who he was talking about.

"The birthday girl, Iris. Do you know her or are you one of Maggie's friends?"

"Yeah, I know her."

"She's a hot piece of ass." He took another swig.

Every protective impulse in Finn's body charged to the surface.

"I fucked it up." He turned toward Finn and flashed a movie star smile. "She always takes me back though. How could she say no to this?" He spread his arms out as if he were a showman about to walk the high wire. "Later, man."

He swaggered toward the gathering around the patio, leaving Finn speechless. Kent Kenny had been someone she'd aspired to emulate, and now she realized he was a complete dick. She pulled herself together and followed Kent. She wasn't going to leave Iris's side as long as that pretty boy land shark was circling.

Iris was chatting happily with Steve and his cute new boyfriend, when she caught a glimpse of someone familiar in her peripheral vision. She'd had a few glasses of wine so her eyes were probably playing tricks. But when she glanced back, there he was. Kent was angling for her, easing his way around the edge of the flagstone patio. For an instant, she had a vision of quickly fleeing for the safety of the house, but instead she froze, and before she could regroup he was there.

Kent leaned forward and kissed her on the cheek.

"Happy birthday, beautiful."

"Kent! You made it." Regina swooped in, giving him a one-armed hug and a quick kiss on the cheek.

Regina had obviously invited Kent. Iris glared at her. It must have been Regina. Maggie never would have asked him to join the party.

"Hi, I brought you a fresh drink." Finn was suddenly at her side.

"Thank you." Iris smiled. She'd never been so happy to see someone. She kissed Finn on the lips. A kiss meant as a signal to Kent that they were more than friends.

"Hey, can I show you something?" Finn motioned toward the house with a tilt of her head.

"Absolutely." Iris smiled thinly at Kent. The expression of disbelief on his face was everything she could have hoped for.

Finn took Iris's hand and they wove through guests until they were in the house. Then she followed as Finn led her down the hallway to her bedroom. Finn closed the door and they were alone.

"Thank you." Iris sank to the edge of the bed. She set her wine glass on the bedside table.

"I thought maybe you needed to be rescued."

"I hope you know I didn't invite him." Iris was furious. "I don't want to go back out there until he's gone."

"I can make that happen."

"Would you?"

"Sure. In fact, it would be my pleasure to do so." Finn knelt in front of her, holding both her hands. "I don't want anything to ruin your party, especially not him."

"Taylor Finn, you are my hero."

Finn grinned. "You wait here while I go uninvite Kent Kenny from this party."

Iris fell back on the bed and let out a long sigh. She did *not* want to see Kent. She wasn't ready to see him. The absolute last thing she wanted was to have Kent and Finn in the same place at the same time. She'd had enough wine for a pleasant buzz, but that had evaporated at the sight of him.

She hadn't meant for Finn to get sucked into her drama with Kent. This wasn't Finn's problem to solve. But she was grateful for Finn's intervention.

Seeing Kent brought everything back, the hurt and betrayal. And it made her question herself. What was she doing with Finn? Was she even ready to be involved with someone, anyone? If simply seeing Kent could send her into a tailspin of regret and self-doubt the answer was probably no.

One thing was certain, she was going to need a lot more wine to bring the fun back to this party. Yes, a lot more wine.

❖

Finn didn't have a hard time finding Kent. He was still standing near the tiki bar, with a small group gathered around him, hanging on his every word. There was no denying that he had real presence. There was no way you'd miss him at a party or even simply entering a room. He had star power.

Once again, the thought, complete with mental imaging, flashed through her head that Kent was Iris's ex. Every time that happened it was like a punch in the gut.

Finn joined the circle. It took a moment for her to get an opening.

"Hey, man, can I talk to you for a minute?" She didn't want to call him out in front of his adoring fans.

He was reluctant to oblige her request, but after an awkward couple of minutes, he did.

"Hang tight, I'll be back."

Maggie caught Finn's arm as she passed by. "Hey, where's Iris?" Then recognition struck. "Oh, hi, Kent."

"Iris is inside." Finn didn't want to say more, and she didn't want Maggie to intervene and derail Kent's exit. Although, it didn't seem as if Maggie was a fan. She gave Finn a knowing sideways glance as she stepped through the French doors into the house.

"So, are you and Iris sleeping together or what?" They'd barely reached the outer fray of the gathering when Kent spun to face her.

"That's none of your business." Finn wasn't one to sex and tell.

"I think it is my fucking business."

"Listen, I know I don't know you, but I'm the one asking you to leave anyway." Finn casually stood her ground. She wasn't intimidated by Kent's size or fame. "Iris doesn't want to see you, and this is her party, so it's time to make a graceful exit."

"I'll leave when I'm ready."

Fuck. She'd assumed he'd have enough class to take a hint, but after the *great piece of ass* comment she should have known better.

"No, Kent. You're gonna leave now and let Iris enjoy her birthday." Finn crossed her arms and stood blocking his return.

"I'm not taking direction from some…redneck."

"I'll take that as a compliment." She'd rather be a redneck than an entitled ass any day.

"Listen, these are my friends too—"

"Kent, she's right, you should probably go." Maggie had appeared out of thin air just as Finn had begun to worry things were about to go sideways.

It was two against one now and this was Maggie's house, so hopefully her request would be more convincing.

"Don't make this a big thing, okay? She's just not ready to see you." Maggie touched his arm as if to remind him that she was a good enough friend to know the whole story of what had happened.

"Okay, whatever." He handed Finn his half-finished beer. "Thanks for the beer, Mags."

Maggie and Finn watched him pull away in his yellow Porsche. Of course he drove a Porsche.

"Your timing was good, thank you." Finn relaxed and turned to Maggie.

"He's not a bad guy, but he really fucked up, and he's probably just now realizing that he had a great thing with Iris." Maggie seemed to register who she was talking to. "I mean, this has nothing to do with you and Iris." She backpedaled. "He never treated Iris right, in my opinion."

"Yeah, I heard a little about what went down." Finn sank her hands in her pockets. She didn't want to mention that Kent had been someone she'd sort of held up as a hero. It sucked to meet your heroes when they didn't measure up.

"I'm sure Regina invited him. She was super invested in their relationship and she's having a hard time letting it go. That happens sometimes with friends. You know, when they get more invested in your relationship than you do. They have a hard time when it ends."

"I know what you mean." Although she wasn't sure she did and now had a bit of distrust for Regina.

"Here, let me take that so you can get a fresh beer." Maggie reached for Kent's cast-off beverage. "I think Iris is still hiding in her room. I'll go let her know the coast is clear."

Finn scanned the back patio and yard. She really wanted this party to be over, but it looked as if it was going to get crazier before it ended. Some guy sprayed another guy with beer while the DJ cranked up the music. Oh yeah, things were just getting started.

CHAPTER THIRTY

Iris opened one eye. The room was extremely bright. Too bright. She sat up and her head began to throb. How much alcohol had she consumed? Possibly too much. After Kent left she was giddy and celebratory, and thirsty. At some point, she stopped counting.

The other side of the bed was empty. Where was Finn?

She was still tired. She slumped back to the pillow.

"Hey, I thought you might need these." Finn stepped from the bathroom fully dressed. She held out a glass of water and a bottle of Extra-Strength Tylenol.

Iris groaned when she sat up again.

"I don't feel so good." She took the water and pills from Finn.

She struggled with the safety top on the Tylenol for a few minutes before Finn relieved her of it and popped the cap. She handed two tablets to Iris.

"Thank you." Iris drank half the water after swallowing the pills and then squinted at Finn. "Why are you dressed already?"

"I'm starting that stunt driving course today. I'm supposed to be there by ten for orientation." Finn sat at the edge of the bed.

"What time is it?" Iris felt around on the bed for her phone and then noticed Finn's amused expression. "What's so funny?"

"You." Finn retrieved Iris's phone from the dresser across the room. "You're a mess."

"Hey, no woman wants to hear that sort of talk first thing in the morning." Iris scowled as the screen on her phone came to life.

She had way too many text messages. It was too early for that and her head was still pounding. She tossed the phone on the bed and scuttled back under the covers. "Last night...did we..."

"Um, no." Finn reached for Iris's hand and stroked it between hers. "I slept in the spare room last night."

"Why?" Iris couldn't help pouting.

"Well, where I'm from, we don't have sex with women who've had so much to drink that they won't remember it in the morning."

"Oh, God, I sound awful." She covered her face with the sheet. "Did I beg?"

"Only a little." Finn tugged the sheet away. "About thirty seconds before you passed out."

"I'm so embarrassed."

"Don't be. You're adorable and, I might add, very affectionate when you're tipsy."

"Wake me up when it's next week." Iris covered her face with her hands.

"I'll call you later, birthday girl." Finn kissed her on the forehead. "Wish me luck."

"Good luck," Iris mumbled.

She heard footsteps, the jingling of keys, and then the soft click as the door closed. Iris tugged the covers over her head and relapsed into blissful slumber.

❖

Rick Crenshaw's Stunt Driving School was held at the Willow Springs Raceway, about an hour and a half north of Los Angeles. Leaving at eight and heading away from downtown, against traffic, Finn figured she'd miss the worst of the morning commute, but the freeway was jammed with cars. She realized pretty quickly that if she took this course for the whole week it wouldn't be realistic to drive from Iris's place. She'd probably need to try to find an inexpensive hotel somewhere closer to the track.

That was a depressing realization. The thought of not seeing Iris at the end of each day was completely unappealing.

The initial orientation was located in a nondescript one-story building just past the entrance gate. There were probably a dozen other people milling about a group of metal folding chairs. There was coffee set up at the back with a few pastries left in a large pink box. Finn helped herself to coffee and scanned the room.

The group was mixed racially and varied in age, but there was only one other woman besides Finn. It was definitely a boy's club sort of gathering. The classes were limited to four students, so the number of people present probably meant there'd be three separate groups.

A man she assumed was Rick Crenshaw entered the space and strode toward the podium.

"Okay, let's find a seat so we can get started." He was like an older version of Kent. He was probably in his fifties but still tanned and fit. He looked like a seasoned body builder.

There were leaflets on the back table near the coffee station. Finn had picked one up as she angled toward a seat in the back row. The flyer was a promotion for the class.

"Welcome, everyone. I'm Rick Crenshaw and I'm lead instructor here. I have a couple of other instructors who will be assisting with this course. Craig, along the back wall. And Adam, seated in the front row." Adam partially stood and held up his hand.

Rick paced in front of the class sounding almost like a motivational speaker. He talked with his hands and made frequent eye contact with his audience. He had obviously refined this speech over the course of a long time.

"Okay, people, actionable item number one…learn what to expect." He paused for effect. "There are some critical things you need to know before jumping into the film industry. The most important one is this. Becoming a stunt driver is easy. Getting work is not."

Finn sipped her coffee. Rick wasn't going to sugarcoat things. She figured that was for the best. Might as well know what she was getting into up front before she committed too much time and money to this.

"The last thing I want to do is turn you away from a career that you're excited about. But I want you to know the truth so that you'll have the best chance at success." He paced several feet and turned back, looking at the gathering of wannabe drivers as he spoke. "If you haven't tried to make it in a freelance environment you might be in for a shock. Nothing is guaranteed, nobody owes you, and you can't expect any handouts. Especially when you're new."

"Is he trying to talk us out of taking this course or what?" The guy next to Finn angled his head closer to her and spoke softly. He was probably ten years older than Finn. He had an accent that she couldn't quite identify. Texas, maybe.

She nodded but didn't verbally respond. At the front of the room, Rick continued.

"For stunt drivers, the market is flooded. Several years ago, the only way to get experience was on a film set actually driving cars. But today there are probably a dozen stunt driving schools that teach professional stunt driving. And as these stunt driving schools pump out graduates every year, the market becomes more flooded with qualified entry-level drivers. This means there's lower pay, more competition for jobs, and you have to work harder to stand out."

Finn was starting to figure out that this whole orientation was a reality check. One person had left already. And the Texan next to her was showing signs of calling it quits. She was determined to stick it out. After all, she'd talked about doing this for years and she'd driven two thousand miles to sit here and have someone tell her how impossible her dream was. At least she'd stay put long enough to drive the damn course.

It was weird that on some level she knew being a stunt driver would mean working in the film industry. But it never really dawned on her that she'd end up confronting some of the same challenges Iris faced. From listening to Iris talk, she knew that making a living in film was tough, and you had to develop a thick skin. She realized now, making it as a stunt driver would never just be about how well she could drive.

Rick started to write on a white board. He was outlining the day's coursework.

Finn tried to focus. She was feeling distracted and couldn't quite get her head in the game. Maybe more coffee would help.

Twenty minutes later, they were out on the track. Orange traffic cones dotted the blacktop as markers for the various tricks in the curriculum for the day, including the slalom, which was up first. Most everyone in her group did okay. Next up was the forward 180, which required slamming on the brakes and spinning the car 180 degrees. All you really needed to pull that stunt off was a working emergency brake and a reliable transmission.

Finn had done a 180 on the dirt track back home, but this was different. The objective was to do the maneuver in a controlled space and stop on a particular mark. Precision driving was more of a challenge than stirring up dirt just for the fun of it.

The first guy in her group spun in a complete circle. The second guy took out several cones, braked too soon, and only did a ninety-degree turn.

"Okay, Finn, you're up!" The instructor, Adam, signaled.

She pulled forward and he got in the car with her.

"Remember to think of the combination of steering and handbrake as one fluid motion." He fastened his seat belt. "You ready?"

She nodded.

Finn knew she needed to be doing at least thirty miles per hour so that she'd have enough forward momentum to fully rotate the car. She lifted off the gas, depressed the clutch, and pulled the handbrake. Not until she felt the tires lock did she add a full turn of the steering wheel. Once the car was mid rotation, she dropped the handbrake, released the clutch, and hit the gas as she unwound the steering.

Adrenaline surged through her system. Damn, that was fun.

"Nicely done!" Adam was quick to praise the turn.

She parked and he moved to the next student in the class, the fellow from Texas. Finn exhaled and sat for a minute to settle. There was no doubt that the *driving* part of stunt driving was what she loved. It was the rest of the Hollywood game she wasn't sure she was wired for.

CHAPTER THIRTY-ONE

Iris slept in. She finally managed to crawl out of bed and make it to the kitchen for coffee by eleven o'clock. Toast was all she could handle for breakfast. Thank goodness Finn had delivered water and Tylenol earlier or she'd probably be feeling much worse. She never drank excessively and wasn't sure why she'd done it the previous night.

Oh, yeah. Kent.

He was such an asshole and she'd dated him for more than a year. What did that say about her? Had she just been in it for the arm candy? No, in the beginning she'd really fallen for his charismatic charm. Over time, it was hard for him to maintain the facade, but by then she felt invested. She knew now it was a completely wasted investment.

After the second cup of coffee, Iris was feeling more awake. She retrieved her laptop and began sifting through email. A new message from her agent had come through only an hour earlier. The attachment was an appointment sheet that said there was an audition the next day on the Warner Bros. lot with a casting director. The breakdown said they were looking for a female, twenty-five to thirty, long hair, girl next door type, to audition for *Hollywood Vice*. She squinted and read the fine print. Yep, she was the victim. This character was going to get mugged in a parking garage.

The sides for what they wanted her to read were also attached as a pdf. She downloaded the documents so that she could read them later.

She sighed and sipped her third cup of coffee. Well, she might as well take the job if she could get it. Since the series shooting in Atlanta wasn't going to work out, she needed the work. She'd been thinking that she really should talk to Judith about what had happened with Eric, the director. If no one spoke up about it then he'd never change his behavior or be held accountable for it. Iris had nothing to lose because she wasn't going to accept the role even if they offered it.

She held her phone for a minute, considering making the call. Then she set the phone on the counter. Maybe she'd call later, after she showered.

Iris rested her elbows on the island in the kitchen and leisurely sipped her coffee. It was good to be back. It was good to *not* be in constant motion. Although it was weird not to be with Finn. They'd spent every moment together for the past six days. Iris was sorry she'd missed having breakfast with her. Had Finn said when she'd be back? Iris couldn't recall. She reached for her phone again.

Hey, where are you?

There was a long pause, and then Finn was responding, but it took a minute to come through.

I was just the object of police pursuit and got spun around like a top.

I have no idea what that means. Iris tried to picture it, but couldn't.

These are the meaningful things one learns at stunt driving school. Finn replied.

Exciting. But she didn't really think so. *I can't wait to hear all about it.*

No response. Iris waited for a moment, sipped her coffee, still nothing. Maybe Finn was driving and couldn't respond.

Want to have dinner? Text me when you're heading back. Iris rested her chin in her palm.

Dinner sounds good. I can probably meet you by six or seven, depending on traffic.

Iris set her phone aside and returned to her email. A few seconds later, her phone buzzed. She had one more brief text from Finn.

How's your head?

Ha ha, very funny. Iris smiled. Her head was fine, but she feared her heart was headed for trouble. *I'll pick up something for dinner and we can eat in.*

Perfect.

And P.S. don't text and drive. Iris hadn't intended for texting to be one of Finn's stunts while driving.

Don't worry. I'm parked. Watching someone else throw cones.

Sounds dangerous.

I'm at a safe distance. Finn added an emoji with sunglasses.

Iris clicked off with a smile and returned to her long queue of unanswered email.

❖

The day dragged slowly by. Iris blamed the birthday wine consumption from the night before, but she knew that wasn't the only reason she was out of sorts.

After answering email and cleaning up remaining party debris, she'd read through the pdf her agent sent, the side she'd be reading later in the week on the Warner Bros. lot. The part was more of the same. It was a one-time role that probably no one would see or remember. Was this her life?

Maybe this was it; maybe she'd risen as far as she was going to with her acting career. How long would she keep trying before she redirected her efforts to a more lasting profession? Acting and theater had been such a safe place for her most of her adult life. All her friends, all her professional connections, they were all related to acting. How would she ever completely move away from that? If she stayed in Hollywood she'd have to at some point be okay with always being the background character and never the lead. Other actors made decent livings as character actors, extras, neighbors, friends. Her ambition wouldn't quite let it go, or her ego. She knew she was capable of handling a lead role if only she got the chance.

Frustration, anger, bubbled to the surface when she thought of how Eric had ruined her chance to break out and move to the next level. She'd finally gotten a shot at a different sort of role. A part that might have been a game changer for her career. Eric had ruined it for her. She could see the smug expression on his face when she closed her eyes, and her heart began to pound. It wasn't fair. None of this was fair.

She picked up her phone to call Judith but decided not to when she noticed the time. Finn would probably arrive in the next half hour, and she didn't want to be in an even worse mood than she already was when Finn got there. Iris left the pages she'd been studying at the end of the dining room table and searched for her keys. She'd pick up enough food for Maggie to have some too if she showed up.

Today reminded her of that fateful day she'd flown into Atlanta, when everything was going wrong. When she'd begun to second-guess all her life choices midflight. This seemed to be a recurring theme for her. To question how she ended up here. What if she'd made different choices at some point? Would she be further along in her career? If you were on *the path*, the right path, didn't things just fall into place? That certainly wasn't happening. Maybe the universe was sending her a sign.

It should've been easy to pop down to the restaurant, park, get food, and return home. But nothing was easy today. Someone insisted on making a left turn where no left turn was allowed, blocking traffic for ten minutes. Then, there was no parking anywhere near the place Iris had intended to pick up food. In the end, parking chose the meal—Chinese food. There was a bit of a wait to order and then for some reason, the card reader wouldn't work when she tried to pay. Luckily, she had just enough cash for what she'd ordered.

The young guy ringing up her order did a double take.

"Hey, are you the girl from that Doritos commercial?" He grinned.

It was clearly just going to be one of those days. Regardless of her skill as an actor, she was destined to be remembered for nothing more than hair and boobs.

CHAPTER THIRTY-TWO

Finn had been happy to be back in the roadster at the end of the day. The MG was like home, a car she was intimately familiar with. They'd driven through course patterns of cones, done box 90s, reverse and forward 180s, and a bunch of other maneuvers she'd always wanted to try. But not enough to risk damage to her own car to try them.

Finn reflected on the day. She'd gotten to drive like a crazy teenager without consequences, was a passenger—on the high side—in a car balanced on two wheels, and had been spun out with a nudge to her bumper. She'd probably never drive the same again, thanks to this stunt driving class. Finn had learned skills that could probably save her life some day. But one thought nagged at her as she sat in freeway traffic headed back to Santa Monica. A thought that she was almost afraid to fully consider.

After spending the day on the course, she had serious doubts about whether she actually wanted to be a stunt driver. Was she crazy to even think that? This was something she'd been considering forever and now that she was here, she wondered if this was what she truly wanted to do.

Ward would probably talk her into giving it more of a chance. But her gut was sending her some strong signals that this just wasn't the right fit. This wasn't what she'd expected, California wasn't what she expected. Everything about this trip had surprised her, including Iris.

Little by little, as they'd journeyed together, Iris had become everything, and stunt driving had simply become background noise.

Discovering that a stunt driving career in Hollywood might not be what she really wanted wasn't the worst thing. At least she'd gotten the chance to investigate the possibility for herself, rather than daydreaming about it forever without really knowing. She'd have had serious regrets if she hadn't at least tried.

What if this wasn't what she wanted to do? Big deal. That didn't make her a failure, right? Stunt driving or not, that wasn't what defined her. So why was she in such a bad mood?

Probably because without the tease of stunt driving on the horizon she was adrift. Without the dream, who was she? Just another loser who didn't finish college. Just another gear head scraping by driving a limo for rich clients. Oh, yeah, she wasn't even doing that any more.

Jeezus, I am a failure.

Wasn't she?

How could she show up at Iris's and tell her any of this? It was one thing to know it for herself, but Iris would no doubt just think she was a loser who couldn't cut it in the real world. She'd run back to her safe little cabin and hide under her mother's apron. God, she *was* a loser. She'd go back to Georgia and Iris would move on with her perfect, exciting life. She'd probably even end up getting back together with Kent. Clearly, he wasn't giving up on their relationship, and his charisma was probably hard to resist indefinitely.

A sick feeling welled up inside, and for a minute she thought she might have to pull over.

But that was impossible. She was in the middle lane and no one was moving. She had no choice but to sit and wallow. Her thoughts spiraled. She felt stuck, trapped.

Finn finally arrived at Iris's place a little before seven o'clock. Her mood hadn't improved. She tapped lightly with the antique door knocker, and within a minute, Iris appeared.

"Hi, you didn't have to knock." Iris stepped aside for Finn to enter.

Finn had hoped for a different greeting, maybe even a kiss, but Iris seemed distracted.

"I wasn't sure if Maggie would be here or you might still be out. Anyway, I didn't want to assume."

"Well, your timing is good. I just got back with the food." Iris walked toward the kitchen and Finn followed her. "I got Chinese food. I picked out a few different dishes so we can each have a little of everything."

"Sounds good." Lunch had been a granola bar and a soda, so Finn was in need of real food. Maybe food would improve her mood.

Iris had already set plates on the table for them, and she began opening the white boxes of carryout so that they could figure out what was in each. Normally, Finn would have used chopsticks, but she was fatigued and feeling lazy, so she opted for a fork instead.

"How was your day?" Finn spooned a sampling from each container onto her plate.

Iris kept avoiding eye contact. Finn wondered if she'd gotten into an argument or something. Had Kent shown up again? Finn gripped her fork and waited for Iris to answer.

"My day was okay, I mean, once I actually got out of bed." Iris groaned. "I still can't believe I drank that much. That was so unlike me."

"Well, you only have your thirtieth birthday once." Finn sampled the food. It was good and she was hungry. Seconds were definitely on her agenda. "Maggie hosted a great party. I hope I was famous enough to be there." Finn couldn't help thinking of her encounter with Kent.

"No one is famous. Everyone is just trying to make it, you know?" Iris sounded depressed.

"Except for Kent. He's pretty famous."

"Yes, but I certainly didn't invite him. Besides his ego only allows space for one star, himself."

"Yeah, Kent was a bit self-focused, but probably not the only one." Finn found it hard to picture Iris in deep friendships with the people she'd met the previous night.

"I suppose people can be a little into themselves, it is LA after all. That's what the Hollywood culture can be like here." Iris cocked her head as if she were weighing some heavy thought.

"You mean, lack of culture, right?" Finn's comment sounded harsher than she'd intended. She hadn't intended to take her foul mood out on Iris.

"What do you mean?" Iris furrowed her brow.

This was the first time since Finn arrived that she had Iris's full attention. And now she wasn't sure she wanted it because clearly, Iris was not in a good mood either. Maybe she should stop talking. She was feeling insecure and defensive, not a good combination. Or possibly a great combination for saying the wrong thing.

Iris regarded Finn from across the table. Why was Finn coming down on her friends? She waited impatiently for Finn to explain.

"I just mean I heard people talking about Burning Man, and eating out, and the best tattoo shops. There didn't seem to be a lot of substance there." Finn backpedaled and focused on her food, serving herself a second helping of cashew chicken and rice.

"Oh, so you're the person who's an authority on culture now?" Iris was annoyed by Finn's gruff assessment. Who was she to criticize a group of people she'd only met once? "Oh, that's right, there's a lot of culture happening in Watts Mountain."

Iris's comment struck a nerve and she immediately regretted it. Finn stopped shoving food around her plate and glared at Iris. She hadn't really meant to say something unkind about Watts Mountain, but Finn pissed her off, and she was already feeling bad about herself. She didn't need Finn heaping more on top of her long list of failings. Her mouth was a step ahead of her brain and she couldn't stop herself from taking some of her frustration out on Finn.

"Wait, I'm confused. Now you're talking about me?" Finn set her fork down and looked at Iris.

"No, I mean, yes…you were making fun of my friends, weren't you?"

"I wouldn't say I was *making fun*. It was more of an observation."

Finn's observation had sounded more like a judgment to Iris. And she was in no mood to let it slide. She'd had a shitty day of career disappointment. She was getting nowhere. Her life was completely stalled. She was doomed forever to be a supporting actress, nothing more than the occasional victim for a crime drama. And now Finn had the gall to be judgmental of her friends?

"Do you hear what you're saying? You're saying my friends are shallow."

"Well, they kinda are, aren't they? It's not the end of the world if they are. They're your friends, not mine."

"Well, you must think I'm shallow too. I mean, if I'm friends with them, then I must be, right?" Was that what Finn really thought? Was Finn lumping Iris in with the whole of Hollywood and everything that was wrong with it?

"No, of course not, but you must have something in common with these people, otherwise, why would they be your friends."

Finn seemed so sure that she was making a completely rational point. Her borderline condescending attitude infuriated Iris.

"I don't understand why you're so bothered by what I'm saying. I made an observation about the people I met at your party, and you took a jab at Watts Mountain. Why don't we just call it even?" Finn was angry now too.

Iris was trying not to let Finn's comment bother her, but it did, and her defenses and her insecurities were ratcheting up.

"Maybe the real problem here is that you and I don't have anything in common with each other." Iris wasn't hungry any longer. She shoved her plate to the side.

"What? What the hell are you talking about?"

"If you think my friends are so shallow and beneath you—"

"No, that's not what I said. You're twisting my words." Finn was pissed. "If you want to know the truth, yes, I think most of the people at that party seemed shallow. There, are you happy?"

"And I suppose your redneck friends back in Georgia are deep and cultured, but they just work at a garage for the fun of it."

"I guess I'm finally finding out what you really think of me."

"And what you really think of me." Iris crossed her arms and sat back in her chair.

"Was I nothing more than a free ride to California?" Finn's question was laced with fury.

Finn's stomach churned, her appetite was long gone. She figured she knew the answer to that question already. Did she really need the insult of Iris's confirmation?

"Was I nothing more than a free place to stay while you attended that driving class?"

"I guess we both got what we were after then, didn't we?"

"If that's what you really think then you should leave." Tears began to gather along Iris's lashes, and her voice trembled.

"Don't worry, I'm not about to stay where I'm not wanted."

Luckily, Finn had slept in the spare room the previous night so her stuff was already in one spot and fairly organized. She stormed from the table. The chair scraped loudly against the tile floor when she stood up. She briskly repacked the few items strewn on the bed. When she strode toward the door, Iris was standing beside the table, hugging herself. She made no move to stop Finn, and when Finn jerked the door open she almost collided with Maggie.

"Oh, are you—"

"Sorry." Finn brushed past Maggie.

She tossed her bag onto the passenger seat and pulled away from the curb without looking back. A couple of blocks away, she parked, unsure if she wanted to scream or cry. She pounded the steering wheel with the heel of her hand trying to relieve some of her anger. What the fuck had just happened? She'd been played, that's what. She'd known this whole thing with Iris was too good to be true. Too easy. Women like Iris didn't end up with women like her. She'd been living in some dreamscape for the past week, but now Iris was back with her friends and Finn didn't measure up. There was no way she could measure up.

Finn took a few deep breaths and tried to calm down.

Now what?

She sat for a moment and considered her options.

Finally, she decided to drive back toward the track, get a hotel, and figure out her next move.

Iris watched Finn blow past Maggie in her rush to leave. She felt furious and dazed at the same time. The entire exchange with Finn had spun completely out of control. Maggie looked back and forth between Finn's angry retreat and Iris before closing the front door.

"Iris, honey, what happened?" Maggie swept her hands up Iris's arms, still folded across her chest.

"Finn and I had a fight." She sniffed and swiped at a tear. She wasn't crying because she was upset, but because she was incensed. She was livid.

"Was it about Kent being at the party? I told Finn you didn't invite him." Maggie urged Iris to sit down.

"No, it wasn't that." Iris didn't want to tell Maggie what Finn had said about all her friends being shallow. "It was about so much more than that. I don't think we're right for each other."

"But you...you guys seemed so into each other. I don't get it. What changed?"

"I think she's not who I thought she was." Iris braced her elbows on the table and covered her face with her hands. "And I'm definitely not who she wants to be with."

"I'm sure that's not true." Maggie touched her arm. "It's a lot to meet someone's whole friend circle all at once. Maybe Finn is just feeling a little overwhelmed...a little outnumbered."

Iris wished that was the case, but that wasn't what Finn had said.

"You should have some food." Iris shoved a plate in Maggie's direction. "I'm not really hungry anymore."

"Just give things a little while to cool off and then call Finn. I'm sure you guys can talk this out." Before Maggie could serve herself some food, there was a knock at the door.

Iris's heart sped up. Maybe Maggie was right. Maybe Finn had come back to apologize. They could talk it through and everything would be okay. Maybe Finn hadn't meant those awful things she'd said. Maybe Iris had misunderstood.

Maggie opened the door.

"Hi, girls, I thought I'd stop by and see how hung over the birthday girl was." Regina strolled in with a bright wheat-grass-green beverage from the juice bar. She took off her sunglasses and squinted at Iris. "Are you crying? What's wrong? What'd I miss?"

"Finn and Iris had a fight." Maggie got an extra plate from the kitchen and set it on the table for Regina. "There's lots of food. Want to join me? Iris is fasting."

"It's my fault isn't it?" Regina took the chair next to Iris. She crossed her legs and leaned forward like an attentive talk show host. "Listen, I would never have texted Kent about the party if I'd known about Finn. I shouldn't have invited him...really. I'm sorry. I just thought, oh, I don't know what I thought. You guys were such a cute couple."

"It's not your fault. This had nothing to do with Kent." Iris shook her head. "You guys eat. And can we talk about something else?"

"Oh. My. God." There was an expression of horror on Regina's face as she looked down at her leg. "Did I just see cellulite on the back of my calf?"

CHAPTER THIRTY-THREE

Driving while angry might not have been Finn's smartest move. Luckily, there wasn't as much traffic as she retraced her earlier route. She'd white-knuckled the steering wheel to the point that her left hand had begun to tingle. Her right hand was required to shift gears so at least there was blood flow to her fingers.

The Motel Six near the track was the perfect fit for Finn's mood—sad, cheap, and run-down. She had just parked the roadster when she noticed the Texan from her class outside his room, drinking a beer. After their initial encounter, she'd learned that his name was Tommy and he'd been working as a long-haul trucker but was looking to switch to a more glamorous, fun career. Tommy the Texan, it had a nice ring. He was a beefy guy, a little thick in the middle. He probably played football in high school and now consumed the same number of calories without all the exercise or the teenage metabolism. Tommy and Finn, as the token southerners, had bonded during the day. Southernism trumped any other thing they might not have had in common.

"Why so sad? Did Chevrolet stop making trucks?"

"Somethin' like that." Despite her dark mood, Finn almost laughed.

"I picked up some beer if you want one." He tapped a small cooler on the breezeway near his feet with his boot heel.

"Yeah, thanks." Budweiser wasn't her favorite, but she wasn't feeling picky. She looked at Tommy while still holding the lid open. "You ready for another one?"

"Nah, I'm still good."

There were faded outdoor chairs along the front wall, covered by the overhang. The cheap plastic chairs matched the rest of the decor. She took the seat next to Tommy and stretched her legs out. This day had not gone the way she'd anticipated. Nope, not at all.

They were quiet for a minute, watching cars come and go and people unloading their stuff. Cars on the freeway provided constant background noise. This hotel wasn't a destination. This was the place people stopped when they couldn't drive any farther and needed to sleep. It was after nine and fully dark.

It was strange to sit outside in the summertime and not have to fight off mosquitoes. The only bugs out and about were a small gathering of moths around the outside light at the edge of the overhang.

"So, you gonna stick this thing out?" The first ten minutes of the class, Tommy had hinted that he might not stay for the full course. She wondered if he'd changed his mind now that the first day of entry-level stuff was behind them.

"I don't think so." He sipped his beer thoughtfully. "I learned a lot today, but I ain't got the luxury of freelancing the way Rick described it. I gotta have a steady paycheck."

"I was sort of thinking the same thing." Finn had been reconsidering everything on her drive from Iris's place.

"Yeah, I've got a kid and child support. I can't be foolin' around hoping work will come my way."

It'd be so much easier to launch a career as a stunt driver if you were like Kent, who came from old California money. At least that's what she'd read about his background. If he didn't get work, it wasn't as if he was going to miss a meal or lose his house.

"Too bad neither one of us is Kent Kenny." She knew she sounded bitter, maybe even jealous. She figured as soon as she was out of the picture Iris and Kent would get back together. Regina was right, they made a cute couple, and obviously he fit in with Iris's friends much better than she did. And as it stood now, Finn had nothing to offer.

"He's all hat and no cattle."

"Really, you think so?" Finn couldn't help smiling. Only someone from Texas would say that, but she appreciated the sentiment.

"Yeah, he's a pretty boy actor who just happens to do his own stunts. He got every break in the world. He's an actor first and a stunt driver second."

"You don't think he's a good driver?"

"Maybe." Tommy paused as if he were doing math in his head. "But how much of that is talent and how much of it is hype because he's an actor."

"Who knows." Finn shook her head. Kent probably got a break in lots of ways based on his looks alone. Must be nice to be that pretty. Even thinking the word pretty reminded her of Iris, and her stomach took a turn south.

"Exactly. Who knows is right." He crushed the empty can and reached for another beer, kicking the cooler top closed with his foot. Maximum gain with the least effort. "Guys like us have to work five times as hard to get to the same place."

"Yeah, I'm afraid you're right about that." Finn was amused by the fact that he'd lumped her in with the guys. That had happened her entire life, so she was used to it. Her more masculine appearance seemed to inspire men to share more than they would with a woman they had some interest in dating. They tended to treat Finn like *one of the guys*.

They sat for a few more minutes not talking while a grumbling family of four checked into the room next to Finn's.

"So, what's your plan then? Are you going to finish the course or are you out of here?"

"I'm out of here tomorrow." He slouched in his chair. "I've got a line on a flatbed truck, a big rig. I'm going to use what I would have spent on the rest of the class as a down payment. And then I reckon I'm goin' back to truck driving. I already got one guy who's paying me to haul a car to Georgia for him after I pick up the truck."

"How much would you charge to haul a car that far?" Finn was formulating a plan.

"Five hundred." He looked at Finn. "You thinking of shipping your vintage MG back?"

"Yes, actually, as of about an hour ago." Finn sipped her beer. She could get herself and her car back to Georgia for what it would cost her for only one more day of Rick Crenshaw's stunt driving class. Maybe she should just cut her losses and do exactly that, if Tommy could help her out. If she stayed in California much longer she'd be too broke to pay attention. As it was, she was already way over what she'd budgeted for the trip.

"Well, I wouldn't charge you five hundred. I'd do it for four."

"Tommy, I'm gonna take you up on that." She extended her hand and he shook it. "It was an adventure to drive Scarlett out here on the old roadways, but that's too much mileage for her. I'd rather not drive back to Georgia." It would certainly cost a lot more than four hundred dollars for gas, food, and hotels. Plus, the thought of retracing the journey without Iris wasn't appealing. There would be a million things along the way to remind her of what she was never going to have.

"I'm going to get the truck tomorrow at eight. I could come back here and we could load your car after that. I'll have my vehicle, your MG, and then I'm picking up the other car in Palm Springs."

"That sounds good to me. If you bring it anywhere close to Atlanta I can pick it up."

"I'm taking the Palm Springs car as far as Dawsonville. It's a classic Ford and there's some collector who's buying it." He tossed his empty can into the cooler. "Will that work?"

"That's perfect. My folks' place isn't too far from Dawsonville." Now all she had to do was find a plane ticket. "I better go figure out a flight home."

"Have a good night."

"You too."

Finn rolled her shoulders and kicked her shoes off. She stretched out on the bed with her laptop looking for the cheapest fare back home. She found a flight out of Burbank that only made one stop in Houston. She hesitated for a moment. She was about to purchase a ticket and be gone. Did she want to sit with that for a minute and think about whether she wanted to see Iris before she left?

There was no doubt she wanted to see Iris. But she was too angry. If she did see Iris she'd likely say even more things she'd regret. Plus, Iris had made it pretty clear what she thought of Finn and all her uncultured Watts Mountain kin.

She hit the purchase tab.

The deal was done.

Tomorrow night she'd be back home, where people cared about you for who you really were, not the clothes you wore or how much money you had. The California scene was definitely not for her.

She reached for her phone. No messages from Iris.

Finn sent a text to her brother. She'd need a ride from the airport in Atlanta since she'd be without wheels. It was after midnight on the East Coast so he probably wouldn't respond until morning. She tossed her phone onto the bed and started channel surfing. She was too wound up and angry to sleep.

Iris tossed about in bed. It was late, but she couldn't sleep. Her head would not keep quiet. Everything that had happened in the past week replayed in a loop every time she closed her eyes. And to make matters worse, she couldn't stop thinking of how it all felt, how good it was to be close to Finn. And how crushed she'd been by what Finn had said. How had everything gone so wrong so fast?

It was probably a miracle they hadn't had a fight sooner. Small car, long, hot drive. Plus, they hardly knew each other. Actually, reflecting back, they'd gotten along remarkably well considering all those factors. Being together had been so easy. Maybe too easy, because the minute the real world intruded everything fell apart. The first time there was any conflict things had blown completely apart.

This was exactly what had been so frustrating about Kent. He'd go from zero to a hundred and then leave before anything got talked through. Trying to work through any disagreement with him or navigate compromise was infuriatingly impossible. He was always right and would never apologize. Iris always had to be the one to walk things back, to make things okay again. Well, she wasn't going to do it any longer. She wasn't going to be that person. Finn could call as easily as she could. Communication worked both ways.

Did Finn really say she was shallow?

Finn definitely said basically that about her friends. And then she said something derogatory about Finn's friend Ward and Watts Mountain in general, which Finn probably interpreted as a criticism of her parents.

Iris sat up with her elbows on her knees and her face in her hands.

What was wrong with her?

Was she a shallow, horrible person?

Iris tried her best to rewind the conversation and replay it accurately. She tried to discern what had actually been said and what had simply been misinterpreted. It was an impossible task alone. She really needed to talk to Finn

She reached for her phone. It was two in the morning. She'd have to wait.

Iris slumped back onto the bed, sighed loudly, and rolled onto her side.

CHAPTER THIRTY-FOUR

Finn figured that maybe she'd finally drifted off for a little while around five in the morning. Her alarm on her phone chirped at seven, so that she could pack and be ready to check out when Tommy returned for the car.

Since there was no way to draw up an official contract or invoice for shipping the car, they'd agreed that Finn would only pay half up front. Then she'd pay the other half of the fee when Tommy delivered the car in Georgia. It would take a few days for him to get there.

It was weird that she'd only just met Tommy but was now about to trust him with one of her most prized possessions. She had a good gut feeling about him. And she usually trusted her gut. So why was her gut all twisted up about Iris?

Finn was still so angry that she could hardly stomach toast for breakfast. Actually, it was hard to decipher whether she was more angry or hurt. Sometimes those things got all mixed together and one was like gasoline for the flame of the other. Not only that, but her gut was at war with her head. Her gut told her that Iris cared about her. Her gut told her that Iris didn't mean what Finn thought she'd meant when they'd argued. But her head had a different opinion. Her head remembered all the words and wouldn't let them go.

It was good that she had so much to coordinate for her return trip. Those tasks gave her head something else to focus on for a while. She wanted to focus on anything but the argument with Iris, because dissecting that was completely exhausting.

By noon she was at the Burbank Airport, waiting at her gate. The ongoing war that her gut was having with her head had ruined any chance of an appetite, so lunch was a bust. She choked down a granola bar and sucked on a bottle of water while she waited for her flight to board. She checked her phone screen about every thirty seconds hoping for some sort of text from Iris, but nothing.

So now for the hard question. Was she really going to get on a plane and leave California without calling Iris? There was no way that Iris could possibly know she was leaving. Iris probably assumed that Finn was at the driving class for the rest of the week, and that they'd talk at some point later in the week. Maybe even meet to talk in person. Only now there was no way an in-person chat was going to happen. Finn had taken care of that.

She was starting to have second thoughts. Had she acted too rashly? A one-way ticket was the ultimate one-sided argument, leaving no room for rebuttal.

The announcement for pre-boarding, for anyone traveling with small children, came over the loudspeaker. Exhausted parents crowded the gate with kids and car seats in tow. And then the announcement for passengers in zone one. Still no message from Iris. Zone two began to board, then zone three.

Fuck.

Finn held her phone in her hand and stared at it. She had to make the call. She knew she'd regret it if she didn't. Sometimes a decision came down to doing the thing you thought you'd regret least.

She hit the call button and waited. Iris didn't pick up. Finn decided that was for the best. She listened to the outgoing message. Just the sound of Iris's voice twisted her stomach into knots and made her chest ache. She focused on sounding confident about her decision to leave, and hoped she could pull it off.

The phone vibrated on the glass tabletop and Iris jumped. Iris had chosen an outside table, hoping the combination of sunshine and coffee would brighten her mood. She'd been on edge all morning, jittery from lack of sleep and too many tears. She'd stopped for a coffee before showing up at the Warner Bros. lot. Soon she was due to read for the part that Judith had sent via email. This was a terrible day to do any reading. She was a mess and wasn't sure she could focus well enough to stay in character.

She picked up her phone to see who was calling. Her heart sped up when she saw that it was Finn.

Finally, Finn had called. Iris had literally checked her phone every minute since the previous night hoping that Finn would text or call or something. Now that the phone was ringing she was afraid to answer it. She hesitated for too long and the call went to voice mail. Should she ring Finn? No, she'd listen to the voice mail first and gauge Finn's mood before calling her back.

She sipped her coffee until the voice mail registered. Iris took a deep breath and then listened.

"Hi, Iris...I don't really know what to say, or what you want to hear, but I didn't want to leave without calling." There was a long pause and lots of noise in the background. "I'm sorry things turned out the way they did." Another loud noise. Was she at the airport? "My flight is boarding, so I've got to go...I guess...I guess that's it. I don't know what else to say. Okay, bye."

Finn was leaving? Nausea threatened to overthrow her stomach. She sank back in her chair. Was that it? They'd had this amazing week, and after one stupid argument Finn was over it? Iris's brain tried to synthesize all the thoughts spinning through her head. This just didn't make any sense. The class Finn had planned to take was supposed to last for a week, right? What had happened besides their argument to make Finn change her plan so abruptly and completely?

Iris replayed the voice mail three times, as much to try to glean any hint of what Finn was really thinking as to hear Finn's voice.

She decided to call Finn back. She had to talk to her and find out what was really going on. The thought of not seeing Finn made her feel sick and a little desperate. This was not at all how she thought things would go.

Finn's voice mail picked up right away. That probably meant she had already turned her phone off. Iris hung up without leaving a message. She held the phone in both hands, summoned her courage, and hit *call* again.

"Finn, I got your message." She took a breath, trying her best to sound calm. "Please call me."

She couldn't bring herself to say much more than that for fear her words would be choked off by tears.

"Excuse me." A man slid into the chair across from her. He was nice looking, probably in his late twenties. He reminded her of her useless lab partner from college. Not dumb, but preferring to use his looks to get others to help him with notes and homework.

"Yes?" The last thing she was in the mood for was small talk from a stranger.

"Can you settle a bet between my friend and me?"

"Probably not." She wasn't in the mood for games either.

"Are you the girl from the Doritos commercial?"

"No, sorry."

He shrugged and returned to the table where he'd left his friend. How long was that stupid commercial going to haunt her?

She put on her sunglasses, turned toward the street, and tried to focus on finishing her coffee. The two guys eventually left, and an older couple, who looked like tourists, took their table. She heard them talking with an unmistakable southern accent and she almost burst into tears.

Her cell phone buzzed. She sniffed and checked the screen, hoping, by some miracle, that it was Finn. But it wasn't. She exhaled slowly before she answered.

"Hi, Judith."

"I'm so glad I caught you before the appointment on the Warners lot."

"Why, what's wrong?"

"Oh, nothing's wrong. In fact, I've got great news." Judith paused. "I got the call just now from the series filming in Atlanta. You got the part."

"What?"

"You got the lead. Congratulations, Iris. This is going to be a great role for you. I can feel it."

Judith sounded genuinely excited. If Iris weren't utterly depressed about Finn, she'd be excited too. But she'd already decided she couldn't take the part even if she got it. Now she had to break the news to Judith. But before she got the chance Judith started talking again.

"Yes, they apologized for taking so long to get back to us. I guess I was wrong about the production delay. I had taken a guess that it had something to do with rights to the book. Turns out they had to find a new director."

"A new director?"

"Apparently, there were several complaints filed with the production company about Eric Gilet's conduct on the previous series he directed. The showrunner and the casting director for this new series, both women, refused to work on the project until Eric was off the show."

Iris was in shock.

"Iris? Are you still there?"

"Um, yes…sorry…I'm still here."

"It's surprising, I know. But not that surprising, right?"

"It's an incredible surprise." Iris shivered. From nerves or excitement? She wasn't sure. "Who's the new director?"

"A woman. I'll find her name. I had it, but now her name escapes me. I'll send it to you."

"Thank you, Judith. Thank you for believing in me."

"Hey, you deserve this. You've earned it." She could almost hear Judith smile through the phone. "I'll get back to you with details as soon as I have them. I just couldn't wait to give you the good news." The sound of shuffling papers came through the phone. "Oh, and I'll let them know you won't make it to the reading today. You're booked. Okay, bye for now."

"Good-bye, Judith. And thanks again."

Iris clicked off.

She got the part. She was going to Atlanta, without knowing where she stood with Finn. Did fate love her or hate her? At this point, it was impossible to know for sure.

CHAPTER THIRTY-FIVE

The flight from Burbank to Houston was miserable. Finn spent the entire time cataloguing all the ways she'd failed. This was failure on an epic scale. This was colossal failure, the kind of failure that people don't bounce back from. This was the sort of fiasco that would dog her once she got back to Georgia. She'd never escape it. There was no doubt that Ward and her parents had told everyone that she'd gone to California to follow her dream. Only to discover that the dream was a nightmare and she'd turned and run home at the first sign of trouble. This was not the sort of thing her father would end up bragging about at the corner store.

She needed to decide right here and now that none of it mattered.

That would be the only way to survive it. She simply needed to convince herself of two things—that the dream of stunt driving didn't matter and that Iris didn't matter.

That last part was going to be the toughest because she knew there was no truth in it. Iris *did* matter. Finn could hardly think of anything else except the hurt look on Iris's face when she'd stormed out of the house. That's all she could see every time she closed her eyes. Sure, Iris had said hurtful things too, but Finn didn't have to turn tail and run like a coward.

Of course, that's exactly what she was, an emotional coward. She knew that about herself. If she were an honest person she'd have warned Iris about that up front.

Maybe it didn't matter. Maybe Iris had just been in it for fun and nothing more. Now Finn was second-guessing everything, and it was all becoming a big pile of confusion inside her head.

The layover was short in Houston. She was going to have just enough time to grab a sandwich from one of the airport kiosks and search for her connecting flight. She turned her phone on as she wove through oncoming pedestrian traffic. She almost toppled over someone's rolling bag who'd come to a stop to read the arrivals and departures screen. When she looked at her phone again she saw that she had a missed call and a message from Iris.

Call me, was the gist of the message.

The very loud Houston airport was not the ideal place to have a conversation that you weren't sure you were ready to have in the first place. Finn needed a little more time to figure out how she was feeling. Hearing Iris's voice set off cascading emotions, some of which she had no control over. She had the intense urge to reach through the phone and hold Iris. But she'd made sure that wouldn't be an option by booking the first flight she could get and leaving. In hindsight, possibly not the most mature decision.

The plane reached its cruising altitude, headed for Atlanta. Finn tried to eat the very dry turkey sandwich she'd nabbed during her sprint though the terminal. In her haste, she'd forgotten to grab condiments. The sandwich was dry and flavorless just like her life was going to be without Iris.

Finn needed to think about other things.

She had other problems besides screwing up things with Iris. She needed a job. She realized that she'd been far too cavalier about the whole stunt driving thing. Even if she'd finished the course and stayed in Southern California, who knows how long it would have taken for her to actually get a paying gig on a movie. She'd have had to find other work in the meantime. It was clear to her now that she hadn't really thought things through. The ease of living in the cabins, barely paying rent to her parents was a luxury hard to re-create and probably impossible to find in California.

Reflecting back, there were a lot of things she really liked about working for the limo company. Maybe she should consider becoming an Uber driver. In the short-term that would give her cash to figure out what was next. Maybe she'd start her own limousine business. Then she could fire asshole clients, instead of the other way around. She could supplement her monthly income by racing again with Ward. She had options, she just needed to be reminded of what they were.

The point was, she was ready to let go of the stunt driving idea, but not ready to give up on cars. Driving was her passion, and she wasn't prepared to lose everything in her life that she loved simply because one part of the dream had been foolish.

Hiring out as a driver was an honest living. There was no shame in it.

Finn was in the window seat. As if to endorse her newly hatched plan, a ray of sunlight broke through the clouds and bounced off her tray table. Yeah, this idea had potential. For the first time in almost twenty-four hours, she was a tiny bit hopeful. She still wasn't sure what to say to Iris, but she had two more hours of flight time to try to figure it out.

Iris sat down with her laptop as soon as she returned home. An email from Judith contained all the info about the series. She read through the details. Filming started in a couple of days. Probably since the production had been delayed they were anxious to get things moving. So was Iris. Although, unless she could sort things out with Finn she feared everything about the trip to Atlanta would simply be one big cross-country reminder of how screwed up things had gotten.

"Hi, you're back already?" Maggie dropped her bag on the kitchen island.

Iris looked up from her seat at the dining room table.

"Yeah, I didn't go to the audition."

"Oh, I'm sorry."

"No, it's a good thing. I got the lead in that new series." Iris had expected to be more excited.

"Wait, what? Really? Iris, that's great!" Maggie hugged her.

"I know, right? I don't think it's quite sunk in yet."

"So, what does that mean, exactly? I mean, you've never done a series before. Is all the filming for the show happening in Atlanta?" Maggie paused, her expression shifted from joy to sympathy. "Oh... Atlanta. Have you talked to Finn yet?"

"She left me a voice mail. And I left her a message, but we haven't actually talked." Iris sighed and sat back down. Maggie sat facing her. "Mags, she flew back to Georgia this morning."

"Whoa...what? Without even talking to you first?"

Iris nodded. She was determined not to cry, again.

"That's really harsh, and unfair."

Okay, now she was going to cry.

"Oh, sweetheart, come here." Maggie scooted closer and put her arms around Iris. "Don't cry. You two will work it out."

"Do you think so?"

"I do, Iris. I really do." Maggie went to the kitchen and returned with a glass of water and the box of tissues from the counter.

She wasn't so sure Maggie was right.

"Thank you." Iris pressed a tissue to her eyes for a minute until the tears ebbed. She sniffed. "Listen, I know that when they shot *Stranger Things* it took six months to do the first season. I could be gone for six months or longer. But I'll still pay rent. I hope—"

"Hey, you're my roommate through thick and thin."

Maggie was the best friend and roommate a person could have.

"Mags, I love you."

"I love you too." Maggie quirked an eyebrow. "But not in a gay way."

"Thank God."

They both laughed.

CHAPTER THIRTY-SIX

Trey was surprised to see Finn back so soon, but to his credit, he didn't pelt her with questions. At least not for the first half-hour of their drive. Finn was starving so they stopped at an all-night diner on the way to Watts Mountain. Finn loved old school diners and now, forever, one of her favorite things would remind her of Iris.

It was nearly ten o'clock by the time she'd gotten her bag and located Trey. It was early enough on the West Coast that she could have called Iris if she'd wanted, but she still had no idea what to say. Maybe by the time she was back at the cabins she'd have something meaningful she could offer to explain her behavior. She was waiting on inspiration or insight to strike. Maybe once she had some food in her system she'd feel better.

"So, are you gonna tell me what happened?" Trey slathered ketchup on his fries.

Finn focused on her burger. She took a huge bite without answering him.

"'Cause, the last time I saw you there was this super hot girl on your arm who seemed kinda into you. I mean, I have no idea why, but still, she seemed into you."

Finn chewed her food slowly, hoping not to choke on it as she tried to swallow around the lump in her throat.

"You were gonna stay in LA and become some hot shot stunt driver." He nibbled on a French fry, then continued. "And now, here you are, without the girl and without your car."

"It wasn't what I thought it would be like." She took a swig of her Coke.

"Which part?"

"All the parts." She took a couple more bites of her hamburger before she explained more. Trey patiently waited. The waitress refilled their drinks. "Iris and I had a big fight and then, well, stunt driving, the class was fun, but I don't think I could ever do it for a living. I think the whole industry is too cutthroat for me."

"Hey, at least you tried it. So now you know. If you hadn't made the trip you'd probably always wonder."

"Yeah, I guess." She took another bite and chewed slowly while she considered it. "Once I knew it wasn't gonna work I decided to cut my losses. I had a convenient offer to ship the car, so I just flew back."

"So, what happened with Iris?" He wasn't going to let her off the hook.

"Her roommate threw her a birthday party and her ex showed up."

"Oh, so she's getting back together with her ex." He nodded sympathetically.

"No, I mean, I don't know. We ended up getting into a fight the next day, about her friends, and then she made some comments about my friends, and, I dunno, things just escalated."

"That was it? You got into a fight about each other's friends?" He braced his elbows on the table and studied her as if she'd said something truly crazy.

"Well, not the way you're making it sound." She sat back, taking a break from her half-eaten burger. "Who someone's friends are says a lot about who they are."

"What are her friends like?"

"Shallow."

"Finn, it's fucking Hollywood. What did you expect?"

"I don't know what I expected."

"Is Iris shallow?"

"No, of course not."

"Finn, I don't think I would have given up on her so easily. I thought you were really into her. And she seemed nice." He finished his fries. "I mean, definitely too nice for you."

"Shut up." She knew Trey was trying to joke and lighten her mood. But hearing herself try to explain the argument just made her sound like an idiot. It had all seemed so much more upsetting, so much bigger, in the moment. "She made a comment about Watts Mountain having no culture." Finn threw out that detail in her defense.

"Isn't she right about that? I mean, unless you consider Turner's Corner store a hotbed of cultural influence."

"Goddammit, I'm an idiot." She covered her face with her hands.

"Yeah, I'm pretty sure you are." In true brotherly form, Trey agreed with her.

It took another hour for them to reach Hideaway Haven. The familiar scent of damp earth and nighttime sounds soothed Finn. She was back in her space, feeling a little defeated but happy to be home.

It was time to call Iris.

She owed Iris some sort of explanation, possibly an apology.

She lounged on the bed with her phone, but she didn't dial the number right away. The first thing she did was scroll through photos from their trip. God, Iris was gorgeous. And dammit, they'd had a really great time together. She had the pics to prove it. She was about to click back to her contacts list but touched Instagram with her thumb by accident. The last feed she'd looked at popped up before she could click off. For some reason she'd looked at Kent's profile after the party at Iris's. She remembered now that she'd pulled it up to unfollow him, but had gotten interrupted and hadn't thought to circle back and delete him from her feed.

The photo that greeted her was a selfie of Kent with his arm around Iris with the hashtags: beautiful and good times.

What the fuck?

Was that a recent photo? It was impossible to tell.

She clicked over to Iris's feed, but Iris hadn't posted a new photo since the party. There was a shot of Maggie, Regina, and Iris posing with drinks.

She'd almost summoned the courage to call Iris, but not now. Seeing the photo of Iris and Kent together was like a gut punch. The burger she'd practically inhaled at the diner threatened to come back to haunt her. Finn tossed her phone to the other side of the bed. She'd wait for Iris to call her. She wasn't the only one who needed to apologize or explain herself.

CHAPTER THIRTY-SEVEN

Forty-eight hours had passed since Iris left a message asking Finn to call her. It seemed clear that Finn didn't want to talk to her. Fine. So be it. If whatever they had between them couldn't survive one single argument then it was best that it ended now while Iris still had her heart intact.

She'd been busy anyway. Iris had a lot to organize before leaving for Atlanta, including a grueling five-hour visit to the California Department of Motor Vehicles. She would never allow her license to lapse again, ever. The only thing more demoralizing than being continually recognized as Doritos Girl was spending practically the whole day at the DMV securing a new driver's license.

The rest of Iris's time before departure was spent packing and hanging out with Maggie and Regina. They'd both promised to come to the Deep South for a visit while she was there. Iris had been very nervous about the flight, after her most recent trip to Atlanta. Regina had offered her a Xanax, but she'd declined. She needed to manage her terror without the aid of a sedative. It wasn't as if she could drive back and forth from Georgia to California by herself. She had to muster her strength, mind over matter. The chance to see Finn again was what gave her courage to fly across the country. She focused on Finn and faced her fear.

A damp blanket of humidity embraced Iris as she exited the terminal. Her hair immediately gained weight and mass.

She'd packed two suitcases for her extended stay in Atlanta. The driver towed both of them toward the town car in short-term parking, while she followed carrying a smaller overnight bag. This trip was already better than the last one. For starters, the plane hadn't almost crashed, she'd been upgraded to extra leg room, and the studio had sent a car service to pick her up. Wouldn't it have been poetic if the driver waiting for her had been Finn? But that was a little too Nora Ephron. Besides, as far as she knew, Finn was no longer driving for the limo service.

Iris had the night to herself before they started filming the next day. She expected the days to be long. It took somewhere between sixty and ninety hours to shoot one hour of television. She'd tried her best to mentally prepare for what she expected to be an exhausting schedule.

The town car moved slowly through evening rush hour traffic toward the hotel. Iris watched midrise buildings pass by her window. Her phone chimed in her purse.

It was a text from Regina.

Hey, where are you? Check Kent's feed. He's posting photos of you again. #stalker

I'm in ATL. Just landed. Which photo? He'd done this off and on since they split. Some sort of weird throwback down memory lane on social media.

Regina responded. *From last year, 4th of July at the beach.*

Iris sighed. How could she tell Kent to stop? He was just trying to get her attention. If she texted him to ask him to stop then he'd have already won because he'd know she was looking at his Instagram feed. He would assume she cared, which she didn't.

I'm going to ignore him. Iris refused to play his game.

Want me to comment and tell him to fuck off?

Iris smiled. Her friends always had her back, shallow or not.

You're sweet, but not necessary.

I'm so sorry I told him about your party. Forgive me? Regina wanted everyone to have a good time. Sometimes that meant she texted before really thinking things through. She really was so sweet and lighthearted that she could almost get away with anything.

You're forgiven. Iris added a smiling emoji.

Good luck tomorrow! xoxo

Thanks. xo Iris clicked off.

Iris resumed sightseeing out the window. She was still holding her phone when it vibrated a few minutes later. She figured it was Regina again. Her heart seized when she saw Finn's name on the screen. She took a deep breath and answered.

"Hello?"

It seemed like minutes before Finn spoke, but it was probably only a few seconds.

"Hi." It was so good to hear Finn's voice even though it made her a little queasy at the same time.

Iris waited.

"Iris, are you still there?"

The sound of Finn's voice turned Iris's insides into a molten mess. She'd worked hard to remain angry, and only a few words from Finn was melting her resolve.

"Yes, I'm still here. I didn't expect to hear from you." That was the truth.

"I should have called sooner, I…I just didn't know what to say. I still don't."

How about, I'm sorry?

"You're back in Georgia?" Iris was still hurt that Finn left California without saying good-bye. And she wasn't sure she wanted to tell Finn she was in Atlanta, yet. She needed to know that what she'd felt from Finn was more than a matter of proximity or convenience, more than just a road trip romance.

"Yeah, I'm in Watts Mountain."

Finn had been so desperate to find out if Iris was back with Kent or exactly what she was up to that she'd started following the Twitter feed for the new sci-fi series Iris had auditioned for. Everyone who was a fan of *Firefly* seemed to be avidly following the show's development so there were lots of bits of fan-centric news on Twitter. The studio had been posting production and casting updates so Finn knew that Iris had gotten the part. She knew that was a big deal and wanted more than anything to help Iris celebrate her success. She wondered if Iris was going to tell her she was coming to Atlanta, if she wasn't there already.

"I'm sorry I left without seeing you…without saying good-bye." Finn wasn't sure if she could genuinely apologize for everything, but she definitely had regrets about that.

"I was pretty upset by the way you left." She could hear the hurt in Iris's words, but otherwise, Iris wasn't revealing much.

Finn heard a male voice in the background but couldn't make out what he was saying. Iris wasn't alone. Finn should end this painful call before it got any worse.

"I can tell you've got someone there." Finn tried to mask her frustration. "Maybe you could call me back sometime if you feel like talking."

"Okay."

Finn was puzzled by how little Iris was saying. Maybe because someone else was listening? Or maybe she had nothing to say to Finn. Maybe what they'd had really was nothing more than a friendly summer fling. That hurt.

"Bye." Finn knew she probably sounded as defeated as she felt.

"Good-bye."

Finn held the phone in her hand for a minute after she ended that call. She'd made first contact, but that exchange had told her nothing. Iris didn't apologize and didn't share any details about her new gig in Atlanta. That omission had to mean that Iris didn't want to see Finn, right? How else could she interpret that?

"How'd it go?" Ward asked. He was standing on the other side of the car ready with the buffing machine in his hand.

"I have no idea." Finn shrugged and slipped her phone in her back pocket.

"That good, huh?"

"Yeah, that good."

"Does she know that you know she's gonna be in Atlanta working on that show?"

"No, and she didn't bring it up either. I'm guessing that means she doesn't want to see me."

"Or it just means she's still pissed." Ward slid protective goggles down over his eyes.

"Let's get this car ready and in working order." She'd decided to finish refurbishing the Lincoln for hauling passengers. All it had needed was a final coat of paint and they were about to buff that out now. Finn figured it would be sort of a cool thing to show up in a vintage Lincoln. Plus, the car could carry four passengers comfortably in the back seat.

Tommy hadn't arrived with Scarlett yet, but he'd texted from Arkansas to let her know his status.

"I don't know why she wouldn't wanna take you back." The corner of Ward's mouth twitched up as if he were trying not to laugh. "I mean, she's just a movie star, and you're an Uber driver."

"Shut up and buff."

But deep down, she knew he was right.

Nights seemed longer since Finn's return from California. After sundown, the hours just dragged on and on with no distraction from her nightly internal struggle. She was rethinking everything that had happened with Iris. The problem with dissecting every exchange was that it was almost impossible to put it back together in any form that made sense.

Nothing looked good under a microscope.

Especially not Finn.

She was fairly sure she'd been a complete ass and gotten what she deserved, the cold shoulder from Iris. The question that lingered, the question that kept her up at night was whether there was anything she could do to make things right. Finn would give anything if she could go back to that last night at Iris's and do things differently. She'd hurt Iris's feelings. She'd known even as the hurtful words had escaped her lips, but she couldn't stop herself from lashing out. She blamed ego and immaturity, but still, that was no excuse.

She decided to sit on the front steps and drink a beer. Maybe the fresh air would clear her head. The porch light was drawing bugs so she turned it off and sank back to the top step to enjoy the darkness. It was late, probably midnight. The lights in the main house were off, and since it was a weeknight only a couple of cabins were occupied besides hers. Those lights were off too. Finn was alone with the darkness.

The painted planks of the steps were smooth and cool under her bare feet. She flexed her toes and rocked back as she tipped the bottle for another long swig.

She was pathetic.

Iris was her dream girl in every possible way and she'd completely screwed it up. When she lay down at night she could hardly sleep for wanting Iris. She missed Iris's smile, and her magical laugh, and the way Iris made the world seem like a better place.

An owl called in the distance. A haunting sound, like a breathy echo from the darkness.

Finn tried to imagine what might have happened if she'd stayed in California. She couldn't quite figure it out. Every scenario seemed more like a Hollywood-ized version of real life than life itself. Because in the real world, there was no way Iris and Finn could be a couple, not for the long term. Yeah, any way Finn tried to organize things she always came to the conclusion that theirs could only ever be a short-term romance. She should just suck it up and be grateful for the time she had with Iris and move on.

CHAPTER THIRTY-EIGHT

It was two a.m. when Iris looked at the digital clock on the nightstand. She'd ordered room service when she'd arrived at the hotel because she was too tired to deal with going out. But whatever she'd eaten made her so thirsty. She retrieved a bottle of water from the mini-fridge and crawled back under the covers.

She sat in the dark, sipped water, and wondered what Finn was doing. Every night since the big fight, Iris would wake and her first thought would be of Finn—what was she doing, what was she thinking, did she care about Iris?

Deep down, in her innermost thoughts, in the place where dreams lived, Iris held on to the belief that Finn did care. In the light of day, her rational mind would explain that away. Her brain would remind her of all the reasons why she and Finn were completely wrong for each other and why things could never work. But late at night, in the wee hours between asleep and awake, things felt different. It was in those moments that Iris allowed herself to hope.

But their last phone call had been terrible. She'd hardly said anything for fear she'd start crying. If Finn had just come out and apologized would that have made a difference? It wasn't as if she didn't owe Finn an apology too. What she really wanted was to see Finn and talk things out face-to-face. She was sick of talking over the phone and she refused to text about anything this important. Kent had resorted to texting to avoid confrontation right before they broke up. She was holding herself to a higher standard. And with everything else that had gone wrong, at least Finn had the decency to call rather than text.

Iris checked the clock again. A half hour had passed and she'd hardly noticed. She sank under the covers and tried to quiet her mind. Tomorrow was going to be a big day. She needed to stop thinking about Finn and focus on doing good work on set.

She rolled onto her side and swept her palm across the cool sheet on the unoccupied side of the bed. *I miss you, Finn.*

Every time Iris got an acting job she'd be relieved for weeks. She'd let go of lots of pent up anxiety and stress about auditions. As Iris headed for hair and makeup, she relished the sense of elation she was feeling. Good things were happening. Not only had she landed the lead, but she actually really liked the script and the premise of the show. And for the first time, behind the monitors, near where the producer and director sat, was a chair with her name on it. Every time she saw it, a little shiver of excitement raced through her chest.

There were a lot of people to meet during the first days of filming. Iris would be on this show at least through the filming of the first season. It was important to be on friendly terms with the people she'd be spending a lot of time with, drivers, hairdressers, and makeup artists. Hair and makeup was your first stop in the morning and could set the tone for the rest of the day. Iris took care to introduce herself to everyone she met. This was going to be her world, her family, for the next few months.

The assistant director, Jonah, was super helpful. Iris liked him right away. She knew he'd be her main source of information until the actual shooting began.

After hair and makeup, Iris was ushered to a short rehearsal for the first shot. The schedule was a little unpredictable, not every scene was shot in the order it appeared in the script, so she ended up standing around. Iris was glad to have some time to wake up and fully caffeinate. She was struggling to get into the right time zone. Her body was still on California time.

Iris was waiting, in a holding pattern, but it wasn't as if she was truly relaxed. This was more like *active waiting*, because she had to be ready to jump in when called.

She and Camille rehearsed scenes a few times, not for the acting itself, but so the director could figure out the blocking and basic camera setups. So far, Iris liked the director, Talia Grant. Talia was straightforward without being bossy. She knew what she wanted from each scene and gave clear instructions. Iris wanted to deliver a great performance, a performance that Talia would be happy with.

"Okay, that was good." They'd run through the scene a couple of times, and Talia was pleased. "Iris and Camille, you can take a minute."

Iris checked in with hair and makeup for a touch-up. When she came back the stand-ins walked through the blocking, while camera and lighting set up for the next shot. Camille was standing next to her. So far, Camille was great too. Iris hoped the friendly chemistry they seemed to have would continue as the long days on set continued.

After almost twenty minutes, Iris and Camille were called back to shoot. Iris's stand-in walked her through specific marks for changes that had been made for technical reasons. Talia ran through some final performance notes.

"This is the first time you two meet." Talia stood between Camille and Iris. "Iris, your character, Jade, has been struggling to survive and Cleo has just thrown her a lifeline, but with strings attached. You're drawn to each other immediately, but trust is a problem for both of you."

Iris stood next to Camille. There were some details still being sorted out between the director and the AD. This gave Iris a moment to quietly chat with Camille, a moment to get to know her a little better.

"So, have you lived in Atlanta before?" asked Iris.

"No, this is my first time. You?"

Iris shook her head. "I live in Santa Monica."

"I live in Brooklyn."

Talia took her chair behind the monitors. "Roll camera."

The brief window of time for get-to-know-you small talk closed.

The camera guy responded. "Camera rolling."

"Marker," Talia called out.

One of the assistant camera operators held the slate in front of the camera that showed the scene number and take. The sticks of the slate clapped loudly, a visual and audio reference to sync sound and picture.

"Action!"

Iris focused on Camille. This was it, time to prove she'd earned this chance.

The process for making a script come alive was the result of a million moving parts. Lots of talented people collaborating so that she could make this character real. The on-set acting was a tiny portion of the entire day and she had to be queued up, ready to perform when called up. The acting would be intense, and in order to be at her best, Iris had to be in an extremely creative and vulnerable state in the midst of a warehouse full of people. But this was what she'd worked and dreamed for. This was her chance and she was going to bring everything she had to it. Iris took a deep breath and exhaled slowly. She was ready for this. She'd been ready her whole life.

CHAPTER THIRTY-NINE

Where are you off to?" Finn's mother was folding towels on the kitchen table in the main house.

"I told you, I signed up and I'm driving for Uber. That's why Ward and I fixed up the Lincoln." Finn stood in the open door of the fridge. She was hungry, but nothing jumped out at her.

"It's late to start work isn't it?"

It was almost three o'clock. Late by some standards, but given the fact that Finn wasn't really sleeping she figured she was doing pretty well to be dressed and ready for an afternoon start time. People needed rides just as often at night as during the day anyway.

"Mama, the beauty of self-employment is you get to set your own hours."

Her mother huffed and shook her head. She wasn't buying it.

"Why don't you just call Iris and talk things out?"

Finn never realized how being in the closet was a blessing in some ways. Especially where her parents were concerned. Now that everything was out in the open, her mother could freely offer parental advice about how amazing Iris was and how Finn had screwed it all up.

"I have called her. She doesn't want to talk to me." Finn let the door close with a whoosh. Food wasn't going to make her feel any better or dislodge the permanent knot in her stomach.

"That was three days ago wasn't it? It wouldn't hurt to call again. Sometimes we have to work a little harder for the things we really want in life." Her mother smoothed the edges of the hand towel and added it to the neat stack of all white linens.

It had been four days, but who was counting?

"I have to go." Her mother meant well. It wasn't her fault that Finn screwed things up. Finn kissed her on the cheek. "Don't wait up."

The afternoon sun was blazing as Finn reached for her Ray-Bans and turned onto the highway headed toward the Atlanta metro area. Before she got very far her phone pinged. Someone in Dawsonville wanted a ride. She picked them up near Starbucks for a destination at the Mall of Georgia. Not bad. She'd just gotten paid for her drive into the city.

It turned out being an Uber driver was fairly uncomplicated. As long as you had no criminal record and you owned a decent car, a cell phone, and set up the payment function, then you were in business.

The first couple of days, most of the routes had been short hops from the suburbs to shows or bars in the city. The second day, she'd actually done two airport runs. Those were almost an hour each so they paid well. By Friday, she was feeling like a pro and riders got a real kick out of the classic Lincoln with the suicide doors. Big smiles greeted her every time she pulled up to the curb for passengers.

If she did this for very long she'd need a car with better gas mileage, but for now, the *wow* factor was working in her favor.

It was around six when she got a ping for someone needing a ride from Midtown to an industrial park on the west side of Atlanta. This was an area she didn't know very well, and it seemed like an odd destination. Her passenger was standing in front of the W Hotel looking at his phone when she pulled up. He was wearing dark jeans and a snug fitting charcoal T-shirt. This guy looked too fit and too coiffed. The first thought she had was that he looked like he was from the LA area.

"Hi, are you Steve?" She wanted to make sure she had the right person.

"Yes, are you Finn?"

"That's me."

"This is a great car." He slid into the back seat. "I thought the app was wrong about the year when it listed the make of the car."

Finn smiled. "I get that a lot." Finn eased back onto the main street. "The destination you entered is kind of in the middle of nowhere. Are you sure about the address?"

"Yeah, it's a location for a series we're shooting."

Finn's stomach flipped over and nose-dived. Was this guy working on the same show as Iris? She was afraid to ask. And at the moment she couldn't because he was talking on his phone.

Within a block of the drop-off, the neighborhood abruptly shifted from early 1900s wood-sided shotgun houses to white trailers, catering trucks, and modular structures like the ones housing offices near construction sites. In the spaces between the trailers, she got a glimpse of the large staging area beyond—camera equipment, rigging of all kinds, and lots of people.

Finn parked the car.

"Hey, would it be okay if I parked here for a few minutes?" she asked.

"I don't think it'll be a problem. Security may tell you to move it, though, so I would stay close by." Steve got out and started looking at his phone almost immediately as he passed through the security entrance and entered the set.

Finn had never been on a movie set. It looked as if this dilapidated warehouse district had been converted to look like an industrial apocalyptic landscape. Finn stood at the edge of everything where a walkway had been set up between white and yellow barricades. The white trailers that edged the expansive set created a visual buffer so that you couldn't really see the extent of the space until you were standing right next to the barrier.

And then Finn saw her.

Iris was walking toward one of the trailers. She was looking at her phone so she didn't see Finn. Even if she had looked up, Finn was a hundred feet away, and probably the last person Iris would expect to see.

This was it. Finn had to make the first move. Fate and Uber had delivered her right to Iris's doorstep. That had to mean something.

Finn looked at the surrounding trailers. Flowers. What she really needed were flowers. Something, a heartfelt offering, to break the ice. Even in the apocalypse there had to be flowers. She needed to make an impression, and for that, she didn't want to show up at Iris's trailer empty-handed. That's assuming she could get past security in the first place.

❖

Iris was tired but invigorated at the same time. The first few days on the set for *Athena* had been great, but gruelingly long. The lot where they were filming the first two episodes was staged to look like what was left of future earth. And things had not gone well for the planet, or humanity for that matter. Partially demolished and crumbling industrial buildings and carefully choreographed urban debris were all part of the staging in the large vacant lot turned future-scape.

Her final shot was finished, and she'd been released for the day. Iris went through wardrobe and makeup and then signed out. She was actually off for the next two days and was looking forward to the break in the grueling schedule.

Iris's trailer was at the edge of the lot, along with a food truck and several other modular air-conditioned trailers to escape the Georgia heat between shots.

It was Friday and everything was wrapping up for the day. Iris hadn't talked to Finn all week. She'd decided as soon as they were done for the day she was going to find a car and drive to Watts Mountain to see Finn. She was tired of not knowing. It was stupid that they hadn't been able to connect. And she felt sure if they saw each other then she'd know whether there was something between them to be salvaged or not.

She still hadn't told Finn she was in Atlanta. She'd been doing eleven- and twelve-hour days, so it wasn't as if she'd had any down time to see Finn anyway.

She ducked into her trailer for a moment to get her bag and to freshen up. She pulled her phone out to check about getting an Uber. Maybe that would be better than trying to find a car. Funny, there was an Uber driver just outside the security entrance. She was about to enter the address on her phone but glanced up quickly to make sure she wasn't going to walk into someone or trip over power cables. Finn was standing at the barricade watching her. She came to a full stop. As she stared, a smile spread across Finn's handsome face.

Oh shit. She wanted to see Finn, but she'd planned to have at least an hour's drive to figure out what she wanted to say to her when she did. She started walking again, but she wasn't completely sure her feet were touching the concrete.

"How did you know I was here?" She'd purposefully not told Finn.

"I didn't." Finn had a casual stance, with her hands behind her back. "I gave someone a ride and then...I saw you."

"That's ironic, because I was actually on my way to see you."

"You were?" Finn stepped closer.

"Yes, I was."

Finn shifted, as if she'd only just remembered she was holding something behind her back. "Here, these are for you."

Finn held a bag of Doritos in both hands as if it were a bouquet.

Iris couldn't help laughing, which broke the ice a little.

"You shouldn't have." She reached for the bag of chips and her fingers brushed across Finn's. There it was, that delicious tingle of electricity between them. It *was* still there. She hadn't imagined it.

"I just wanted to make you smile." Finn's words were soft, like a caress.

"Want to go somewhere so we can talk?"

"I'd like that."

"Follow me." She took Finn's hand and tugged her toward her trailer. Over her shoulder she spoke to the security guard. "It's okay, she's a friend."

The trailer's interior wasn't anything elegant. It was more like a camper trailer, but without an ounce of character. Everything was gray or beige. Iris invited Finn to sit on the cushion covered bench beside a small table, mounted so that it extended from the wall.

"Can I offer you a drink?" Iris checked the mini-fridge. "It looks like all I have are Diet Coke and water."

"Water would be great."

Finn's throat was so dry she was afraid she was about to lose her voice. Iris returned with two bottled waters. She set one in front of Finn. Iris was as beautiful as ever, but she seemed a little sad. Finn felt responsible.

"You cut your hair." Iris's hair was an inch or two above her shoulders where before it had fallen halfway down her back.

"I needed shorter hair for the part. Too many props getting tangled in longer hair. Apparently, long hair is problematic in outer space too...you know, helmets and zero gravity and all that." Iris coyly tucked her hair behind her ear and glanced at Finn. "Do you like it?"

"I do." Finn took a sip of water and tried to focus on slowing her heart rate. She figured this was it. She'd either say the right thing and fix things, or say the wrong thing and not be able to walk it back.

There was a moment of awkward silence.

"Why don't we agree that things couldn't get any worse." Iris sounded so calm. At least she didn't sound angry any longer.

"Agreed."

"So, we have nothing to lose by being completely honest with each other." Iris's direct gaze warmed Finn's skin.

"Iris Fleming, the woman who bypasses small talk and goes right for the heart of things." Finn smiled. She was grateful for Iris's direct approach. She wanted to know where she stood. She wanted Iris to put her out of her misery. "I'm in." She toasted the air with the water bottle. "Here's to honesty."

"Okay, I'll go first since this was my idea. Here's the truth..." Iris took a breath, looked out the small window beside them, and then turned back to face Finn. Iris was sitting across from her, and the few inches of space that separated their hands on the tabletop were churning with charged particles. It was hard not to reach for Iris's hand. "That night we argued...I was feeling like a failure."

"I felt like a failure that night too."

"So, we tore each other down. Mutually assured destruction."

"I guess." Finn sighed. "After meeting your friends, and Kent, I just felt like I could never measure up."

"Measure up to what?"

"You...your world..."

"The perceived perfection of my life?"

"Something like that."

"Except my life isn't perfect." Iris hesitated. "Especially without you in it."

Finn smiled. She gave in and reached for Iris's hand and loosely entwined her fingers with Iris's.

"What do you have against perfection anyway?" asked Iris.

"Besides the fact that it's usually too good to be true?" Finn leaned forward, resting her elbows on the edge of the table.

"What has perfection ever done to you?"

"Nothing." She raised Iris's fingers to her lips and kissed them. She whispered against Iris's fingers. "I'm sorry." And she truly meant it. Just sitting across from Iris made her heart hurt. She sorely regretted every callous thing she'd said. She'd been a complete jerk.

Iris focused on Finn's lips as they brushed across the back of her fingers making her heart flutter painfully fast. She wanted to climb across the table into Finn's lap. But she knew if she did that, there would be no more talking. And she wanted everything out in the open before things went any further.

"Can we agree that maybe we're okay with perfection?" Iris waited for Finn to meet her gaze and hold it. "Because I think you're perfect."

"Iris, I'm sorry for how I left."

"Did something happen at the driving school?" It just seemed that there had to be something. Something else besides their stupid argument.

"I thought that was what I wanted. I'd been holding this stunt driving dream like it was some holy grail, some unreachable thing. But then I did reach it and it wasn't what I thought it would be. I felt like such a loser. And you...you're living your dream. You didn't need me tagging along."

"If I hadn't gotten this part, I don't know. I was feeling like giving up. I was definitely feeling bad about myself that night. I think we just tapped into each other's insecurities or something and everything escalated." She paused. "I don't want you to think I'm some shallow actor—"

"I don't. I should never have said that. I didn't mean it. I was just lashing out." Finn cradled Iris's hand in hers. "I was angry at myself for chasing some dream I would never catch. Like chasing sunset, always just beyond the horizon, just beyond my reach." Finn looked at Iris with the sincerest expression. "And when I got back here I realized I wasn't chasing sunset, it was you…you were the dream. I don't want to chase anything any longer, except you."

"You caught me." There was a lump in Iris's throat. She tried to swallow around it.

Finn closed her eyes and took a deep breath. "Iris, will you stay with me tonight?"

"Yes." Iris stopped fighting the urge.

She rounded the table and slid into Finn's lap and kissed her, hard and possessively. Finn's hands were at her hips, drawing her close.

"God, I miss kissing you. I miss everything about you, Iris." Finn searched her face. "Will you forgive me for being a complete idiot?"

"As long as you forgive me." Iris wrapped her arms around Finn's neck. "I've been miserable without you. This great, exciting thing happened in my life and you were the only person I really wanted to share it with."

"Why didn't you tell me you were in Atlanta?"

"I was afraid you would only think I wanted to be with you because I got the part…only because I was in town, and that wasn't true." Iris kissed her lightly.

"Want to get out of here?"

Iris nodded.

They left Iris's trailer hand in hand. At the barricade, one of the security guards spoke.

"Do you need me to call a car for you, Ms. Fleming?"

"No, thank you." She looked at Finn. "I've got a driver."

She smiled and squeezed Finn's hand.

❖

Finn's cabin was just as cozy as she'd remembered from the first night. The night with the bear. The night she'd thrown the drink in Finn's face. She was glad she'd been so wrong about Finn. Iris worried she'd talked Finn's ear off on the drive. It seemed like so much had happened in a week. Finn simply smiled and listened.

They held hands on the drive. Every so often, Finn brought Iris's fingers to her lips and kissed them. And every time she did it, a surge of warmth coursed through Iris's body.

It was well after dark when they reached the cabin. Iris wanted Finn so badly. The second the door clicked shut she began to loosen the buttons of Finn's Levi's. They angled toward the bedroom, dropping clothing as they went. Finn was wearing only her y-front briefs when Iris shoved her backward onto the bed. Iris slid out of her jeans slowly while Finn watched. Wearing only her bra and a thong, she crawled up Finn's long frame until she was straddling her waist. Tenderly, she bent down and kissed Finn's chest, allowing strands of her hair to caress Finn's skin. When she looked at Finn, her eyes gave her away. Iris was struck by the frightening fragility of the human experience. Struck by how hard trust was earned and how easily it could be lost.

"You're here." Finn brushed the back of her fingers across Iris's cheek.

"I'm here." Iris kissed her. "It was you I meant to belong to all along."

"Iris, I'm so in love with you."

Iris smiled. She squeezed her eyes shut for a moment and then took a deep breath, breathing Finn in. Her face was close enough that Iris could feel the warmth of her sun-kissed skin.

"I think I've been in love with you since our first date. Since my birthday. I just didn't allow myself to believe it."

Iris rocked back, reached around, and unfastened her bra. Finn swept her palms tenderly up Iris's ribs and then covered Iris's breasts. She captured Finn's wrists and pressed them into the pillow above her head. Her breasts brushed against Finn's, causing Iris to catch her breath. She closed her eyes, savoring the intimate caress of skin against skin.

"Hey, look, I'm taking my hands off the wheel," Finn whispered and caught Iris's lower lip playfully between her teeth.

"Oh, how I love it when you let me drive."

EPILOGUE

Finn lounged in an antique deck chair on the flagstone patio at the back of Iris's house. She was waiting for Iris to get ready. They'd decided to eat out. Finn was in the mood for something casual. There was a place she liked up the coast, just a little bit north of the boardwalk, but she'd wait to see what Iris was in the mood for.

The filming of the first season of *Athena* had wrapped up a week earlier, and they'd driven the Lincoln out to Santa Monica at a leisurely pace. Retracing their original trip, only with a lot more layovers in scenic spots. Ward was in charge of taking care of the roadster until they returned to Atlanta. Six months in Georgia and then three months back in California before filming for the second season started up again.

Finn shook her head. Six months had zoomed by.

Iris put in long hours during the week so they savored their weekends together.

Finn was feeling good. She took a moment to reflect on that. Thinking back to when she'd first returned to Georgia, she'd never have imagined this was where things would end up.

It turned out that she hadn't had to completely abandon her dream of working in the movie industry after all; she just had to shift her focus. She was around the set enough with Iris that after a month she ended up meeting the owner of Cinema Auto. After a few more conversations, she landed a job. Cinema Auto was the largest supplier of car rentals for movies, television, and commercials in the country, and they were right in her back yard. They supplied customized vehicles, automotive fabrications, and car rentals for film all over the country. As luck would have it their headquarters was in North Hollywood, but they also had a full-service facility in Atlanta. Finn was finally able to combine her passion for cars with her interest in movies and turn it into a job.

A year ago, she'd never have imagined that life could be this good, or this fulfilling. Working for Cinema Auto, she got to drive and deliver all kinds of custom and vintage cars all over the place. It was her dream job.

A dream job to go along with finding her dream girl.

"Sorry that took so long." Iris stood on the threshold of the French doors. She was wearing a summer dress with spaghetti straps. "I was texting with Maggie. She said she'll be here next week, but just for a quick two-day visit."

Maggie had been accepted into a three-month art fellowship program for painting in New York. Until she returned, they had the house to themselves.

"You look great." Finn kissed Iris lightly. She dangled her keys from one hand and captured Iris's with the other.

When they reached the car, Finn held the door until Iris slid in.

They'd spent the past six months getting to know each other and planning their future. Every possible scenario was brighter with Iris in her life.

Finn cranked the Lincoln, but before she put it into drive she reached for Iris's hand. "Where do you want to go?"

Iris smiled.

"Anywhere, as long as it's with you."

The End

About the Author

Missouri Vaun spent a large part of her childhood in southern Mississippi, before attending high school in North Carolina and college in Tennessee. Strong connections to her roots in the rural south have been a grounding force throughout her life. Vaun spent twelve years finding her voice working as a journalist in places as disparate as Chicago, Atlanta, and Jackson, Mississippi, all along filing away characters and their stories. Her novels are heartfelt, earthy, and speak of loyalty and our responsibility to others. She and her wife currently live in northern California.

Books Available from Bold Strokes Books

Blood of the Pack by Jenny Frame. When Alpha of the Scottish pack Kenrick Wulver visits the Wolfgangs, she falls for Zaria Lupa, a wolf on the run. (978-1-63555-431-1)

Cause of Death by Sheri Lewis Wohl. Medical student Vi Akiak and K9 Search and Rescue officer Kate Renard must work together to find a killer before they end up the next targets. In the race for survival, they discover that love may be the biggest risk of all. (978-1-63555-441-0)

Chasing Sunset by Missouri Vaun. Hijinks and mishaps ensue as Iris and Finn set off on a road trip adventure, chasing the sunset, and falling in love along the way. (978-1-63555-454-0)

Double Down by MB Austin. When an unlikely friendship with Spanish pop star Erlea turns deeper, Celeste, in-house physician for the hotel hosting Erlea's show, has a choice to make—run or double down on love. (978-1-63555-423-6)

Party of Three by Sandy Lowe. Three friends are in for a wild night at billionaire heiress Eleanor McGregor's twenty-fifth birthday party. Love, lust, and doing the right thing, even when it hurts, turn the evening into one that will change their lives forever. (978-1-63555-246-1)

Sit. Stay. Love. by Karis Walsh. City girl Alana Brendt and country vet Tegan Evans both know they don't belong together. Only problem is, they're falling in love. (978-1-63555-439-7)

Where the Lies Hide by Renee Roman. As P.I. Camdyn Stark gets closer to solving the case, will her dark secrets and the lies she's buried jeopardize her future with the quietly beautiful Sarah Peters? (978-1-63555-371-0)

Beautiful Dreamer by Melissa Brayden. With love on the line, can Devyn Winters find it in her heart to stay in the small town of Dreamer's Bay, the one place she swore she'd never remain? (978-1-63555-305-5)

Create a Life to Love by Erin Zak. When sixteen-year-old Beth shows up at her birth mother's door, three lives will change forever. (978-1-63555-425-0)

Deadeye by Meredith Doench. Stranded while hunting the serial predator Deadeye, Special Agent Luce Hansen fights for survival while her lover, forensic pathologist Harper Bennett, hunts for clues to Hansen's disappearance along the killer's trail. (978-1-63555-253-9)

Death Takes a Bow by David S. Pederson. Alan Keys takes part in a local stage production, but when the leading man is murdered, his partner Detective Heath Barrington is thrust into the limelight to find the killer. (978-1-63555-472-4)

Endangered by Michelle Larkin. Shapeshifters Officer Aspen Wolfe and Dr. Tora Madigan fight their growing attraction as they work together to destroy a secret government agency that exterminates their kind. (978-1-63555-377-2)

Incognito by VK Powell. The only thing Evan Spears is focused on is capturing a fleeing murder suspect until wild card Frankie Strong is added to her team and causes chaos on and off the job. (978-1-63555-389-5)

Insult to Injury by Gun Brooke. After losing everything, Gail Owen withdraws to her old farmhouse and finds a destitute young woman, Romi Shepherd, living in a secret room. (978-1-63555-323-9)

Just One Moment by Dena Blake. If you were given the chance to have the love of your life back, could you ignore everything that went wrong and start over again? (978-1-63555-387-1)

Scene of the Crime by MJ Williamz. Cullen Mathew finds herself caught between the woman she thinks she loves but can no longer trust and a beautiful detective she can't stop thinking about who will stop at nothing to find the truth. (978-1-63555-405-2)

Accidental Prophet by Bud Gundy. Days after his grandmother dies, Drew Morten learns his true identity and finds himself racing against time to save civilization from the apocalypse. (978-1-63555-452-6)

Daughter of No One by Sam Ledel. When their worlds are threatened, a princess and a village outcast must overcome their differences and embrace a budding attraction if they want to survive. (978-1-63555-427-4)

Fear of Falling by Georgia Beers. Singer Sophie James is ready to shake up her career, but her new manager, the gorgeous Dana Landon, has other ideas. (978-1-63555-443-4)

In Case You Forgot by Fredrick Smith and Chaz Lamar. Zaire and Kenny, two newly single, Black, queer, and socially aware men, start again—in love, career, and life—in the West Hollywood neighborhood of LA. (978-1-63555-493-9)

Playing with Fire by Lesley Davis. When Takira Lathan and Dante Groves meet at Takira's restaurant, love may find its way onto the menu. (978-1-63555-433-5)

Practice Makes Perfect by Carsen Taite. Meet law school friends Campbell, Abby, and Grace, law partners at Austin's premier boutique legal firm for young, hip entrepreneurs. Legal Affairs: one law firm, three best friends, three chances to fall in love. (978-1-63555-357-4)

The Last Seduction by Ronica Black. When you allow true love to elude you once and you desperately regret it, are you brave enough to grab it when it comes around again? (978-1-63555-211-9)

Wavering Convictions by Erin Dutton. After a traumatic event, Maggie has vowed to regain her strength and independence. So how can Ally be both the woman who makes her feel safe and a constant reminder of the person who took her security away? (978-1-63555-403-8)

A Bird of Sorrow by Shea Godfrey. As Darrius and her lover, Princess Jessa, gather their strength for the coming war, a mysterious spell will reveal the truth of an ancient love. (978-1-63555-009-2)

All the Worlds Between Us by Morgan Lee Miller. High school senior Quinn Hughes discovers that a broken friendship is actually a door propped open for an unexpected romance. (978-1-63555-457-1)

An Intimate Deception by CJ Birch. Flynn County Sheriff Elle Ashley has spent her adult life atoning for her wild youth, but when she finds her ex, Jessie, murdered two weeks before the small town's biggest social event, she comes face-to-face with her past and all her well-kept secrets. (978-1-63555-417-5)

Cash and the Sorority Girl by Ashley Bartlett. Cash Braddock doesn't want to deal with morality, drugs, or people. Unfortunately, she's going to have to. (978-1-63555-310-9)

Counting for Thunder by Phillip Irwin Cooper. A struggling actor returns to the Deep South to manage a family crisis, finds love, and ultimately his own voice as his mother is regaining hers for possibly the last time. (978-1-63555-450-2)

Falling by Kris Bryant. Falling in love isn't part of the plan, but will Shaylie Beck put her heart first and stick around, or tell the damaging truth? (978-1-63555-373-4)

Secrets in a Small Town by Nicole Stiling. Deputy Chief Mackenzie Blake has one mission: find the person harassing Savannah Castillo and her daughter before they cause real harm. (978-1-63555-436-6)

Stormy Seas by Ali Vali. The high-octane follow-up to the best-selling action-romance, *Blue Skies*. (978-1-63555-299-7)

The Road to Madison by Elle Spencer. Can two women who fell in love as girls overcome the hurt caused by the father who tore them apart? (978-1-63555-421-2)

Dangerous Curves by Larkin Rose. When love waits at the finish line, dangerous curves are a risk worth taking. (978-1-63555-353-6)

Love to the Rescue by Radclyffe. Can two people who share a past really be strangers? (978-1-62639-973-0)

Love's Portrait by Anna Larner. When museum curator Molly Goode and benefactor Georgina Wright uncover a portrait's secret, public and private truths are exposed, and their deepening love hangs in the balance. (978-1-63555-057-3)

Model Behavior by MJ Williamz. Can one woman's instability shatter a new couple's dreams of happiness? (978-1-63555-379-6)

Pretending in Paradise by M. Ullrich. When travelwisdom.com assigns PR specialist Caroline Beckett and travel blogger Emma Morgan to cover a hot new couples retreat, they're forced to fake a relationship to secure a reservation. (978-1-63555-399-4)

Recipe for Love by Aurora Rey. Hannah Little doesn't have much use for fancy chefs or fancy restaurants, but when New York City chef Drew Davis comes to town, their attraction just might be a recipe for love. (978-1-63555-367-3)

Survivor's Guilt and Other Stories by Greg Herren. Award-winning author Greg Herren's short stories are finally pulled together into a single collection, including the Macavity Award nominated title story and the first-ever Chanse MacLeod short story. (978-1-63555-413-7)

The House by Eden Darry. After a vicious assault, Sadie, Fin, and their family retreat to a house they think is the perfect place to start over, until they realize not all is as it seems. (978-1-63555-395-6)

Uninvited by Jane C. Esther. When Aerin McLeary's body becomes host for an alien intent on invading Earth, she must work with researcher Olivia Ando to uncover the truth and save humankind. (978-1-63555-282-9)